THE CHIANTI FLASK

THE CHIANTI FLASK

MARIE BELLOC LOWNDES

With an Introduction
by Martin Edwards

Poisoned Pen
PRESS

Published by Poisoned Pen Press, an imprint of Sourcebooks, in association with the British Library
P.O. Box 4410, Naperville, Illinois 60567-4410
(630) 961-3900
sourcebooks.com

The Chianti Flask was originally published in 1935 by William Heinemann, London and Toronto.

Library of Congress Cataloging-in-Publication Data

Names: Lowndes, Marie Belloc, author. | Edwards, Martin, writer of introduction.
Title: The Chianti flask / Marie Belloc Lowndes ; with an introduction by Martin Edwards.
Description: Naperville, Illinois : Poisoned Pen Press, [2022] | Series: British library crime classics
Identifiers: LCCN 2021023603 (print) | LCCN 2021023604 (ebook) | (trade paperback) | (epub)
Subjects: GSAFD: Mystery fiction.
Classification: LCC PR6023.O95 C45 2022 (print) | LCC PR6023.O95 (ebook) | DDC 823/.912--dc23
LC record available at https://lccn.loc.gov/2021023603
LC ebook record available at https://lccn.loc.gov/2021023604

Printed and bound in the United States of America
SB 10 9 8 7 6 5 4 3 2 1

CONTENTS

INTRODUCTION

THE CHIANTI FLASK OPENS AT A MOMENT OF COURTROOM drama. A quiet, enigmatic young woman called Laura Dousland is on trial for murder. She is accused of poisoning her elderly husband, Fordish Dousland. The couple's Italian servant, Angelo Terugi, chief witness for the prosecution, is on the stand. His evidence is potentially damning, but in a crucial intervention, Laura challenges him from the dock.

At the heart of the puzzle of Fordish Dousland's death is the Chianti flask that held the wine containing the poison which killed him. But the flask has disappeared, and all attempts to trace it have come to nothing. Sir Joseph Molloy, the barrister who is defending Laura, contends that the deceased took his own life, and he calls Laura's friend and former employer, Alice Hayward, to tell the court about Dousland's suicidal tendencies. The defence case is also strengthened by evidence given by a young doctor, Mark Scrutton. When Laura herself is called into the witness box, not only does she decline to cast any suspicion on Terugi, she expresses the view that Terugi genuinely believed he was telling the truth when making a series of allegations against her.

The jury delivers its verdict, but this represents simply the "end of the beginning" of Marie Belloc Lowndes's novel. Her prime focus is not on the trial itself, but on its aftermath. She charts the implications of a murder charge, both on the person accused and those close to her. Is it true that there's no smoke without fire?

The bulk of the story is devoted to Laura's behaviour in reaction to the stress of the case, and on the uneasily developing romance between her and Mark Scrutton. The author demonstrates with subtlety and skill that a person such as Alice Hayward, who appears to be extremely generous and kind-hearted, may in fact be capable of doing great harm, simply as a result of flaws in her character. This book is in essence a psychological study written from a subtle feminist perspective, but Marie Belloc Lowndes also maintains the reader's interest by keeping secret the explanation of Fordish Dousland's death. Only in the closing pages is the mystery of the Chianti flask finally unravelled.

Marie Belloc was born in London in 1868. Her father was a French lawyer; her mother, Bessie Parkes, was a prominent advocate of women's rights. A love of literature ran in the blood. Bessie was a poet and her friends included George Eliot and Elizabeth Barrett Browning. Marie and her brother, Hilaire (who became a noted man of letters and collaborated with G. K. Chesterton), spent their early years in France. After their father's death, they divided their time between France and Britain; traces of this cultural duality can be discerned in Marie's writing.

In 1896, Marie married Frederick Lowndes, a journalist who would ultimately chalk up more than forty years on the staff of *The Times.* Two years later she published a biography of the Prince of Wales. From that moment, there was no stopping her. Stories and nonfiction poured from her pen until her death, almost half a century later.

She was a convivial woman, and very well-connected in London society, as is evident from the posthumous compilation of her diaries and letters produced by one of her daughters, Susan Lowndes. Her wide social circle encompassed, at different times, Oscar Wilde, Henry James, George Meredith, Hugh Walpole, H. G. Wells, and H. H. Asquith. Although she began with nonfiction, she had always longed to write fiction, and no less an authority than Robert Browning commented favourably on her first published short story.

When Frederick received a legacy of two thousand pounds, he encouraged her to try her hand at a novel, and the result was *The Hours of Penelope,* published in 1904. This gave her an early insight into the realities of authorship: "all it brought me in was nine pounds, though I am sure that William Heinemann did his very best for it… he had hoped to sell ten thousand copies. He did sell under a thousand…"

She described her early novels as "studies of character, rather than studies of crime," and that keen interest in human nature lifted her fiction out of the ordinary when she sought to make crime pay. She was fascinated by real life mysteries, and in 1912 she obtained a ticket to sit in on a high-profile murder trial. Frederick and Margaret Seddon were accused of poisoning their lodger Eliza Barrow for financial gain. Marie recorded her fascination with their behaviour during the trial: "the way in which they constantly talked to one another, and his laughter at anything in the proceedings which could be considered as comic, such as the pompous way in which an old gentleman took the oath." Seddon did not, however, have the last laugh; although his wife was acquitted, he was found guilty and hanged.

The Chink in the Armour, published in 1912 (and filmed a decade later as *The House of Peril*) was one of Marie's earliest ventures into crime fiction. A year before that book appeared, she'd contributed to *McClure's Magazine* a story that she later expanded into the novel which remains by far her best-known work.

The Lodger, which appeared in 1913, is a gripping story inspired by the Whitechapel murders, and it sold half a million copies when marketed for sixpence by the Reader's Library. The book has been filmed and adapted for television and radio on numerous occasions; the most famous movie version dates from 1927 and was an early success for Alfred Hitchcock. The Royal Academy of Music commissioned Phyllis Tate to write an opera based on the book, with a libretto by David Franklin, and the result was premiered in 1960; it was subsequently broadcast on the radio, and a CD of the performance is now available. In recent years, the opera has been translated into German. Few crime novels have enjoyed such a varied afterlife over the course of more than a century.

Marie continued to switch regularly between fiction (novels, short stories, and plays) and different forms of factual writing (memoirs, biographies, a study of the Lizzie Borden case, and a book of *Noted Murder Mysteries*, published under the pen-name Philip Curtin). As a crime writer, she remained productive throughout the Golden Age of Murder between the two world wars, but her approach was distinct from that of younger detective novelists such as Agatha Christie, Dorothy L. Sayers, and Margery Allingham. Her focus was on "whydunit," examining criminal psychology in a leisurely manner reminiscent of Edwardian era fiction, rather than "whodunit," and the creation of convoluted puzzles. That said, she did occasionally venture into detection, creating a detective called Hercules Popeau, who attracted rather less attention than Christie's Hercule Poirot.

Letty Lynton, inspired by the sensational Victorian trial of Madeleine Smith, was filmed in 1932 with Joan Crawford, although litigation resulted in the movie disappearing from sight. *The Story of Ivy,* originally published in 1927, was eventually made into a film called *Ivy*. Sam Wood directed, Joan Fontaine was cast in the lead role, and Hoagy Carmichael wrote the theme song. The movie was released in June 1947 and is now regarded as a capable example of film noir.

Marie died in November of the same year; the last rites were administered by a priest who happened to be "Roman Catholic Chaplain to Broadmoor Criminal Lunatic Asylum." As her daughter Susan noted, the priest had become a friend during Marie's short illness, and it is clear that this was a woman whose talent for fiction was matched by a gift for friendship. *The Chianti Flask,* first published in 1935, is a relatively obscure novel which has long been out of print, but it provides a good illustration of her style and her abiding interest in crime and its consequences.

—Martin Edwards
www.martinedwardsbooks.com

"In love the heavens themselves do guide the state,
money buys lands, but wives are sold by fate."

I

"All that you say is true, Angelo, but it happened another time, when your master was angry with you, and when he had hidden—"

And then the voice broke, but each human being there knew that the words which had been left unspoken were "the Chianti flask."

As the wailing pleading tones had echoed through the court, every eye had become focused on the frail young woman who stood in the dock. She had a slight girlish figure, and looked strangely small; the smaller as just behind her was a stalwart prison wardress.

During the days the trial had already lasted, the prisoner had looked unnaturally pale. Not unbecomingly pallid, but of a whiteness that appeared luminous, as does a white camellia seen in a dim light. And now as she sensed that eager, questioning, enveloping gaze, she crimsoned deeply.

Angelo Terugi, the man in the witness-box, who was chief witness for the Prosecution, was tall, lank, and dark. He was a Venetian, and had been servant as a boy to a British family in Italy. He spoke good English, but it was clear that he was pitiably nervous. Up to now he had looked straight before him, not once glancing towards the dock. In answer to that urgent cry, however, he quickly turned his head and threw a deprecatory look at the lady who had been the wife of his employer, and who was now being tried for her life on the accusation of having caused that employer's death.

Meanwhile, taken entirely by surprise, Counsel for the Prosecution had stayed the next question on his lips, and during that interval, which seemed considerably longer than it really was, a heavy silence brooded over the Assize Court.

The sleepy cathedral town, within a few miles of the sea in southern England, had sprung into pulsing life, for there had been enacted the drama of the Dousland case, and there also Laura Dousland was now being tried on the charge of murdering her husband, Fordish Dousland. Indeed, the eighteenth-century building known as the Assize Court, Silchester, had become, for the time being, the centre of the world to hundreds of thousands of the prisoner's fellow-countrymen and countrywomen, because there was in the story those elements of mystery and strangeness which fascinate most thinking minds.

The centre of the mystery was a Chianti flask; it had contained the wine in which the poison which had caused Fordish Dousland's death had almost certainly been administered. That flask, according to the evidence of Angelo Terugi, had disappeared during the night of Fordish Dousland's death. The Italian, in his first statement to the police, had asserted that he had searched for this flask of wine everywhere he could think of, inside and outside the house, on two occasions—the morning after his master's death, and two days later, when he had been called upon to return the empty flasks to the wine-seller, who had brought a new provision of the Chianti by road from London. Two dozen flasks had been listed, but only twenty-three had he been able to produce.

And now, while this man's examination in chief was nearing its end, had come that surprising intervention from the dock.

In the long history of British trials for murder, no woman prisoner had ever so interrupted a witness; and that Laura Dousland should do such a thing would have seemed inconceivable to any of the people who had known her during her working girlhood, or as the young wife of an elderly retired lawyer. Even Sir Joseph Molloy, the famous Irish advocate retained for her defence, who had an astounding knowledge of human nature, would have supposed her quite incapable of such an outburst. Still, deep in his heart, Sir Joseph was not sorry that his client had done so improper and unexpected a thing, for the Italian's evidence was serious, and might even be considered damning—if true. But was it true? The prisoner's passionate protest made many a man and woman doubt it, and doubt it very much, both at the time it was made, and for ever after.

Counsel for the Prosecution instantly felt the change of feeling in court, and also perceived that his witness had been considerably affected by that appeal from the dock. So it was in quiet gentle accents that he resumed his interrogation.

"Tell me in your own words what happened the afternoon and evening before Mr. Dousland's death."

"I went away, sir; to London."

"It was your weekly evening out?"

"Yes, sir, and before I start I get ready the master's supper."

"What time were you supposed to be back?"

"When I like, sir."

"As a matter of fact what time were you back that night?"

The Italian hesitated. "A wheel of the coach turned soft, so I return late. I do not know at what exact time, as I say to the police."

"Never mind what you said to the police. Would it have been after midnight?"

Terugi nodded.

"Please say 'yes' or 'no.'"

"Yes, sir."

"Cast your mind back to Mr. Dousland's supper. Can you remember what it consisted of that evening?"

"Spaghetti, sir, which I cook ready for Mrs. Dousland to make hot. Mr. Dousland was very particular about his food, so I leave it in the oven."

"How did you usually serve your master's supper?"

"On a tray, sir."

"Did you get a tray ready on this occasion?"

"Yes, I did do that, sir."

"What did you actually put on the tray that evening? Can you remember what was on it?"

Terugi waited for what seemed a long time. But at last he replied in a positive tone: "Biscuits and butter, sir. Also two plates—a big plate and a little plate. Also a glass for wine—" and then he stopped, and fidgeted somewhat in the witness-box.

"Did you put anything else on the tray besides the objects you have enumerated?"

"Yes, sir. I put on the tray a flask of the Chianti."

"You have no doubt that you put the wine on your master's tray on that occasion? The night before his death took place?"

"Of that I am quite sure, sir. I do swear that. It is the truth."

The Judge leaned forward. "Surely you realise that everything you are now saying is on oath?"

"Oh, yes, your Eminence, I am swearing all the time," replied the witness, and there was "laughter in court."

"What happened when you came back to the house in the late night or early morning?"

The Italian looked puzzled. "I do not remember."

"There was nothing unusual when you came in?"

"No, sir."

"I presume the house was in darkness."

"Yes, sir. I go to bed, for I feel a little sick."

"What happened the next morning?"

"I was sound asleep when there comes a knock on my door. It is Mrs. Dousland, and she calls out to me that Mr. Dousland he is dead in bed."

"What did you do then?"

"I get out of bed, and as I dress myself I think, 'Ah, poverina! this is a great trouble.'"

"What did you do after you were dressed?"

"I go down to the kitchen."

"What did you see there?"

Again the Italian fidgeted uncomfortably before he answered: "I see the tray on the table."

"May I take it that on the tray were the remains of Mr. Dousland's meal?"

"Yes, sir. But not much left."

"Was anything missing from the tray?"

"Yes, sir."

"What was missing?"

"With permission, I say the Chianti was missing. There was no wine there, and I think to myself 'this is strange.' I look about the kitchen and in the cupboard. But the flask he has gone."

The speaker made a dramatic gesture with his right hand, apparently indicating that what he had searched for had vanished into the air.

"Did you point out to Mrs. Dousland that the flask of Chianti was not on the tray?"

"No, sir, for I was rattled, as they say here."

And then again there was some foolish tittering in the court.

"Did you go on searching for that particular flask of Chianti?"

"Yes, sir, for when they bring new Chianti from London I have to give back the empties. So I looked again for that flask, but I did not find it anywhere."

"Was a money allowance made on each empty flask?"

"Yes, sir, fourpence, always."

"That was probably the reason why you made a second search for the flask?"

"Yes, sir, for my master he love money very, very much."

And now had come the moment when Angelo Terugi was about to face the ordeal of cross-examination at the lips of the prisoner's formidable advocate. Fortunately for himself the Italian knew nothing of Sir Joseph Molloy's reputation, and of how often that gentleman had been compared to a huge tom cat playing with a baby mouse. But the serried mass of men and women in the court was looking forward with cruel pleasure to the duel about to take place. They had little doubt but that Sir Joseph would reduce the self-confident foreigner to a state of abject terror and, as like as not, force him to eat his words.

To the disappointment of many of those present, Sir Joseph began by handling the witness in a gentle, and even a pleasant, manner.

For a few moments he looked fixedly at the slim, still young, man, and then he said in an almost casual tone: "In your own interest, Terugi, as well as in that of the prisoner, I feel compelled to raise once more the question of the Chianti flask."

There was a long pause. Then Mrs. Dousland's advocate said firmly: "I believe you are an excellent servant, and that you prepared your master's tray both with care and, I may add, with kindness. But I am instructed that your memory is at fault, and that you made a serious mistake in asserting that you put a flask of Chianti on the tray that night."

He paused, and looked sternly, searchingly, at the man before him.

"I make no mistake, sir. No, I did not."

"Is it not a fact that about three weeks before your master's death you placed a partly-filled Chianti flask on a tray which was taken up to Mr. Dousland in his bedroom?"

Sir Joseph paused, and the Italian, after what seemed considerable hesitation to those who listened, with obvious reluctance replied, "I did do that, yes."

Still speaking in a considerate, even kindly, tone, the Irishman asked quietly: "What happened on that occasion?"

Terugi's face flushed. "Mr. Dousland he think I drink his wine. That was a damn lie."

"Did Mr. Dousland tell you of his suspicion?"

"No, sir. He just hide the flask, and in Mrs. Dousland's bedroom, where I never do go."

"How was this fact brought to your knowledge?"

"I say when I come for the tray, 'Where is the wine,

madam?' Mrs. Dousland she tells me Mr. Dousland 'as it. She is embarrassed, for I am no thief," his voice rose to a shrill scream. "I tell her I go away, but she say: 'Stay, Terugi, for I know you are a good man. You never do a fault.'"

There rose a murmur of sympathetic laughter, and Terugi smiled contentedly.

"Then Mrs. Dousland persuaded you to stay?"

"Yes, sir, and Mr. Dousland, he say he trust me, and he is sorry for what he done."

"Now according to my instructions, you have confused those two occasions—the occasion when a flask of Chianti undoubtedly did disappear from off your master's tray, with what took place the evening before his death. My instructions are that you cannot have put the flask of Chianti on your master's tray on that second occasion, for the good reason that all the wine in the house had been finished a couple of days before. I now put to you that you confused those two separate occasions."

"I made no confusings, sir. The Chianti he had not all been drunk up. I inform myself and see there was some left in the flask, perhaps a quarter." The Italian waited a few moments, and then he exclaimed excitedly: "I do swear that the morning my master die I do search everywhere, and I do not find the flask."

"I ask you now a solemn question, and I beg you to pause before you answer it. Assuming your statement to be true, was there not a special reason why you felt—shall I say disappointed?—over the disappearance of the Chianti flask on the morning following Mr. Dousland's death?"

Sir Joseph fixed his eyes on his witness, and a look of perplexity flashed across the Judge's face. But Counsel for the Prosecution smiled within himself. Was "Joey," as the great

Sir Joseph was known to his legal brethren, going to shake this honest Italian's testimony? He began to think he was.

Meanwhile a dusky colour had come over Terugi's olive face, and it was plain the question disturbed him.

"I repeat my question. Why were you so specially anxious on that agitated and distressful morning as to the whereabouts of what you desired to find—the partly full flask of wine?"

Terugi stared at the questioner without speaking.

"Come, Terugi, answer."

The Italian muttered: "I do not know."

"I have a witness, as a matter of fact the baker who called at 2, Kingsley Terrace that morning, who will swear that you told him you were disappointed not to find that there was a little wine left in any of the flasks which were about to be called for from London. Do you agree to that statement?"

"The truth is, sir, that I felt what they call here bad, ill, shaken. My master, he had been quite well—"

The Judge leaned forward: "Surely not quite well if he had his dinner in bed?"

Counsel for the Crown intervened, "Mr. Dousland was not ill, my lord. If I may venture to ask your lordship to refer to your notes, I think you will find that it was that gentleman's habit to have his last meal on a tray, not only in the dining-room, but quite often in his bedroom."

"Aye, aye, I remember you explained this was so in your opening speech, Sir Edward. I have a note of it. Proceed, Sir Joseph."

The famous advocate continued.

"Now, Terugi, you have just told the jury that you felt what they call here bad, ill, shocked, as a result of learning that your master, who had been quite well, had died suddenly in the night."

He waited a moment. "No doubt you felt that a little—"

"Sir Joseph?" murmured the Judge.

But Terugi followed the lead which ought not to have been given to him. "Yes, sir, I say to myself, 'a little wine will do me good.'"

There was a ripple of laughter at that frank admission, and the Italian scowled. To his mind, what he had just said was not at all funny.

"That is why I look in a special manner for that Chianti flask. I knew Mr. Dousland only drink a little wine, and Mrs. Dousland only water. So to myself I exclaim, 'I will have a swig of the Chianti, and that will make me feel better!' So I look and look to find the flask."

Sir Joseph put up his hand, but now that the witness had started talking of himself, it was as though he could not stop.

"I look at last in the cupboard where the empty flasks wait to be taken away. I even count them all, to be sure, and there I count the twenty-three and not the twenty-four."

"I put it to you that, according to your own statement at the inquest, your master's wine-glass had not been used. That surely proves you are mistaken as to there having been any wine on the tray."

The Italian hesitated. He looked round the court. "I do think, sir, about that wine-glass—"

But before he could say what he thought, Sir Joseph had pounced upon him. "You have no business to think, or rather you have no business to tell us what you think. You have made a mistake, haven't you? What I require from you is a plain 'yes' or 'no.'"

Angelo Terugi made no answer to that, and the

Prosecuting Counsel noticed a look of distinct relief zigzag both across the olive-tinted face, and the fair face of Sir Joseph, too.

And then the Judge again intervened.

He did his often difficult work admirably, but he had earned the nickname of "The Intervener" because he was apt to take a hand in any case being tried before him, especially when a man or woman was being tried on a charge of murder.

Now he asked the witness: "Tell us, in your own words, exactly what happened on the other occasion on which a flask of Italian wine did undoubtedly disappear. Do you recollect quite clearly what did happen then?"

"I do indeed truly remember what happened, your Eminence. I will never forget it, for I was so furious that I, Angelo Terugi, should be believed to be a thief."

"Yet you have just admitted," said the Judge sternly, "that you intended, and indeed were anxious, to drink what wine remained in the bottle, or flask, on the morning following your master's death?"

The Italian straightened himself, and it was with some dignity that he answered: "The condition was different, your Eminence. For me to have taken Mr. Dousland's wine with him alive would have been a steal. But for me to want to drink some wine when I have had a terrible shock is not wrong. Willingly would I have asked Mrs. Dousland's permission, and surely she would have said, 'By all means, Angelo, you drink that wine.'"

The Judge made no comment on this bold answer. He simply inclined his head towards Sir Joseph Molloy, and the cross-examination went on.

But the man who was fighting to save Laura Dousland

did not return to the vexed question of the Chianti flask. He next cross-examined the witness with regard to certain matters which had arisen during Terugi's examination-in-chief. These matters all concerned the married life of Fordish Dousland and the woman now accused of his murder.

In his original statement to the police Terugi had declared that the couple were not on really good terms. He had vouchsafed his belief that Mr. and Mrs. Dousland would have been far happier had they possessed religious faith to support them in the ordeal to which married life subjects its votaries. He had also declared that Italian husbands were more devoted and even more faithful than were English husbands. This statement when read out by Sir Joseph in a satirical tone had provoked loud laughter. Even the members of the jury had smiled.

Sir Joseph now went back to his first suave and even kindly manner.

"Come, Terugi! Can you give me even one instance when you overheard anything which could be called a quarrel between your master and his wife?"

The witness made no immediate answer to that question. He looked undecided and uncomfortable. At last he said, "I must examine my thoughts."

"I press you as to this, for I have several witnesses who will swear that Mr. and Mrs. Dousland were an affectionate couple. I will, however, put my question in another way. Did you ever see Mrs. Dousland lose her temper with Mr. Dousland?"

At once came an eager: "No, I never see that, sir." But before Sir Joseph could speak again the man added: "But my master he often lose his temper with Mrs. Dousland."

"In what way did he show this?"

And then Angelo Terugi, who was becoming very tired and somewhat dazed, muttered: “I do not know how to explain.”

“I am calling a lady who will assert that Mr. Dousland was passionately attached to his wife; his affection for her being indeed so strong that he disliked her leaving home even for a day or two. Were you aware of that fact?”

“Oh yes, sir! Mr. Dousland—he was jealous—very jealous!”

There ran a shrill titter round the court. It was a cruel titter. The women present found it difficult to believe that any man could have had cause to be jealous of the prisoner in the dock. She looked, to feminine eyes, though years younger than her age, which was thirty-two, quite lacking in sex appeal.

“Jealous? What d'you mean? This is a serious allegation, though an allegation, let me point out, against your late master, not against his wife.”

“It is true, sir. It cause me much shame, for my master to behave so.”

“Of whom was Mr. Dousland jealous? Can you name the gentleman, Terugi?”

Every sound was stilled in the crowded court and every human being there held his or her breath. Was what had been up to now completely lacking, namely, a motive for secret murder on the part of a wife, about to be revealed?

Even Sir Joseph Molloy felt as he had not felt for years in a court of law, exceedingly disturbed. But he made up his mind in one flashing moment to face the new statement boldly.

And then came so unexpected an answer to his momentous question that it caused a burst of loud laughter from many of those in court. And it was laughter which, in spite of the Judge's frown, ended, on the part of some of the men present in loud guffaws.

"Mr. Dousland was jealous of all gentlemans," was what Angelo Terugi replied.

"When asked who came to the house, you said there had been no visitors in your time. Was that statement true, or do you now assert that various gentlemen came to the house?"

"No, sir. But Mr. Dousland he say very angrily one day to Mrs. Dousland, 'I will not let you visit—'" and then Terugi hesitated: "It is a place where lovers live," he concluded.

"What place d'you mean by that?" exclaimed the Judge.

Sir Joseph said gently: "I can supply the name, my lord. The witness must mean Loverslea, the estate of Mr. and Mrs. Hayward, Mrs. Dousland's close friends and former employers."

Amusement and disappointment struggled for mastery in the minds of those present who had hoped for some startling revelation.

"Terugi is so far right inasmuch as Loverslea was a love-nest of Charles the Second," interjected Prosecuting Counsel.

"Was the place which Mr. Dousland objected to Mrs. Dousland visiting called Loverslea?" the Judge addressed the witness.

The Italian looked bewildered. He had not understood a word of the short quick discussion, and still less why the Judge, whom he dimly felt to be in the position of an arbitrator, the gentleman called "Sir Edward," whom he had thought till now to be his protector and friend, and Sir Joseph Molloy, his enemy, had all smiled broadly at one another. It was clear that they were all in league together, and just now were making fun of him, Angelo Terugi! He felt he had been insulted, and he was angered with all these Englishmen who had questioned, cross-questioned, and now had actually laughed at him. Also he felt honestly shocked that there had crept all at once a spirit of levity into a trial for murder. He had always had a kindly feeling for Mrs. Dousland, and he had been dismayed when it had been explained to him that he was to be a witness for the Prosecution.

Suddenly, now, he decided he would not be badgered and browbeaten any more.

"Faz d'una mosca un elefante!" he exclaimed in a loud voice, albeit he was speaking to himself.

"What is it you say?" enquired the Judge.

Every eye was fixed on the witness.

"Repeat what you said, Terugi," commanded Sir Joseph Molloy in a stern voice.

But the Italian remained silent. Then he saw that the Judge was looking at him with what appeared, to his excited mind, a terrible and threatening expression. So, reluctantly, came his answer: "I only remark in my own language that it is folly to try and make an elephant out of a fly, your Eminence."

Everyone present felt that the Italian had scored.

The rest of the evidence for the Prosecution, though it took up many hours, was comparatively unimportant.

Dr. Grant, the elderly physician who had come to the house in response to Mrs. Dousland's telephone call, cut a poor figure in the witness-box, for he had to admit that though he had at once thought Dousland's death presented suspicious features, he had signed a certificate stating the cause to be heart disease. Again, he had waited three weeks before he had communicated his suspicions to the Coroner, and he had only done so because that gentleman happened to be a friend of his.

This was the only remaining witness for the Crown over whom Sir Joseph Molloy took any real trouble. By a series of apparently innocent and simple questions, he made it quite clear to the Judge, and he hoped equally clear to the jury, that Dr. Grant was violently prejudiced against the prisoner. Now such prejudice in a British Court of Law always acts, illogical though it may appear, in favour of a man or woman on trial for his or her life.

The opening speech for the Defence was short, and took the form of a submission on Sir Joseph Molloy's part that there was not, and never had been, sufficient evidence against Laura Dousland to make it right or reasonable that she should have been arrested on a charge of murder. Instead of attacking the evidence for the Prosecution, her advocate put the whole of his powerful intellect to proving that what evidence there was told equally against Angelo Terugi. This man, he asserted truly, was obviously innocent. His master, though mean and penurious by nature, had yet raised his wages twice, and had promised to pay, should he stay a whole year in his service, half Terugi's holiday return-ticket to Italy.

Having disposed of Angelo Terugi, Sir Joseph turned to the only other person in the case, Fordish Dousland himself.

"I shall put before you," he said in an emphatic tone, "a witness of the highest honour and credibility, who will tell you that this man not only threatened to commit suicide, but was extremely indignant when his threat was not taken seriously."

At the close of Sir Joseph Molloy's speech, the Judge observed: "Do I understand you to mean that I ought to tell the jury that they cannot convict?"

"I mean, my lord, that they ought not to convict."

"That they cannot reasonably convict?"

"Exactly, my lord. That is my point."

Many of those, even members of the Bar, who had listened with close and careful attention to the opening speech for the Defence, thought it doubtful whether Sir Joseph would call the prisoner to give evidence in her own defence. But their doubts were soon set at rest, for he now observed in almost casual tones: "I am of course going to call the prisoner. Indeed from the first she has been eager for me to do so. But before calling Laura Dousland, I propose to call that lady's friend, Mrs. Alice Hayward."

There then stepped up into the witness-box a pleasant-looking, and what the Scotch call a sonsie, middle-aged woman. She was very well dressed, and wore some fine, if unobtrusive, jewels.

Mrs. Hayward took the oath in a quiet steady tone, and with downcast eyes. But when answering Sir Joseph Molloy's questions, she lifted her head and looked both at him, and now and again at the jury, with what was obviously an honest desire to tell the truth, the whole truth, and nothing but the truth.

"You are the wife of Mr. John Hayward of Loverslea?"

"Yes."

"You confirm the fact that the prisoner, Laura Dousland, at the time Laura Dalberton, was governess to your two daughters for five years?"

"Yes."

"What was your opinion of the young lady?"

"The highest opinion. From the first we all became extremely attached to her. She was exceedingly kind-hearted, most conscientious, and scrupulously truthful. In spite of her youth—she was only twenty-three at the time—when I had to be absent from home for some time, nursing my mother through her dying illness, I left my household, which is a considerable one, in her entire charge."

"Was Mr. Fordish Dousland a friend of yours and of your husband?"

"My husband and Mr. Dousland had been at school together, and they had always kept up to a certain extent their early acquaintance. So when Mr. Dousland wrote to Mr. Hayward and said he was looking out for a place to live at on his retirement, we asked him to come and stay with us at Loverslea so that he might look at our part of the country."

"That, I understand, is how he met his future wife?"

"Yes, it was, and Mr. Dousland fell in love with Miss Dalberton, I think I may say, at first sight. But she did not accept his first, or even his second, offer of marriage; in fact, she hesitated for some months before she consented to become his wife."

"I suppose you yourself became more or less intimate with him during his courtship?"

"That is so, though we did not ask him to stay again in our house, as we thought it best for Miss Dalberton that she should not be compelled to see too much of him before she had made up her mind. But he took lodgings in the neighbourhood, and both Mr. Hayward and myself were touched by his great devotion to Miss Dalberton. In fact I strongly advised her to accept his offer of marriage."

"And now, Mrs. Hayward, I come to a serious point. Did you, even then, regard Fordish Dousland as an eccentric man?"

"He was eccentric, even then, as to his dislike of meeting people."

"Did that dislike of company grow on him?"

"Decidedly yes. When they were first married, he and Mrs. Dousland would sometimes come and stay with us. But during the last two years of his life, he not only refused our invitations, but he was extremely annoyed when I tried to persuade Mrs. Dousland to come alone for a few days. In fact she only did so once."

There followed a long pause, and it was in an absolutely silent court that Sir Joseph asked his next question.

"Did you ever hear Fordish Dousland say anything about finding life worth living?"

"Yes; he declared that he did not find life worth living."

"When did he say or declare that?"

"He said so frequently during the weeks Laura Dalberton persisted in refusing his offer of marriage. He not only said that life would not be worth living if she refused to marry him, but he seriously threatened to commit suicide."

"Did you take this threat seriously?"

"Not when he first said it. In fact I remember very well, though it is a long time ago, bursting out laughing, and also how angry my laughter made him. He told me that his grandfather, when a widower, had suffered a love disappointment and, as a result, had committed suicide. He said that he had made up his mind to follow that example if Laura Dalberton persisted in her refusal."

"From what you said just now, I gather that after the marriage you did not see as much of Mrs. Dousland as you would have liked to do?"

"That is so, for I was exceedingly fond of her. In fact I regarded her, and still regard her, as my dearest friend. The fact that she was living here, at Silchester, which is only about an hour by car from Loverslea, added to my feeling of disappointment at seeing so little of her."

"Did you form the impression that Mr. Dousland was jealous of his wife's affection for you?"

Mrs. Hayward hesitated. "To that I regret I have to say yes. Mr. Dousland was also undoubtedly jealous of my two daughters' affection for his wife, and of hers for them."

The cross-examination of Mrs. Hayward by Counsel for the Crown provided the second startling sensation in the trial. But it opened quietly enough.

"Am I right in saying that during the last two years, Mrs. Hayward, you saw little or nothing of Mr. and Mrs. Dousland? Will you answer 'yes' or 'no' to my question?"

"It is impossible to answer 'yes' or 'no' to your question, for I saw Mrs. Dousland as often as I could. We sometimes met at a tea-room when I had motored here, to Silchester, for the afternoon. I do a good deal of household shopping in this town."

"Do you agree that Mr. and Mrs. Dousland got on less well as their married life went on?"

The witness hesitated, then she said firmly: "Mrs. Dousland never complained to me of her husband, apart from the fact that she found it difficult to satisfy him with regard to the kind of food he preferred. He liked foreign, or rather Italian, food, and it was a great relief to Mrs. Dousland when he engaged Angelo Terugi. Mr. Dousland enjoyed talking Italian, and from then on he did the housekeeping."

"I put it to you that Mr. Dousland was known to have changed in his manner to his wife. Were you unaware of this change?"

"Mr. Dousland was deeply disappointed at their being childless. Of that I was aware, for meeting my husband casually, he actually spoke to him of the matter."

"I must ask you not to repeat anything said to anyone but yourself."

Prosecuting Counsel smiled a wry smile, and then he quoted the famous dictum: "'What the soldier said is not evidence.'"

There was laughter at that, and the lady in the witness-box felt a surge of anger sweep athwart her. She turned towards the Judge.

"May I say something, my lord?"

"Only if it has a direct bearing on the case."

"I think, and I hope, it has."

"What is it you wish to say, madam?"

"I wish to say that, remembering Mr. Dousland's threat of suicide, I felt seriously concerned, the more so that Mrs. Dousland had confided to me that she thought their childless condition was making Mr. Dousland more and more strange and morose. Though I did not tell Mrs. Dousland so, I became full of foreboding."

The Judge observed: "You mean that you were afraid that the disappointment of being childless might make Mr. Dousland feel his life not worth living?"

"Yes, my lord."

And then, raising her voice, the witness exclaimed in quick, passionate tones: "I am convinced that Fordish Dousland poisoned himself! Further, that Laura Dousland could be suspected of murder is to me, who have now been closely intimate with her for ten years, monstrous, as well as wickedly absurd."

Sir Edward looked, as well he might, extremely disturbed, as well as angry. His further cross-examination of Mrs. Hayward suffered in consequence. The only point that he made, but it was a good point, was that the witness was obliged to admit that, during the last months of his life, the presence of the Italian servant had made a great difference, if not to the happiness, then to the comfort of Fordish Dousland. He also elicited the fact that Mrs. Hayward had come to regret deeply the marriage of her friend.

The next witness for the Defence was a young doctor named Mark Scrutton. He had been a golfing acquaintance of Fordish Dousland, and one day had come home with him, the reason being that Dousland had felt ill on the course. He had made a cursory examination, finding nothing very wrong, and had made out a prescription. All this entirely as a friend. Then, not very long before Mr. Dousland's death, he had called one Sunday afternoon, and brought some plants for the garden of 2, Kingsley Terrace, he, the witness, being a keen gardener. On that occasion he had been told that there was apparently a nest of rats in the empty house next door, and he had suggested the purchase of a new kind of vermin killer. The peculiarity of this stuff was that it caused a speedy and painless death. In his presence Mr. Dousland had told Mrs. Dousland to send for a tin. That tin had undoubtedly provided the poison which had caused Fordish Dousland's death.

"Do you recall any special circumstance connected with this vermin killer?"

"Yes."

"Describe the circumstance."

"Mr. Dousland questioned me closely and intelligently as to the effects of the poison. He seemed especially interested in the painlessness of the—well—I suppose I may call it the process."

"Did he ask if this painlessness would apply to the administration of a dose of this vermin killer to a human being?"

"Yes, he did."

The Judge intervened, and it was the last time he did so.

"Did you notice any sign of jealousy on the part of Mr. Dousland? I mean jealousy of his wife?"

"Not the slightest sign, my lord," came at once the surprised reply.

In his cross-examination of this witness Counsel for the Crown only brought out a fact already more or less obvious to anyone who had listened closely to Dr. Scrutton's evidence. This was that Mrs. Dousland had been present when the conversation as to the effects of the poison on a human being had taken place.

II

After the prisoner had exchanged the dock for the witness-box, Sir Joseph Molloy waited a perceptible moment before he began his examination. He had thrown her a quick glance, and had noted with satisfaction that her appearance would undoubtedly impress both Judge and jury favourably; a fact which was partly owing, as he was well aware, to a word or two he had exchanged with Mrs. Hayward when he had first met that lady before the opening day of the trial.

"You must see that our poor young friend looks her best during these days of ordeal," he had observed. "I mean of course with regard to her wearing becoming widow's mourning, and so on. A pretty hat is generally a great help."

"Do you really think, Sir Joseph, that the jury are likely to be influenced by the sort of clothes worn by Laura Dousland during the trial?" The tone had been contemptuous.

"I don't think it—I know it," he had barked out in his booming voice. "It isn't only the jury, it's the Judge, and for the matter of that, the gentleman I shall call my learned friend—I mean Sir Edward Burke. Being but men, after all, they are naturally influenced by the appearance of a woman prisoner."

Mrs. Hayward had looked shocked, and indeed disgusted. All the same she had carried out his order, for such it had been, and the prisoner, in her deceptively simple black chiffon frock, and the becoming hat which framed her face, had appeared on each of those long hot days when she had stood in the dock, a singularly appealing figure.

After having given all those concerned in the matter plenty of time to make themselves acquainted with his client's pleasing appearance, Sir Joseph began his examination by taking Laura Dousland briefly through the various events of her past life. They were simple, unimportant and, in a way, pathetically uninteresting events.

Her mother had been killed in an accident when she was a child, and her father, the only survivor of one of the oldest territorial untitled families of England, had run through his inheritance as a young man, and died when his only child was eighteen.

The then Laura Dalberton had been given no training of any sort, and so she had had to take, in the way of work, what she could get. For a long while she had been mother's help to a clergyman's wife; that lady had been kind to her, and it was through her that the then Miss Dalberton had procured a better position as governess to one little boy. But after two years the child had been sent to school and, fortunately for herself, she had come across Mrs. Hayward, who had at once engaged her as companion-governess to her two daughters. With Mr. and Mrs. Hayward she had lived for five years, in fact till her marriage to Fordish Dousland.

"It was because you wished to remain in touch with

Mrs. Hayward that your husband bought a house here, in Silchester?"

"Yes."

"It is a fact, is it not, that the bulk of your husband's income came from a share in a legal business, and that the income stopped at his death?"

"Yes."

"What was this life income?"

"It averaged six hundred a year."

"He had savings?"

"Yes."

"What did they amount to?"

"Fourteen hundred pounds."

"Was your husband insured?"

"No."

"Then the interest on fourteen hundred pounds is all you can look forward to in the way of income?"

"There is the house which my husband bought."

"Has it been valued?"

"Yes."

"What is its value?"

"Twelve hundred pounds."

"Should you sell the house for that amount, all this means that you will have, if your money is carefully invested, round about a hundred pounds a year?"

"Yes."

"During your four years of married life were you on good terms with your husband?"

"I think so."

"Did you regard him as eccentric, and unlike other men?"

"He was unlike any man I had met till I knew him. But I do not know that I should have called him eccentric."

"In what way was he unlike the ordinary Englishman of his class and kind?"

"Since he left college he had always spent every holiday in Italy. He was devoted to that country, and more than once after our marriage I urged him to pay a short visit there, even if, as he said, he could not afford to take me."

"He refused to leave you even for a short time?"

"Yes."

"I put it to you, Mrs. Dousland, that Mr. Dousland was distinctly strange in some of his ways. How did he occupy himself?"

"He was very fond of going to sales and auctions. In fact, almost the whole of our house was furnished in that way."

"Do you mean he never bought anything in a shop?"

"No furniture in our house, apart from what I bought with my own money, came from a shop. It was all bought by him at sales."

"In the opening speech for the Prosecution, you heard my learned friend state that you had had a good deal of domestic worry till your husband engaged an Italian, Angelo Terugi. I take it that is correct?"

"Yes."

And then to the surprise of those who listened to her clear, yet low-toned and apathetic answers, the witness added: "I suggested he should put an advertisement in the *Daily Telegraph* for an Italian servant; and we had several answers. My husband went to London to interview the applicants, and he decided Angelo Terugi was the best."

"Was Angelo Terugi a success—I mean as a servant?"

"Yes, certainly. My husband liked the Italian cooking, and for my part, I had nothing to complain of as regards his housework."

"And now I must ask you to tell me your version of what I suppose I must call the Chianti flask mystery."

For the first time in answer to a question Mrs. Dousland remained silent.

"Will you tell the jury what you think of Terugi's assertion that the Chianti flask disappeared from the tray on which he had placed it the evening before your husband's death."

Slowly and with obvious reluctance came the answer. "I am quite sure there was no flask of wine on the tray that night. It is my impression that the last bottle of the wine had been finished two or three days before that evening."

"What makes you feel so sure of that?"

The witness answered in a low voice: "Because I remember that Mr. Dousland that very evening was much annoyed that I had forgotten to order a fresh provision. That was why I at once wrote and gave the order for more to be sent."

"To what do you attribute the fact that Terugi is so positive that he did place the flask on the tray?"

"I think he is honestly mistaken, and that he believes he did put the flask on the tray."

"His assertion does not affect your belief that there was no flask there?"

"No."

"If, as a matter of fact, there was a flask on the tray, and it did disappear, what do you suppose happened to it?"

An impressive silence hung over the court for some moments. Everyone present was listening intently for the answer to that question. But those who hoped that some light might finally be thrown on the mystery were disappointed, for at last the witness said slowly: "I can form no opinion as to what could have happened to it."

"You have heard, and no doubt you knew before I said

so, that I am instructed that Terugi may well have confused what happened on the morning following your husband's death with a scene which occurred on another morning, when he missed the flask of wine from off a tray he had prepared for Mr. Dousland's supper."

In answer to that, Mrs. Dousland made a statement which took several of those present by surprise, and which certainly proved of value to the defence.

"I should not have thought of it myself, but my solicitor asked me if there had been a previous occasion when a flask of the Chianti had disappeared. I then recalled the fact that my husband one evening suspected Angelo Terugi of having drunk some of the wine, and that because of this suspicion, he hid the bottle which had been on the tray on the bottom of a hanging cupboard in my bedroom. Terugi, who was out that night, missed the flask when he went and got the tray the next morning, and was very angry when he learnt that Mr. Dousland had hidden it."

"Do you agree that a flask of Chianti as a matter of fact was missing when two dozen empty flasks had to be returned to the wine merchant?"

"I suppose so."

"You have been in prison for three months. Are you now ready to answer what my learned friend may ask you relating to this case?"

"Yes."

Counsel for the Crown began his cross-examination in thoughtful, serious tones.

"What age was your husband when he died?"

"Sixty-six."

"Did he remain as passionately devoted to you after his marriage as he was before?"

"I—I am afraid not," and the witness showed by her tone that the question had distressed her.

"I am sorry to have to follow up your answer by asking if it is not true that when your husband was no longer passionately in love with you he became morose, and was sometimes very unkind in his manner to you?"

"He had always been what I suppose is called morose, but I do not know that he meant to be unkind. He was certainly very disappointed we had no child."

And then the witness broke into convulsive sobs, and the Judge directed that she should sit down. She was offered a glass of water, which, however, she refused.

Her agitation was so great that Sir Edward Burke suggested in a kindly tone that she might prefer to postpone the rest of her cross-examination to the next day. But at that suggestion she shook her head, and said that she would be quite ready to go on in a few moments, and so she was.

"Sir Joseph Molloy elicited the fact that during the last few months of your married life, everything went better because of the presence in the house of this Italian manservant. Do you confirm this fact?"

"Yes. One reason why my husband was what I suppose some people would call unkind now and again, was that he so disliked the type of English general servant I was compelled to employ after my marriage."

"And now I must ask you certain questions concerning this bottle or flask of wine, which Terugi persists in declaring was placed by him on the tray on the night before your husband's death, and of which since then no trace has been found. Can you suggest any reason why he should tell a lie about this matter?"

"I can suggest no reason."

And then came a question to which Sir Joseph Molloy at once objected.

"Do you believe he drank the remains of the wine, and then hid, or in some way destroyed, the flask, in his fear that his master should find out what he had done?"

There was a sharp interchange of words between the two Counsel, Sir Joseph insisting that this was not a fair question. But at last it was allowed, only to elicit the tame reply: "I am much more inclined to believe that Angelo Terugi has made an honest mistake."

"When you went into your husband's room and found him dead, did it occur to you that he had committed suicide?"

The Judge leaned forward to hear the almost inaudible. "No such thought crossed my mind."

"I presume you think so now?"

"I suppose so."

"You were aware that there was this peculiar new kind of poison in the house?"

"Yes, for I ordered it myself the day that we were told of it by Dr. Scrutton."

"Of course you knew where it was kept?"

"No, I had no idea where it was kept."

The re-examination of the prisoner took but a few minutes. It was plain that she had produced an excellent impression, and her counsel desired to do nothing to dull or dim that impression. But he elicited the fact that Fordish Dousland had told his wife to lose no time in sending for this special vermin destroyer.

Next day came the final speech for the Defence. It was extremely short—the shortest speech, indeed, that Sir Joseph Molloy had ever delivered in a court of law.

He contented himself with making it clear that there was nothing that could be called real evidence against Laura Dousland, and he held up old Dr. Grant to bitter scorn.

Then he marshalled what he was careful to insist on were the facts, as supported by actual evidence, in a masterly fashion, drawing from them what appeared to be the inevitable conclusion that the prisoner's husband had committed suicide.

Perhaps the most striking passage of his speech was that in which he reminded the jury that they had been given ample opportunity of considering the credibility of the two principal witnesses, Angelo Terugi, and the prisoner herself. And he also reminded them that Mrs. Dousland—in that showing herself a high-minded, scrupulously honest gentlewoman belonging to that passing world, the old English squirearchy—had scorned to throw the slightest suspicion on the good faith of the Italian manservant. Indeed, she had gone out of her way more than once to declare her belief that Angelo Terugi thought he was telling the truth, when he had made certain assertions which would have told against her very gravely, had there been any real evidence to support the contention of the Crown that murder, and murder most foul, had been committed.

Sir Joseph concluded with boldly demanding "an acquittal for this innocent woman, with regard to whom there has already been a most cruel miscarriage of justice."

The closing speech for the Prosecution was studiously fair. In fact, the decision was left completely to the jury, and, to the disappointment of many of the men and women in his audience, Sir Edward Burke scarcely touched upon the mystery of the Chianti flask. But those members of the Bar who were listening intently to each of his measured sentences, realised that he had now come round to the belief Angelo Terugi had made an honest mistake, and that, as had been asserted by the prisoner, no wine had been placed on the tray on the evening preceding Fordish Dousland's death, owing to the simple reason that the provision of Chianti had been exhausted a day or two before. That Mrs. Dousland had ordered a couple of dozen flasks the very evening before her husband's death, had been proved by the Defence.

He concluded with the words: "British law is very merciful. But with regard to a case of murder, it is justice, not mercy, that matters. The verdict rests entirely with you, gentlemen. It is your duty to act according to the conclusion at which you have arrived after carefully considering the evidence. If you think the evidence is not conclusive, I say do not hesitate to acquit the prisoner. Give effect to the results of your deliberations. Once you have done that, you will have done your duty, and justice will have been done."

Following in a sense the lead of Counsel for the Crown, the Judge also left the great decision, as to whether the prisoner should be declared innocent or guilty, to the jury. He, however, went over the whole of the evidence in detail, although those who heard him found it impossible to divine which way his own mind inclined. He did bring out, however, what he evidently regarded as a matter of fact, very clearly. This was that the question lay entirely between the dead man and his wife, and that no suspicion could, or should, rest on Angelo Terugi. He quoted Laura Dousland's own admission that the greater part of her married life had been unhappy. She had been for four years a young woman tied to a husband over thirty years older than herself, and Terugi, although an unwilling witness, had admitted that he had often heard his master speaking in an unkind way to his mistress. On the other hand, apart from the obvious truth that the two had not been really happy together, no motive had been suggested why this young and gently-nurtured woman should have committed so fearful a crime.

Turning then to the question as to whether Fordish Dousland had taken his own life, the Judge reminded the jury of what Dr. Scrutton had stated on oath, concerning the conversation which had taken place when he had unfortunately advised the purchase of the poison which had undoubtedly been the cause of the death concerning which there had now been held two investigations. It was clear from the medical man's evidence that Fordish Dousland had shown a morbid interest in the action of the new poison, and had specially enquired if its action was also painless in the case of a human being.

The Judge also recalled Dousland's threat of self-destruction made to Mrs. Hayward, should the girl, with whom he was then passionately in love, refuse to become his wife. Not only had he uttered that threat, but he had shown himself angry and surprised when his listener had refused to take it seriously. To quote the actual words used in the summing-up: "Fordish Dousland no longer loved his wife. He was bitterly disappointed of his desire to have a child. It is possible that he felt life was no longer worth living, and that he made up his mind to take his life without considering the pain, the distress, and above all the suspicion, that his wicked and selfish act was likely to leave behind him."

The Judge concluded what had been a model of what a summing-up ought to be, that is, a clear, lucid statement of all the circumstances which have been revealed at a trial, by impressing on the jury that they must be satisfied beyond all reasonable doubt that Mrs. Dousland had poisoned her husband.

"Are you satisfied that you can find a verdict of wilful murder against her? Although she is a woman, she comes under the same laws as everyone else. If she is guilty of murder she must pay the same penalty as any man. Be not moved by sympathy, be not moved by fear. There must be men among you who would have given much not to have been in this case. I have the same feeling. But we are all bound under our oaths—the oath that I took, and the oath that you took—to do justice. Justice means to acquit her, if you have a doubt. Justice means to convict her, if she is guilty.

"Gentlemen, may you have strength given you to come to the true conclusion. This woman cannot be tried again. May you have strength given you to do that which is, and will be, justice, if you do it on the lines which I have indicated to you. Then, whatever the result may be, you will have at all events the testimony of a clear conscience."

The jury were absent forty minutes, and there swept a wave of pessimism through the court. Almost every man and woman present on this, the last day of the trial, felt increasingly anxious and doubtful. Here and there stood or sat a man who thought the verdict should be "Guilty." Among such were the Coroner, and the members of the Coroner's jury, who had decided that Laura Dousland must be sent for trial. But so strong was the feeling for the prisoner, that this small minority kept their innermost thoughts to themselves.

At last there came a stir through the packed court. The slight sable-clad figure reappeared in the dock. Laura Dousland looked grave but unafraid, though in her set white face only the dark eyes which were her one fine feature, appeared alive.

As the jury came filing back, only a very stupid spectator could have had any doubt as to their decision.

"Gentlemen of the Jury, are you agreed upon your verdict?"

There was a pause. Then the foreman of the jury answered: "We are."

"Do you find Laura Dousland guilty, or not guilty, of wilful murder?"

"Not guilty."

"Let the prisoner be discharged."

A moment of tense silence, and then followed a scene unknown in modern criminal annals, for both men and women leaped up on the benches and chairs, so as to see the clearer the little figure who still stood, rigid, in the dock, staring as if fascinated, not at the jury, to whom she owed her life, but at the Judge, who, robed in scarlet and ermine, was gazing in surprise at the scene.

"Clear the court!"

No one appeared to take any notice of the stern injunction. But it had an effect.

The gate of the dock was swung open, and there followed a rush of the now freed prisoner's friends and sympathisers, from every part of the court, while Laura Dousland was being assisted kindly, and even tenderly, down the three steps by a wardress who had always firmly believed in her innocence.

Sir Joseph Molloy elbowed his way through the dense crowd. He took the now trembling young woman's hand in his, and bent to hear her whisper, "I know it was you who saved me from being hung."

But there was no fervour or excitement in her almost inaudible voice. She looked dazed, and there rose in the great advocate's breast a feeling of authentic pity of a kind he had never felt for any other woman with whom he had come in contact during his long career.

"What you must do now is to go away for a long rest, my poor little friend. And earnestly, most earnestly, do I beg of you to put the past behind you, and forget—everything."

He gazed feelingly into the large dark eyes, out of which, now, all the light and life seemed to have gone, and there came back to him a vivid recollection of the interview he had insisted on having with Laura Dousland on the eve of her trial for murder. She had told him, then, that she did not care what happened to her. And she had exclaimed, in answer to his forcibly uttered words of rebuke: "You don't understand—you can't know—how terrible everything has been for me, and for so long a time. If you did know, you would not wonder that I don't care what happens to me now."

He had left her, feeling very uneasy, and yet through the long weary days of her trial, she had shown no signs of the morbid misery which had possessed her during his anxious hour with her in the prison. And when there had come the dread ordeal of the witness-box, and she had answered first his own questions, and then those far more probing interrogations in the course of the cross-examination conducted by the Counsel for the Crown, she had appeared entirely composed.

Meanwhile, in another part of the court a distressing scene was taking place. Mrs. Hayward, who had looked so strong, and had proved herself so confident, when giving evidence for her friend, had slipped down on the floor in a dead faint, as the words "Not guilty" had been pronounced by the foreman of the jury.

Dr. Scrutton had been standing between her and her husband during the torturing time of waiting for the verdict, and he had at once applied restoratives. Then, when she had revived, he had helped to get her out of the hot stuffy atmosphere of the Assize Court by a back way to a street where stood the motor-car which had been waiting all morning in readiness to bear Laura Dousland away to Loverslea, the Haywards' beautiful home—if, that is, all went well.

John Hayward had never doubted, not even for a fleeting moment, that his daughters' one-time governess would be cleared of the charge which, if hideous, seemed to him as it had done to all those who knew her, incredibly absurd. But Alice Hayward, especially yesterday and to-day, had felt filled with awful forebodings, and every miscarriage of justice of which she had ever heard and read, had risen full of silent menace before her as she had listened to the closing speech for the Prosecution and to the Judge's summing-up.

She had gazed into the stolid impassive faces of the twelve jurymen, and it had seemed to her awful indeed that the freedom or shameful death of a fellow human being should rest with that group of self-satisfied looking, mentally-limited men. So it had come to pass that as the minutes, which seemed like hours to her fevered brain, wore themselves away, her state of fear and of suspense grew more and more tense, till the sudden relief brought with it blackness, followed by oblivion.

Thus it was that neither Laura Dousland's only real woman friend, nor Dr. Scrutton, who, if not a friend, had given on her behalf evidence of inestimable value, were among the group of people who were now pressing round the freed prisoner, several of them moved to hysterical tears by their joy at her acquittal. From the Market Square outside came waves of roaring exultation, and at last, a police official, Inspector Jarrett, muttered something aside to Sir Joseph Molloy. At once that gentleman raised his voice: "Now all you dear kind people—fall back and let Mrs. Dousland get away. She deserves a rest!"

He and Inspector Jarrett each took Laura by an arm, and swiftly they led her through the part of the court reserved for the officials connected with the legal conduct of the cases being tried there. Behind the bench which had just been quitted by the Judge, the inspector unlocked a narrow door leading first into a small antechamber, and then into a low passage which led into a quiet thoroughfare which was now deserted, save for some half-dozen cars.

"I'll send one of these chauffeurs to find a taxi, and I'll take you where you want to go!" exclaimed the inspector to the ex-prisoner.

"My car is the one over there," said Sir Joseph quickly. "It can take Mrs. Dousland wherever she likes; but then it must come back here, for I've got to go to London. My wife, who has her own motor, is staying on with my daughter, till to-morrow, with Mr. and Mrs. Hayward at Loverslea."

Meanwhile, the woman by his side was standing with bent head, and taking no notice of what was being said. But a moment later she was half carried, half pushed, into a luxurious car, and Inspector Jarrett took his place beside the chauffeur.

Now he had in his pocket, as it happened, the latchkey to No. 2, Kingsley Terrace, where the tragedy had taken place. He himself had searched the house from garret to scullery, in the hope of finding the Chianti flask round which had then seemed to centre so much mystery. But he was now convinced that there had been no such flask on the tray which had been prepared for Fordish Dousland on that fatal night. Foreigners, according to his idea, seldom tell the truth, and never when it is to their advantage to tell a lie. He believed that Angelo Terugi (what a name for a man!) had of course drunk up what remained of the wine. Why he might even have taken the missing flask to refresh himself when on the way to London on his weekly holiday? What more natural that at the police-station the Italian, afraid of admitting the truth, had lied? Once the chap had done that, he had had to stick to his lie, and no doubt it was Terugi poor Mrs. Dousland had had to thank for the cruel wicked way she had been treated.

He, Inspector Jarrett, had had the job of arresting her; and now it seemed to him a kind of poetic justice that it was he who should escort her back to her home after her triumphant acquittal.

They had soon left the centre of the cathedral city where stood the Assize Court, and they were now driving through the outskirts of the town, moving rapidly down dreary-looking, ill-kept roads. At last, "Those three houses standing over there by themselves are Kingsley Terrace, and we are bound for the middle one," observed the inspector to Sir Joseph's chauffeur.

The three narrow houses were built of brown bricks, and the windows and canopied front doors had surrounds of weather-stained, grey, painted stucco, and looked unutterably forlorn and ugly.

The centre house, that is number two, looked in better condition than its neighbours, for someone had kept the front grass plot tidy, and had clipped the quick-growing hedge which hid the black railings. But the eight steps leading to the front door were dirty, and the red paint on the door had become discoloured.

The smart chauffeur could hardly believe his eyes. Had the lady who had become such a heroine, and whose acquittal was now blowing such a gale of rejoicing and delight over the whole of Silchester really lived in this poverty-stricken-looking house? It seemed incredible to him. Yet, like so many other things that appear incredible, it was true.

The motor stopped before the mean-looking little iron gate, and the police inspector, stepping down, opened the door of the car. A moment later Laura Dousland stood in the sunlight, looking so pale and ill that he wondered if he had been right to bring her to a place which must be so full, to her, of tragic memories.

He felt relieved when she said: "I'm quite all right now," and smiled a wavering smile.

"It seemed best to bring you home, ma'am, for a little while at any rate, because I don't suppose that anybody would think of looking for you here. If you'd gone anywhere else, even to the Deanery, all the reporters would have been after you. You don't want to be seeing any newspaper chaps just yet, do you, Mrs. Dousland?"

"Oh no, no," she murmured, as he was opening the gate.

She hadn't cared where she was being taken, so long as she could be alone when she got there. The Haywards had intended carrying her off to Loverslea, and hazily she wondered, now, what had become of them. The Dean of Silchester had been keenly interested in her case, and had become one of her strongest public supporters. His wife had come to see her twice in prison, and had vied with Mrs. Hayward in expressing, even in public, her firm belief in the poor young woman's innocence. So no doubt, Mrs. Dousland would have been warmly welcomed at the Deanery had she gone there from the Assize Court. But she was oh! so relieved to know that she was to be alone, even here, for at any rate a little while.

Inspector Jarrett was now helping her up the steep steps which led to what had been for four years her front door.

"I've got to get back to the Assize Court as quick as possible, Mrs. Dousland. For one thing Sir Joseph Molloy wants his car, and for another I must get in touch by 'phone with Mr. Hayward. I suppose you know what happened to Mrs. Hayward?"

Laura looked startled. What could have happened to that good stalwart friend of hers?

"Mrs. Hayward was so fearfully anxious about the verdict, that the 'Not guilty' was hardly out of the chap's mouth when she fell down in a faint. What's more, Dr. Scrutton had quite a job bringing her round, for she's by way of being a stout lady, and I don't suppose her heart's any too good."

For the first time since the return of the jury into court, Laura Dousland showed emotion; there even crept a little colour into her pallid cheeks. "What a dreadful thing—I *am* sorry," she murmured.

"Why yes, ma'am, I expect you are. Otherwise—why she'd have been the first, wouldn't she, to offer you her congratulations? Mr. Hayward, now I come to think of it, did say he'd come back for you the minute he'd taken her home. But it's a good step to Loverslea, and I must try and get in touch with him, or he'll not know where to find you. If I leave you now, I'll catch him all the sooner."

He unlocked the door, and then held out the latchkey, with a somewhat shamed expression on his honest face.

"Now, is there anything more I can do for you, ma'am? Would you like me to get you a glass of water from downstairs?"

She shook her head. "I shall be quite comfortable. I had some water while I was waiting for—"

She did not complete the sentence, while she had been waiting for the jury to come back. Oh! how she had longed then to be alone.

She put out her hand blindly, seeking the handle of a door on the right of the narrow passage. But it was the inspector who found the handle and, opening the door, ushered her through into the sitting-room.

"I'll sit down in here for a little while," she murmured.

If only he would go away! Yet he, too, had been wonderfully, oppressively, kind, and indeed she felt grateful to him.

She made a determined effort to appear unconcerned, though everything seemed to be spinning round her, "I'm afraid I've given you a lot of trouble, first and last, inspector? Will you thank Sir Joseph Molloy for having allowed me to use his car?" she said quietly.

"Why, certainly I will, ma'am."

He looked round him dubiously. He had realised, during the minute search of this house he had made weeks ago, what a—well, *horrid* was the only word he could think of in connection with this room. It was over-full of furniture, but nothing matched, and everything seemed queerly incongruous. Fordish Dousland must have been an odd sort of elderly gentleman, and no mistake.

"Will you be all right here?"

"Perfectly all right," and then she asked a half-question which struck him as strange. "I suppose Angelo Terugi isn't living here now?"

"As a matter of fact, he has been sleeping here, Mrs. Dousland. We didn't quite know what to do with him, as he was the leading witness for the Prosecution. He declared, too, that he had a right to three months' notice."

"That was true," she said quickly.

"I don't think he's had much of a time, for there's been a very bitter feeling against him in the town; all Silchester has been for you, ma'am, if you understand my meaning."

"I know that," she said, "and—and I've felt very grateful to everybody."

"I'll say good-bye now, Mrs. Dousland. I hope that your troubles are quite over, and for ever, too."

She muttered an inaudible "Thank you," and then he left her, standing in her own drawing-room, and with her own latchkey in her hand.

All the same, as he shut the front door behind him, Inspector Jarrett felt uneasy. He wished he could have brought some kind-feeling woman along with him to cheer up that poor soul a bit.

III

Laura did not sit down, tired and giddy though she felt, after Inspector Jarrett had left the house. She continued standing, and as she heard the car move away from the front gate she slowly looked round the room.

The air struck dank and even chill, on this summer day, for each of the two narrow French windows was tightly closed. Everything about her appeared at once familiar and unfamiliar, and awoke memories of past days which had been full of pain, and even of despair. She told herself that it was something to know that those days, at any rate, had gone for ever, though the release had been bought at so awful a cost.

Fordish Dousland's mysterious death had taken place during the night of January the twenty-seventh. His widow had been arrested on March the tenth, it was now June the ninth; and the three months had been filled with such long drawn-out misery and shame, as well as extraordinary happenings, that they had seemed like years.

Suddenly a sensation of fear clutched at her heart. Why

had she been brought here? She could not remember, and she thought it the stranger because it had been arranged by Mr. Hayward that after her acquittal—never once had he budged from his firm belief that her innocence would be triumphantly vindicated—she should go straight with him and his wife to Loverslea, the beautiful historic country house, about thirty miles from Silchester, which he had bought some ten years before. Then she remembered what she had been told about Alice. Alice Hayward had fainted. What an amazing thing! But soon someone would come here and take her to Loverslea. She was to stay there as long as she liked, "getting over it all," as Mrs. Hayward had put it.

And now, suddenly, Laura Dousland recalled that phrase, and there came over her face a bitter expression. What did the woman who had uttered those kindly, confident words know of what "all" had meant, and would mean, as long as life endured? Yet in a sense she had put up so brave a fight for the sake of John and Alice Hayward. It was because they believed so absolutely in her innocence, and had thrown themselves with such passionate zeal into all that concerned her defence, that she had battled as she had done, not only during those long days of what someone had called her full-dress trial, but during the nightmare waking hours spent by her under remand, in prison.

The opening of the trial—but she had not troubled to let anyone know the truth as to that—had been a relief. And the standing in the witness-box answering the questions put to her, had appeared child's play in comparison with what she had had to endure during what had been called the preparation of her case.

At last she made her way to a couch her husband had bought at the last sale he had ever attended. It was deep and roomy, and had gone for what Mr. Dousland had called at the time "a mere song."

She sank down on to it, feeling all at once very weak. She had found it impossible for many days to eat in a normal way, though the food sent into the prison had been more to her liking than the Italian dishes of which her husband had been so fond.

At times, though not as often as is, according to their own admission, the case with most of those men and women who are about to be tried on a charge of murder, she had been haunted during her nights in prison by a terrifying vision of shameful and cruel death. But that vision had not risen even once to unnerve her during the course of the trial. During the last few days she had been curiously unafraid and, for the most part, as if deadened to all that was going on about her.

Now she tried to remember how exceedingly kind people had been to her during that time of fear, of suspense, and of horror. Every member of the big provincial firm of lawyers engaged on her behalf had behaved as if he was her friend. As for her fellow-townspeople, there had actually been talk of a defence fund being raised in Silchester. But though she had expressed and had felt true gratitude for all the sympathy lavished on her, she had often reminded herself how much a thousandth part of the interest and kindness lavished on her now, would have meant to her during the four dreary years she had lived in their midst.

As a bride she had been in fleeting touch with quite a number of people in the cathedral city. But the Douslands lived in a new quarter, in an unattractive house, and the master of the house appeared ungenial, and cared for none of the things that interested the other men of his age in

Silchester. That was the reason why in no case had acquaintance continued or ripened into friendship.

The fearful drama of an arrest for murder, and the early passionate advocacy of a popular newspaper in favour of an innocent woman who had been victim of a gross miscarriage of justice, had alone caused the neighbours of one who was gently nurtured and attractive, to feel and show interest in her personality.

But now Laura no longer desired friendship or human companionship. All she craved was peace and solitude. In her prison cell she had been alone for long hours; yet she had never felt alone, for at all moments of the day and night someone had the right to intrude upon her, either from a wish to "cheer her up" (Oh! how she had come to hate those three words!) or from a hidden, sadistic curiosity.

But as Sir Joseph Molloy had impressed on her, during those few moments when he had held her hand clasped closely in his, she must force herself to forget all that had happened in the last few months. That, maybe, she could achieve, but there were other happenings she could never forget, and now this cheerless sitting-room brought back a flood of turgid memories.

Many a time, when sitting here staring into the gas fire, she had thought with bitter anger of how Mrs. Hayward had almost forced her to marry Fordish Dousland. Alice Hayward, a happy woman, married to the lover of her youth, who was a normal, kindly-natured man, had spoken with all the valour of ignorance when she had said to her young governess: "After all, what have you got to look forward to? This man adores you, and marriage means security."

Laura had never told, and now she felt less inclined than

ever to tell, her friend at what cost that security had been bought.

Laura Dousland was exceptionally intelligent; and as she had been entirely thrown on herself since the day she had begun to earn her living, she had fashioned her own philosophy of life, and made up her mind, when still in her early twenties, about much which remains uncertain and nebulous with most women.

As Laura Dalberton, she had abandoned all belief in revealed religion, but, naturally reticent, she had kept her unorthodox views strictly to herself. Also, the average British father, sufficiently old-fashioned to prefer a home education for his daughters, would not care to entrust that education to an agnostic. Though the Haywards themselves motored off to golf early on most Sundays in the year, they expected their governess, as a matter of course, to take their children to the parish church. During the weeks and months of his courtship, Fordish Dousland had always accompanied the schoolroom party, and Laura had been somewhat surprised to find, after their marriage, that the thought of going to church never even crossed his mind. Now and again she herself would attend the cathedral services, but that was only to escape for a while her husband's perpetual presence about her.

Suddenly she heard the door behind the couch on which she was sitting swing open, and a tremor ran through her. What if she were wrong, and there is, in truth, a life beyond the grave? Were that so, it would be like Fordish Dousland to return and confront her with cold, mocking eyes.

Everything that had happened to her since his death had

been so strange, so unexpected, and so terrible, that nothing, she felt, should surprise her any more.

She sat quite still, and then she felt a violent commotion go through her ailing weary body, for it was the Italian, Angelo Terugi, who had so nearly sworn her life away, who walked round the edge of the couch and stood before her. How foolish of her not to have remembered that he was still sleeping here, and so must have a latchkey admitting him to the house!

She looked up into his dark, inscrutable face.

"If the signora pleases, I will go away to-day."

She was conscious of an intense feeling of relief, a relief so acute that it was almost pain. But years of self-repression had taught Laura Dousland never to show what she was really feeling; so all she said was: "You must do whatever suits you best, Angelo." She waited a moment, then added, with an effort: "I know you have had a trying time, and I will, of course, give you an excellent character."

"I voyage to Venetia, signora, and after a leetle holiday, I find an English family. I have my good characters here," and he brought out of a pocket two or three crumpled-looking envelopes.

She flushed painfully. That meant that he did not want her to give him a testimonial.

"I think your wages have been paid week by week?"

"Mr. Hayward, he has been a very kind gentleman."

He was looking down at her now with a curious expectant look. She had never seen that look on Angelo Terugi's face before; it made her feel oddly uneasy.

"I thought perhaps the signora will give me a little present. It costs a great deal of money for me to return to Italy."

Ah! that was it. He wanted money. And then she

reminded herself again that he had been put to a great deal of unpleasantness all these weeks. She had grown to know the man, and even to like him, during the months he had been in her husband's employment. Always he had treated her with deference and respect; very differently, that is, to the women servants who had succeeded one another at almost monthly intervals during her married life. Yes, poor though she was, Angelo Terugi should be given a present, and a good present, too.

"I know you have had a great deal of trouble, and I will give you the utmost I can afford," she said firmly.

"Thank you, signora."

She wondered what he would expect, also what she could afford, and at last she said: "I will give you fifty pounds."

A look of satisfaction, even of joy, flashed into his face. She had never seen him look so pleased. He, too, no doubt, had led a strangely repressed life.

"I cannot give you the money to-day, but I think I can give it you to-morrow."

She was telling herself that Mr. Hayward would most certainly advance her fifty pounds, if she found she could not yet draw on the comparatively small sum of money which would remain after she had paid the costs of her defence.

"I will either send you the money, or ask you to come out to Loverslea. You know there is a coach line close to the park gates?"

Laura Dousland had always been kind, and thoughtful for the comfort of those about her. That was one of the things which had endeared her to her various employers in the old days. She was always willing to do more than her bond called for.

She felt as if the blood was now coming back to her brain;

that fearful feeling of being as if stunned was gradually leaving her; but with the return of life came pain.

She held out her hand to this man whose insistence on the disappearance of so apparently unimportant an object as a flask of wine had nearly brought her to an agonising and shameful death. Yet, even so, she held out her hand with a friendly gesture.

"If I don't see you again, Angelo, I should like to say good-bye to you now."

Did he hesitate a fraction of a second before he put out his long brown hand? She thought so, and felt a touch of pain. But when his fingers met hers, he exclaimed in a concerned tone: "The signora is cold—very cold!"

She tried to smile, "I am more tired than cold, Angelo, and after a rest I shall be all right." Something prompted her to add: "I shall have to work, of course, for Mr. Dousland's income stopped when he died."

There was something else she longed to say to this man. Yet the thought of saying it frightened her, and while she was hesitating, the Italian turned away and left the room. As he closed the door Laura remembered how pleasant she had found his quiet, noiseless ways, after the rough impudent woman who had been his predecessor.

She lay back and shut her eyes. She felt passionate relief in the knowledge that soon Angelo Terugi would be out of England, and that he intended to get a situation in Italy. Almost all responsible people insist on a personal character or reference, and when Angelo had first come into the room she had told herself with dismay that for a time, at least, he would be connected with her unhappy story, and that without any fault of his own. How fortunate that he had had the shrewdness to realise how uncomfortable that would be for himself. She wondered if he realised that all England had rung with his name ever since a Chianti flask had come to be associated with the case. Indeed, it was a popular newspaper who had first discovered the importance of Terugi's statement as to the disappearance of the wine.

The telephone bell rang, and she started violently. Then she stood up and, trying to regain some measure of composure, walked across to the instrument. As, however, she took up the receiver, her heart lightened, for it was John Hayward's voice, which exclaimed: "Is Mrs. Dousland there?"

"It's I—Laura," she breathed.

The Haywards had begun to call her by her Christian name when her engagement to Fordish Dousland had been finally achieved. After having been for five years "Miss Dalberton," she had suddenly become "dear Laura," just because she was going to be married. She had sometimes since remembered, with a bitter sensation of self-contempt, what pleasure that trifling fact had given her.

"Whatever made you go back to that awful house, my dear girl? Still, I'm glad you did, as now I know where to find you. We couldn't think where you'd gone, or how to track you down, especially as you've so many friends and admirers in Silchester! It was Alice who said she thought it quite on the cards you had gone—" he hesitated a moment before he brought out the word "home."

Even he, unimaginative as are most men of his class and generation, realised how painful must be this poor soul's associations with the ill-built uncomfortable mid-Victorian house where she had spent the whole of her married life.

He went on quickly: "Alice fainted right away when she heard that 'Not guilty'! She hadn't slept a wink all night, and

I didn't sleep much, for she *would* talk, starting new hares all the time about that Chianti flask mystery, as everyone calls it. Yet, as I told her again and again, the truth's not hard to come by, is it, my dear? *That bottle of wine was never there.* That's the top and bottom of it, isn't it?"

He waited a moment, but as his invisible listener said nothing, he called out: "I'll come and fetch you right away! Alice is simply aching to see you."

"Thank you," she said gratefully.

But John Hayward had not finished yet. "By the way, we'll have to think about getting rid of that house of yours. I'm afraid you won't get as much as Dousland gave for it. Still, we'll talk it all over in the next few days, for there's all the time there is, now, thank God. So long, my dear—"

As Laura walked back towards the couch, her foot slipped, and she nearly fell down on to the floor. She had never been over-strong, and now she was physically very weak.

Wearily she lay down again and, as she did so, the door opened and Angelo Terugi again entered the room.

He held a hot bottle in one hand, and a rug in the other. The woman lying on the couch knew it was his hot bottle, his rug. Silently he came up to her, put the bottle near her feet, and then covered them with the rug; and it was as if this kindly act of charity unsealed a spring in Laura Dousland's heart. Tears coursed down her face, and Angelo, the while, stood looking down at her, while on his grave dark countenance there came an expression of deep concern and pity.

"*Poverina*," he muttered, and then again, "*Poverina*."

She made a great effort, and drying her eyes exclaimed: "Angelo, I feel I must say something to you!"

"Yes, signora?"

"Surely you know that there was no wine on the tray you brought upstairs the evening before—" and then with a perceptible gasp she ended her sentence, her question, with "—Mr. Dousland died?"

He looked at her deprecatingly.

"I did not remember, signora; but the police they force me to say 'yes,' that the flask was there."

She said gravely: "I felt sure it was the police made you say that."

"Then the signor he did hide the wine? There was some in the flask that day—that I do remember," and he looked down at her fixedly.

"Yes," she said in a low voice. "Mr. Dousland hid it after lunch, in the locked cupboard in the dining-room."

For a few moments they gazed at one another, and she thought he was going to say something more. But he stood mute till, at last, he crept silently from the room. A few moments later she heard him going upstairs to his ill-furnished attic.

Lying back she again closed her eyes. She was glad that she had forced him to admit what she had felt sure all along was the truth. That he had been badgered, that is, by the police into telling that dangerous lie.

She closed her eyes, and there came back to her with uncanny vividness all that had happened on the wintry morning after she had gone into her husband's room and found him lying dead.

She seemed to see herself, as if it had been someone else, going up the steep uncarpeted stairs that led from the lobby into which opened Fordish Dousland's room, to the Italian's sleeping place. She saw that woman, who appeared at once so like and so utterly unlike the woman she now felt herself to be, knock on the unpainted wooden door of the attic, and heard that now stranger exclaim: "Angelo! Please get up and dress at once, for something terrible has happened—Mr. Dousland is dead."

What had followed after that? Slowly, now, all that had taken place immediately after she had called Angelo Terugi came back. But this time she no longer mentally watched her own wraith. Memory took the place of visualisation.

In the telephone-book now lying by the instrument in a corner of this room, she had sought, in her fear and distress, for the name of the young doctor who had been to the house a couple of times. Then she had remembered that his number was under another name.

It had taken her a little while to find it, for she was feeling very agitated, indeed terrified. And when she had got through, it was only to be answered in an old man's fretful voice. "Dr. Scrutton is out. Can I do anything for you? I'm Dr. Grant."

Ah! something ought to have told her that this was the voice of a potential enemy. But instead of saying, "I'd rather wait till Dr. Scrutton comes in," she had called back: "I'd be glad if you would come as soon as possible, for I'm afraid—"

And then that cross voice had barked out: "What are you afraid of? I can't hear you. What's the matter? I'm not up yet."

Desperately she had answered: "I'm afraid my husband is dead."

Without a word of sympathy or of kindness, Dr. Grant had asked for the address, and then after what had seemed a long, long time he had arrived and told her that yes, Fordish Dousland was dead. Looking back, she knew, now, that he had been both suspicious and puzzled that morning. But she hadn't known it then.

There had followed three weeks of what had seemed almost unnatural peace, at Loverslea with Polly, her favourite ex-pupil, as only company, for Mr. and Mrs. Hayward were at Monte Carlo. But the very day after the return home of the master and mistress of the house, the police inspector from Silchester had motored out there, and in their presence she had learnt of the exhumation of Fordish Dousland's body, of the result of an examination made by the public analyst, and of her presence being required at the inquest which was about to take place.

She did not now remember much of the enquiry held by a Coroner who had already made up his mind as to her guilt, for she had fallen ill—sufficiently ill with a high temperature and an irregular pulse to make it impossible for her to be present on the concluding day of the inquest. It was owing to this perhaps merciful fact that her arrest had taken place at Loverslea.

Though both the Haywards had been astounded at the awful charge brought against their one-time governess, and though they had both begun from the first moment to try and establish her innocence, it was the wife who had thrown herself with passion into the case. It was she who had constantly interviewed the lawyers who had been engaged on Laura's behalf, and she who had insisted that Sir Joseph Molloy should be chosen as Counsel for the Defence. If Alice Hayward had persuaded her friend to marry Fordish Dousland, she had also gone far to save her life when her friend had been accused of having murdered that same man, Fordish Dousland.

At last Laura rose from the couch, and stood trying to gather up courage to face life again.

There was a panel of looking-glass let into the wall of

the sitting-room between the two windows. It had cost practically nothing, for the mirror gave a slightly distorted reflection. She had always shrunk from seeing herself in it; still, it would serve, now, to show her how the long ordeal she had just endured had told on her appearance.

Walking across to the mirror, she placed herself with her face to the light, and looked at herself searchingly.

It was the first time Laura Dousland had done such a thing for—it would be scarcely an exaggeration to say for years. Among the instructions Sir Joseph Molloy had given her friend, Alice Hayward, she knew there had been that she must procure a becoming black dress and hat, so as to look her best when in the witness-box. Mrs. Hayward had spoken of this advice, or rather order, with scoffing contempt. Still, the pretty frock and hat had been procured, and she, Laura, was wearing them now. But gazing intently at her reflection in the glass, she realised that she appeared fearfully worn, old, and ill.

At no time of her life had she thought much of her looks or, indeed, of herself, in the way most girls and women think of their outward appearance. Yet, now and again, sometimes at long intervals, a man had felt for her so violent an attraction as, for the time being, to appear, nay, maybe to become, what is called mad. But her husband's crazy passion had not outlasted many months of married life, and at first she had felt bewildered by the change in him. Then suddenly she had known the reason.

His love had turned to something like hate because there had been on her side no response of the kind for which he hungered. Even so, to the end of their joint life, enough had remained of that greedy earthy passion to cause him to feel jealous of even a few smiling words bestowed on another man. Once, to her indignant anger, he had tried to make her say that John Hayward had "liked" her. Also he had found it impossible to believe that she had never been in love, and that what he called her coldness towards him was in no way her fault.

Fordish Dousland discouraged visitors, but now and again some man who had belonged to his professional life would propose himself to lunch or tea, and then it became her duty to provide a better meal than usual. But never was such a guest invited to sleep even for one night at 2, Kingsley Terrace.

John Hayward had given his old schoolfellow as a wedding present a life membership of the best golf club in the neighbourhood, and Dousland was wont to go there now and again. But the only fellow-member he had ever brought home with him had been Dr. Scrutton, and that only because he had felt ill when on the course. Indeed, it was the doctor who had suggested accompanying him home.

When for the second time Dr. Scrutton had come to Kingsley Terrace he had brought some bulbs with him, for he was a keen gardener, and on the occasion of his first visit he had evidently been surprised at the bareness of the garden behind the house. Laura remembered the second time Mark Scrutton had come, because she and he had worked really hard, planting the bulbs in the small narrow border which ran round the paved garden, as well as in the carved marble Italian well-head her husband had bought at a sale because it reminded him of Italy. In that queer narrow paved garden there were various pieces of statuary, including a marble faun and an old Roman stone head of Hercules.

Turning away from the mirror, she went up to what had been, and in a sense still was, her bedroom, for she shrank from taking to Loverslea any of the clothes she had worn in prison. Also she knew that in a cupboard in that room was a fitted suitcase. It had been a wedding present from one of the Haywards' acquaintances, a rich bachelor named Hal Ford, who at the time had been in thrall to a married woman. He had felt much attracted by the young governess and, to the surprise of her employers, had expressed both wonder and regret at her marriage. Mrs. Hayward had been astonished at the value of his gift.

As Laura opened the door of the bedroom, she stopped on the threshold, for everything therein roused in her a sensation of repugnance, even of loathing. Yet many of the young matrons and girls who had come to Loverslea, when she was leading her placid life there as governess to Emma and Mary Hayward, would have thought it a delightful room, for this bed-chamber was in astounding contrast to the rest of the ill-furnished house.

The most prominent object was the bed. It was low and wide, with a satinwood painted head, and on it lay a pale pink satin eiderdown, covered with an embroidered muslin coverlet. The dressing-table was also of satinwood, inlaid and painted with amorini; and on the thick costly pile carpet stood four painted chairs. There was a narrow swinging mirror, and a hanging cupboard, copies of good old pieces. Everything there had come from a London shop famous for its luxurious bedroom furniture.

Mr. Hayward had given her a handsome cheque as wedding present, and at her future husband's suggestion, the whole of that money, with more added from her savings, had been spent over what was to be her bedroom in the house he had just bought at Silchester, without allowing her any say in the matter.

To the bride's naïve astonishment, this room had been the first to be furnished, and even now she still remembered the man who had brought the furniture from London exclaiming, with a laugh: "You'll have to have a grand drawing-room to live up to this 'ere apartment, missy!" She had already begun to suspect that the rest of her new home would not "live up" to her bed-chamber, but she had not known she would come back from her honeymoon to an almost bare house, with a husband whose only real pleasure was to attend sales, and pick up what he called "bargains."

Laura Dousland also recalled the first time Alice Hayward came to Kingsley Terrace after the marriage, and her look of incredulous amazement when she had entered this room. But true to British upper-middle-class tradition, all she had said was: "That looks a very nice and comfortable bed, my dear. I always say beds and bedding are what really matter in a house."

With memories of the past crowding on her, Laura walked slowly across towards the deep cupboard, passing on the way the door which led into what had been her husband's room.

She stayed her steps and looked at the door. No one had known, and no one would ever know, anything of the more intimate side of her married life. Her only woman friend, indeed her only friend in the world, had been and was Mrs. Hayward, and she was not the kind of person to whom even a natural babbler would offer confidences of a certain kind.

Slowly, and moving about the room as if she were an old woman, she packed the suitcase in readiness for her stay at Loverslea, and she had only just finished, when she heard the sound of the horn which belonged to the car Mr. Hayward always drove himself. Oh! how her spirit, and even her body, shrank, from the thought of meeting the big jovial man. Even so, she hastened out of the room, for if she waited upstairs till the bell rang, Angelo Terugi would go to the front door, and then might come trouble, for both the Haywards thought extremely ill of the Italian, and would have liked, had such a thing been in any way credible, to believe him to have been the secret poisoner of his master. As she reached the hall she heard the bell.

"Ready? That's good! I hope you'll never enter this beastly house again, Laura. In fact, I'm going to see to it that you don't."

John Hayward spoke in a hurried, rather awkward, way. Owing to his wife having fainted, he had not been among those who had crowded round the dock just after the "Not Guilty" had rung triumphantly through the Court House. And now, as the door opened, and he took in every detail of her slight, sable-clad figure, and her tragic-looking face, he felt she would shrink from congratulations on what, after all, had been a foregone conclusion.

"How about your luggage, my dear?"

"I've only got this," she said in a low voice.

He looked down, surprised at the newness, as well as the smartness, of the sealskin leather suitcase.

"Mr. Ford gave it me as a wedding present, and I've never had occasion to use it."

She looked at him gratefully, feeling that it was so good of him, so truly, delicately, kind, to make no allusion to the fact she was now a free woman, and had been what his wife called "vindicated."

He said heartily: "I felt sure you'd rather I came alone to

fetch you, though Alice was disappointed. Inspector Jarrett told you she fainted in the court, didn't he? That nice chap Scrutton said she must keep really quiet for a bit. Besides, we've got a houseful, as I expect you know—"

And then he checked himself. How could poor Laura know that? But she soon would, the more so that everyone at Loverslea was aching to see her.

Suddenly he glanced through an open door which gave into the paved garden. He hadn't been in this house since the quite early days of the Douslands' married life, for at no time had he had anything in common with his old schoolfellow.

"Your garden looks quite foreign, doesn't it? What's the thing in the middle? That round thing?"

"An Italian well-head; it came from Minstead Park. So did that marble faun. I've often thought of that strange and lovely book when looking at it."

John Hayward wondered what book she could mean. Though there was a charming room called the library at Loverslea, the owner of that library and of its well-furnished bookshelves very seldom opened a book, and he had an honest contempt for any work of pure imagination. He had elected to join his father's great business at the age of eighteen, instead of going to college, and he had never regretted his choice. His only regret in life—a regret that he kept hidden in his heart—was that he had no son to tread exactly in his own footsteps.

IV

THEY DROVE ALONG IN SILENCE, THE MAN AT THE wheel avoiding the narrow streets and bye-ways round the cathedral close, where Laura Dousland would be bound to be recognised. Though he kept his eyes well on the road, as a good driver should, now and again he cast a side glance towards the unnaturally still figure sitting by his side on the wide seat of his fine Daimler.

He felt as though she was a stranger, for she seemed a different person to the young woman who had been for five years a familiar inmate under his roof. Even then he had always thought her curiously quiet and reserved for a girl still in her twenties, and he had been secretly amused as well as very much surprised, when his queer old schoolfellow, Fordish Dousland, had fallen for her in the extraordinary way he had. Often and often, during the last few weeks, he had felt consciously glad that he had never pressed the then Laura Dalberton to marry Dousland, though, of course, at the time he had been well aware that his wife was strongly for the marriage. For one thing, even the most commonplace man knows a good deal more concerning any fellow-man than does even the cleverest, shrewdest woman. He knew that he ought to have said: "That man is queerer than you think, Alice! Why, the way he is going on, now, proves that he will never make a good, let alone a decent, husband, to any nice girl."

True, his wife would not have believed him—but he ought to have said that, all the same.

He felt that the woman sitting by his side preferred silence to speech, and his mind swung back to the events of the morning.

"At any rate, all's well that ends well!" That was what he had exclaimed, when he had got his Alice safely back to their delightful country house, after that alarming faint of hers. Fortunately for himself, he hadn't taken this affair to heart in the way she had done. Still, he, too, had done his best, and his best was very good, for poor Laura Dousland. Also, he intended to go on doing his best.

Alice had spoken to him an hour ago as though she hoped their poor young friend might stay on with them for an indefinite time. As to that he hadn't said anything, though no man was likely to feel particularly anxious to have a permanent visitor in his house, and especially not a woman about whom there still hung as much interest and unhealthy curiosity as was felt about this unfortunate soul. He had observed: "I expect she will long to get right away, and forget it all," to be at once answered: "She's got no one to go to, John! I do think it will be our duty to keep her until she is fit to go out again." And he had nodded kindly, while in his heart telling himself that it would not be easy to get Laura Dousland any kind of job. The wise thing to do, so he and her lawyers had agreed yesterday, would be for her to change her name, and go out to a colony. There, with any decent luck, she would in time probably have a chance of making a happy marriage.

Everyone he and his wife knew had been absolutely agreed that such an attack on one who was as clearly innocent as Laura Dousland, had never been known. Several of her supporters had even recalled the half-forgotten Dreyfus case in connection with the affair! But Dreyfus, for his misfortune, was a Frenchman. They had all felt that any Englishman, and how much more any Englishwoman, naturally feels absolutely safe from a monstrous miscarriage of justice. He, John Hayward himself, had never doubted that Laura would be acquitted. Unluckily his wife had not felt that certainty, and during the last two days of the trial he had been amazed and troubled at her state of suspense and wretchedness. For one thing she possessed that passionate love of abstract justice which has become more a woman's than a man's trait, in our modern civilisation.

Such were the thoughts and memories that drifted through this kind man's mind as he drove Laura Dousland the thirty miles which separated Silchester from the place where he was about to offer her a home and shelter.

When within sight of the great gates of the fine property he had acquired when his father's death had brought him in a large sum of ready money, he slowed up, and turning round exclaimed: "Alice is simply living for the moment when she'll greet you as a free woman, Laura! Though Dr. Scrutton said she ought to keep quite quiet for a bit, nothing would serve her when she got back here, than to go up almost at once to the King's Room to see that everything was ready there for you—"

Loverslea had been built by one of Charles the Second's early mistresses, and the fine apartment known as the King's Room had always been kept more or less as a show-room, though as long as Mrs. Hayward's old mother had lived she had always occupied it when staying with her married daughter. Since her death no one had slept in the Carolean four-post bed, or used any of the fine, frail-looking pieces of walnut furniture which, according to tradition, always passed with Loverslea to any new owner.

Laura felt extremely surprised, and even distressed at this mark of favour. "I would much rather be in my old room," she murmured.

"I daresay you would, and *I* would in your place. But Alice is determined to do you honour, and it would be unkind to disappoint her by not seeming pleased, my dear," and he smiled at her kindly.

"I—I will be pleased. And Mr. Hayward—?"

"Now then!"

"—I mean John. I want to tell you that I do thoroughly understand all you've done for me, and that I know no one in the world has ever had such friends as you and Alice have been to me."

The words came out in quick gasps, and her listener felt really moved at the passion of feeling the woman now by his side had thrown into her voice. Gratitude, as he had reason to know, for he was a generous-hearted man, is a far rarer quality than most people would be ready to acknowledge.

They were now speeding along the long avenue that led to the rose-red brick manor house, and suddenly he exclaimed: "Why, there *is* Alice!"

Sure enough, framed in the wide doorway, stood the tall buxom mistress of Loverslea and, as the car swept round the stone-paved carriage-way, her husband told himself that she was quite her own strong determined self again.

After having kissed her visitor warmly on each cheek ,she said eagerly: "Listen, my dear—I've managed to get everybody out of the way while you and I have an early cup of tea in the drawing-room before you go up to your room. Once there you'd better lie down for an hour before coming downstairs again. The whole party will be back by five, and of course they're all longing to see you! By the way, dinner will be something of a celebration, for I've asked Dr. Scrutton, and both your lawyers, to come over from Silchester. I'd hoped Sir Joseph Molloy would propose your health, but he had to rush back to London. Lady Molloy and her nice daughter are staying till to-morrow. You probably noticed that they were in court the last three days?"

Laura Dousland opened her mouth, then she closed it. She was recalling the blurred yet terrifying vision of what had appeared to her, as she had stood during the last three days in the dock, of hundreds of eyes filled with a hard and cruel scrutiny. Only the Judge, and now and again the man or woman in the witness-box, had seemed separate entities during the long hours when she had appeared, to all those in court, unnaturally collected and mentally alert.

Her friend led the way through the circular hall, lined with sporting colour prints, and down the broad corridor hung with a Chinese wallpaper which connoisseurs would now and again ask permission to come and view. And, as she followed, Laura felt oppressed with the recollection of the winter day when she had walked between Inspector Jarrett and a policeman along where she was walking now, but of course towards, and not from, the front door.

Still, when she found herself in the drawing-room now

filled with scented flowering plants, and with the four French windows open on the stone terrace, there did come to her burdened heart a slight sensation of reassurance and of comfort.

This room belonged to the only part of her grown-up life when she had been happy. Not ecstatically happy, but still far happier than she had ever been in the dreary years which had elapsed between her father's death and her coming to Loverslea. Yet it was also here, by the carved marble mantelpiece, that she had heard the dread words uttered which accused her of having committed murder.

"Sit down at once, Laura, and let's have a cosy chat before anyone can come in and interrupt us!" exclaimed her hostess.

But the newcomer did not sit down as commanded. She stood still, and in a choking voice exclaimed: "I've tried to tell Mr. Hayward, and now I want to tell you, Alice, how—how grateful—"

"My dear girl—I hope we should have done as much for *anybody* who was treated as you were treated! But John was sensible. He knew you would be acquitted. I wasn't so sure, especially after that Italian brute had had his lying say about the Chianti flask."

Laura put out her hand, and she blindly seized the edge of the mantelpiece. She felt as if everything in the room was whirling about her in a *danse macabre*. "I—I feel so queer. I wonder if I could go upstairs now?" she muttered.

"Very well, I'll take you up at once, and you can have a cup of tea upstairs. We're putting you in the King's Room," and Alice Hayward looked at her visitor with real attention for the first time since Laura had come into the house.

As a result she said in a vexed voice, "You look very pale,

my dear. By the way, what made you go to that horrid house, instead of coming straight here? Everything had been so nicely arranged! I *was* a fool to faint. Such a thing hadn't happened to me for years."

There followed a pause. Laura had let herself drop into a chair.

"Who was it thought of your going to Kingsley Terrace? Surely you didn't ask to go there?"

"I had to go out of the Court House by the back, because of the crowds in the Court Square, and Inspector Jarrett—he was very kind, Alice—went with me. I suppose it was his idea, but there were things, clothes, I mean, I was glad to have a chance of getting before coming here."

"I do hope you weren't there long before John telephoned? I always think it's such an eerie feeling being alone in an empty house."

"I was only alone for a very short time, for Angelo Terugi came in."

"D'you mean you had to speak to that man?"

"How could I help speaking to him."

Would Mrs. Hayward never stop talking? Though Laura obediently called her ex-employer "Alice," she couldn't help always thinking of her by the name she had called her for five years.

"I hoped Terugi would be had up for perjury! Unluckily, Sir Joseph doesn't think that's at all likely. Well? We'll go upstairs now, and I'll have some tea brought there at once."

After they had gone up the stately staircase of the grand old house Alice Hayward went on: "All the servants are so excited, and longing to see and congratulate you! As for cook? You would have been quite touched, Laura; this morning she said to me, 'I didn't sleep a wink, thinking of poor Miss Dalberton!' Isn't it nice to think that Trimley, cook, and Fenman were all here in the old days? But the third housemaid, Jane Wick, will look after you; to-day is her afternoon out; she wanted to stay, but, of course, I couldn't allow that—one has to keep the rules, you know, in a household like ours. So it is Trimley who will make you comfortable now; in fact, I expect she's already unpacked your things."

As she uttered these last words, she opened the door of the King's Room, and stepped aside to allow her now honoured guest to go through it.

The elderly head-housemaid was still engaged in placing the visitor's few possessions in the drawers of a tallboy. She had already put out the tortoiseshell brush and comb, and other fittings of the suitcase, on the dressing-table; and the spacious apartment looked inhabited for the first time in Laura's recollection.

She had often been in the King's Room, for now and again, in her days as governess at Loverslea, she had been asked to take some stranger up here, and she had always enjoyed doing so. Not only was each piece of furniture a museum piece, but over the deep fireplace was a fine contemporary portrait of Charles the Second, and the dark glowing eyes seemed to follow those who came to see what had once been the place within four walls where, during a certain period of his life, he had most delighted to be.

Standing there, now, she recalled the last time she had been in this apartment. It was a fortnight before her ill-fated marriage, and she had accompanied an American historian to the King's Room. They had had a lightsome amusing talk, for she knew far more of the England of the past than did the owners of Loverslea.

"Well, my dear! I'll leave you now in Trimley's hands. I'm afraid I ought to go downstairs, for I've a great many letters to write. I didn't feel up to anything, when I came back in the evening from Silchester the last three days."

She waited a moment: "I hear the telephone! It has never stopped ringing, and when I was at home I always tried to answer everybody myself. One wanted to create an atmosphere of hope and of confidence everywhere—and I think we did help to do that."

Still she lingered, this time near the door. Then: "Trimley? You must make Mrs. Dousland lie down in a few minutes. I want her to be *quite* well and rested, by the time she has to dress for dinner."

After Mrs. Hayward had left the room, Trimley came up and looked at her mistress's now cherished guest with a curiously hard stare. She had not been particularly pleasant to Laura in the old days, for she thought poorly of ladies who have to go out and earn their living. The young governess had had to endure many a small slight, and even intentional rudeness, from the grey-haired woman who now stood waiting as if to hear her pleasure. And then, all at once, Laura knew that Trimley believed her to have been guilty of that of which she had been accused, and that she was staring at her, now, to see what a murderess looks like.

There came over her an awful sensation of shrinking fear of that grim face, but it was in an even voice that she said: "I can manage all right now, thank you; there is no need for you to stay."

"I think Mrs. Hayward would like me to stay, ma'am. You don't look at all well."

"I don't feel well, Trimley; but I can manage to get into

bed without any help, thank you. I understand that the third housemaid is going to look after me?"

She uttered these last words in a firm determined voice. Like many a gentle-speaking and very feminine-looking woman, Laura Dousland had never lacked either moral or physical courage.

Trimley suddenly felt half-ashamed of her suspicion. She was exceptionally intelligent, and though she had never liked the young lady whose pitifully poor-looking clothes she had just put away, the sight of her standing there, looking so like the Miss Dalberton she had known so well for five years, did make her feel that, maybe, she was mistaken as to her belief that Mrs. Dousland had poisoned her husband. The butler, footman, pantry-boy, and the five other maids, had always been definitely convinced of Laura Dousland's innocence, and also violently anti-Angelo Terugi. When the Italian had admitted that he had longed for what he had vulgarly described as a "swig" of his master's wine, he had broken one of those unspoken, draconian rules to which British servants have adhered for centuries.

So it was in a pleasanter tone that the head-housemaid now asked: "Are you sure there is nothing I can do for you, ma'am?"

"Quite sure, thank you."

Meanwhile Alice Hayward had joined her husband in the library, where the master of the house would sometimes take refuge from his wife's visitors.

His first words were: "What d'you think of Laura Dousland? She looks pretty bad, doesn't she?"

"I don't know what to think, John! I didn't expect her to

go mad with joy, for she's always been quiet in a way, but she certainly looks like a ghost to-day. Why, she seemed happier in the dock than she does now she's a free woman! Trimley is putting her to bed till it's time to dress for dinner."

"I wouldn't make her come down if I were you."

"I never *make* anyone do anything, John. But poor Laura must come down to-night, if only because of Lady Molloy. I've got both those lawyers, too, as well as that nice Dr. Scrutton coming; besides, it will do her good to make the effort."

"I disagree *in toto*! You don't want her to fall seriously ill on our hands, do you? She looked awful on her way here."

He spoke with such conviction that his wife felt a little shaken. "I'll 'phone Dr. Scrutton, and ask him to come half an hour earlier and have a look at her," she observed. "He might bring something with him which would buck her up. After all, she'll have to face the world some day, and she may as well begin this evening."

"It's unfortunate," said John Hayward musingly, "that she was taken back straight from the Assize Court to that appalling Kingsley Terrace. Of course, the inspector acted as he thought for the best, and she was too dazed, I suppose, to ask to be sent straight here."

Alice Hayward exclaimed: "That wretch Angelo Terugi actually forced himself in on her! That must have given her a horrid shock, though she wouldn't admit it just now."

"That house should be put up for sale at once; it's a horrid, sinister-looking place. And the garden? Not a blade of grass—all stone and marble! Fordish Dousland was certainly a queer chap."

"No one will want to buy a house associated with such an affair as this yet awhile," said his wife firmly. "I'd wait for some months at any rate."

"I believe you're right, Alice. I hadn't thought of that."

To this she made no answer. Of course, she was right. She always was right, though now and again she suspected, with a touch of exasperation, that John didn't always think so. But he generally let her have her own way, and that, after all, is what matters to a wife, especially if she loves her husband as much as she, Alice, loved her John.

After Trimley had left the King's Room, Laura, for a while, lay almost as still in the vast bed as if she had been what she wished she was, that is dead.

She began gazing intently at the wide expanse of blue sky which now appeared to her one of the symbols of her freedom. Often, in prison, she had thought of Oscar Wilde's lines in "The Ballad of Reading Gaol."

> *"I never saw a man who looked*
> *With such a wistful eye*
> *Upon that little tent of blue*
> *Which prisoners call the sky.*
> *And at every drifting cloud that went*
> *With sails of silver by."*

They came into her mind now, for it was the sight of the illimitable sky which made her realise that she was now really free, and mistress not only of her soul, but of her body, too.

During the time she had spent at Loverslea, immediately after her husband's death, she had found it well-nigh impossible to believe that he had vanished for ever out of her life. Her one-time employers and now good friends, who had seen so little of her during her married life, had come to her within three hours of her discovery of Fordish Dousland's death, and Mrs. Hayward had insisted on taking her away at once from her poverty-stricken-looking house. Everything that usually falls to a dead man's nearest relations had been done by these generous-hearted people, and the widow had not been allowed even to attend the funeral at which John Hayward had been the only mourner.

And oh! how good they had been afterwards, when shame and horror had overwhelmed her as in a swirling flood. At once John Hayward had made himself financially responsible for her defence, and as for his wife, apart from everything else, throughout her trial the prisoner had been perpetually conscious of the presence of her friend, and of that friend's proud confidence, not only in her innocence—that went without need of a word—but in her powers of endurance and of courage.

Always Laura had had a sensitive and scrupulous conscience, and now she felt painfully ashamed of her shrinking distaste of the mere physical presence of Alice Hayward. Why, she even dreaded the sound of the clear voice she had never heard raised once in anger during the nine years she had now known it, save when face to face to some act of cruelty or injustice. In everyday life the mistress of Loverslea belonged to that rare order of being, an absolutely good-tempered woman.

And now, suddenly, that good-tempered woman came back into the King's Room. She had opened the door so quietly that Laura had not heard it open, and for a moment the hostess, without her presence being suspected, saw her guest's side face, and that side face looked so pinched and ravaged that there came across the older woman, and for the first time, an inkling of what the younger woman had suffered, and was still suffering.

"Laura, my dear?"

Though the three words were said in an unusually gentle tone, Laura gave a stifled cry. Then she lifted herself in the canopied bed and, turning her head round, tried to smile.

Meanwhile there suddenly rose from the terrace below the half-moon window, sounds of laughing and talking, and to one of the two now in the King's Room, those sounds appeared oh! so strange and unreal. Laura Dousland had not heard people laughing and talking in that light, care-free fashion since she had stayed at Loverslea three years ago. It made her feel even more remote from ordinary human kind than she had felt that morning in her prison cell.

Mrs. Hayward came up to the side of the bed. It was rarely indeed that she thought her husband was more likely to be right than herself, but as she looked down into the drawn face of the woman lying there, she told herself uneasily that Laura might not be fit, after all, to join the dinner-party which she had planned with such zest. Still, everything in her protested against so bitter a disappointment.

"John wants you to see Dr. Scrutton, and let him decide whether you are fit to come down to-night or not. I can't help thinking that the sooner you take up normal life again, the better it will be—I mean for yourself, but John doesn't agree to that."

She was relieved to hear the submissive answer, though it was delivered in a shaky voice.

"I expect you're right, Alice. I feel better now, and I'll certainly come down. I don't want to see Dr. Scrutton. I don't feel ill, only rather tired."

"Oh, but you must see Dr. Scrutton! In fact I asked him

to come early on purpose. As a matter of fact he's up here—waiting outside the door. But he needn't stay more than a few minutes, so you'll have plenty of time to dress," and as she spoke she turned, and opening the door called out: "Will you come in, Dr. Scrutton?"

A moment later the man Laura Dousland had last seen in the witness-box, giving evidence on her behalf, was looking down into her upturned face.

Mrs. Hayward said briskly: "I'm afraid I must leave you, Laura, for I've just heard the car. That must be Polly coming from the station; she's been travelling practically day and night in order to be home this evening, and she has to go away again to-morrow." To the doctor she exclaimed, "Do stretch a point and allow Mrs. Dousland to come down to dinner? She can go off as soon as she likes, afterwards. It will be a sad disappointment—to me personally, as well, of course, as to everybody else—if you won't let her join us this evening. Dinner has been planned so as to bring together all those who have helped us most during this dreadful time," but to the relief of both the doctor and his new patient, she left the room without waiting for an answer.

"You see that I shall have to go down to-night, Dr. Scrutton?"

Though Laura's voice was low and weak, there was a resolute note in it, and for the hundredth time in the last few days the young man felt a surge of admiration for her pluck. He made no reply to that assertion. He simply took up the thin hand which was lying on the embroidered coverlet, and felt its owner's pulse.

Laura had always had, from childhood, an instinctive dislike of being approached too nearly, yet Dr. Scrutton's close clasp brought with it a feeling of strength and reassurance.

There was something impersonal, authoritative, in his cool, firm touch. Still, when he dropped her hand and said: "Will you allow me to listen to your heart, Mrs. Dousland?" she felt a moment of recoil, and there mounted up to her pale face a painful flush.

"There is no hurry; we will wait a few moments," and he walked across to the window and, turning his back on the bed, he stared, unseeingly, at the beautiful view of down-land, sea, and sky.

He felt moved in a way he had never felt moved before in the presence of any woman patient. And there came to him a memory of the first time he had seen Laura Dousland standing in what had seemed to him, and he was not wont to notice unfamiliar surroundings, the ugliest and most depressing sitting-room into which he had ever been shown. Even then he had wondered what could have drawn two such utterly incongruous people as elderly Fordish Dousland and his young wife together? Apart from all else he had felt surprised at the difference in their ages, for he had thought Dousland older, and Laura younger, than he now knew they both had been, though on this June after-noon she looked piteously young and forlorn.

He came back at last, across the great room now filled with the glow of the setting sun and, with his own face in shadow, he saw her clearly.

The dark curling hair, which she had kept long in def-erence to the wish of her husband, was spread over the pillow, and formed a nimbus round her now drawn-looking face, and he felt as if he was in the presence of a woman who had just gone through a fearful physical, rather than mental, ordeal. So might have appeared a poor creature in mediaeval times who had been subjected to some fearful form of torture, and there came to him the sudden perception that she shrank from even the lightest and most fleeting of human contacts.

"I shan't listen to your heart; it was stupid of me to suggest it. All you require is to be quiet and, as far as may be, alone," he said quietly, and she looked at him with a mixture of gratitude and surprise.

He waited a moment before adding: "That you should get up now and join a large party of men and women all anxious to kill you with kindness is out of the question."

"Is it really?" There was no doubt of the relief in her low voice.

"You must stay on in bed till I give you leave to get up; and I hope you will see as few people as possible."

He had come close up to her by now, and all at once a quick look of secret understanding flashed between them. Each was thinking, and each knew that the other was thinking, of Alice Hayward.

"May I tell your hostess and her daughter that I have forbidden you to talk at all for the next three days?"

"Oh no, you mustn't do that, Dr. Scrutton! Mrs. Hayward has been wonderfully good to me; and Polly Hayward has taken a long journey just to see me for a few hours. After all, why shouldn't I talk to them, if they want me to, and if it's the only way I can prove how grateful I am to them?"

She added, as if to herself: "It doesn't really matter about me, one way or the other."

He felt startled, and puzzled, too. What exactly did she mean by saying that? Surely she knew that she mattered, and mattered very much as it happened, to thousands of people to whom she was, and would for ever remain, if only a name, yet the symbol of that by which all her fellow-countrymen and countrywomen set great store, that is innocence. Yet what would have been eager words of remonstrance were stayed on his lips, for there was a look at once of apathy and yes, of suffering, on her face.

Mark Scrutton's heart felt wrung with pity, and anger, too. How fearful that this sensitive highly-strung creature should have been chosen, out of all the world, to be so cruelly used by what is called fate!

She felt restless under that intent, commiserating gaze, and "Do sit down," she said tremulously.

He fetched one of the old chairs standing near the wall of the room, and all at once Laura turned herself round and smiled as she exclaimed: "Mrs. Hayward doesn't allow anyone ever to sit even for a moment on one of those chairs! You must get the one that's over there, by the dressing-table."

He did what she suggested, amused and touched by her sense of—one couldn't call it duty exactly—was it obedience? to the woman who had doubtless been her benevolent tyrant for five years.

In a sense that trifling episode had destroyed the tension between them. "I want to talk to you seriously for a few moments, Mrs. Dousland. You are a clever woman, or I wouldn't do so."

She looked at him deprecatingly. She had never thought of herself as being clever. Clever women, or so she believed, do not make muddles of their lives as she had done.

"I don't ask you to try and recover your nerve for your own sake, but for that of the people who have been, as you said to me just now, good to you."

As she remained silent, he went on impressively: "You mayn't matter much to yourself, but you matter a very great deal to a great many people. I motored one of your lawyers out here this evening, and he told me he had had dozens of telegrams, and even long-distance calls, from all over the country, sending you messages of congratulation."

And then she surprised him again: "I hope that soon these people will have something else to fill their minds," she said, and there was what seemed to her listener a strange bitterness in her voice. "All I want—all I long for—is to be forgotten by everybody who has ever heard of me."

She waited a moment, then she said wearily: "I'm afraid you think me very ungrateful."

"Of course I don't. But I do feel you ought to leave this neighbourhood. Have you no sensible old friend living abroad to whom you could go in a few days for some weeks of real rest?" and he stressed the "real."

"There is no one in the world, Dr. Scrutton, either at home or abroad, and I am lucky indeed in having such good friends as the Haywards. They are going to let me stay on here, till I am well enough to look for work."

She looked at him anxiously. "That needn't be very long, need it? I'm only tired after all, and I suppose my nerves are still upset."

He made no answer to that, though everything in him revolted at the thought of this poor woman having to look for work among strangers who must surely be told, should they not already know, her tragic story.

"I suppose you have been sleeping very badly?"

She answered at once. "I haven't slept badly up to now. And last night—" she stopped.

"What happened last night?"

"I felt as if my father, who died twelve years ago, was there, close to me, in my cell. If I was a spiritualist I should believe he actually did come to me."

"Are you sure he did not?" asked the young man gravely.

"Yes, I am sure," and she sighed. "I used to believe in a future life when I was young and happy, but I don't believe in it now."

"The more I think about it the more I believe this life cannot be the end," he said, as if speaking to himself.

They looked at one another in silence, and there flashed a strange expression over Laura Dousland's face. She was telling herself how staggered, as well as shocked, Alice Hayward would have been had she heard that admission of unbelief. Without ever having seriously considered them in any real sense, the mistress of Loverslea held to every tenet of the faith in which she had been born and brought up. So far as she ever thought of religious belief with regard to other people, she supposed science to be the foe of religion. Thus she would have heard with genuine surprise the assertion just made by Mark Scrutton, for even she was aware that the young man was more concerned with the scientific than the practical side of medicine.

The door opened, and the woman of whom Laura was thinking came into the room.

"I hope you feel better now, my dear?" Then she turned to Mark Scrutton. "Everyone downstairs is hanging on your verdict, doctor."

And then she felt vexed with herself. She was sorry she had used the word *verdict,* and it was with a real sense of relief she saw Laura had not noticed the slip.

"I'm afraid I'm going to disappoint you, Mrs. Hayward, for my patient mustn't think of getting up this evening. She is worn out."

Mrs. Hayward felt very much vexed, and showed it.

"Don't you think coming down would do her good?"

The doctor shook his head; but she went on: "I think she looks much better than she did just now—and everyone will feel so bitterly disappointed!"

He was stung into replying: "You don't want to have Mrs. Dousland falling seriously ill on your hands?"

How strange that an intelligent woman like Mrs. Hayward—he took her intelligence for granted—should not know that it is always wrong to discuss an ailing person's condition in front of that person.

Not that Laura Dousland was taking any notice of what was being said. She was again staring before her with an apathetic look which made him feel afraid that she had gone through more than she had been able to bear without becoming permanently affected.

He made a sign to Laura's friend, and they walked out of the room together. Once out of earshot he said firmly: "I brought a strong sedative, which I propose should be given at once to Mrs. Dousland. Her condition is serious. She's—" he sought for the right expression and could only find: "—all smashed up, and the best simile I can use is that of a cord which has been stretched too tightly, and is on the point of snapping."

"And yet she has been so marvellously calm and brave—"

As he said nothing to that, Alice Hayward added, in a tone which made him feel a surge of anger: "Surely it's a mistake to encourage her to give way, Dr. Scrutton?"

"No encouragement has been needed," he observed dryly, and she wondered what he meant by saying that.

That night Laura Dousland went through a strange and awesome experience. It was only a dream; but was more vivid than any dream, or nightmare, which had ever come to her, though she had been a highly imaginative child, and later on an abnormally sensitive and highly strung girl. She lived, during that experience, through every moment of the hour preceding the execution of a woman who has been found guilty of murder, and condemned to be hanged by the neck till she is dead.

The place where she found herself was the condemned cell of the New Prison at Silchester, and though she had of course never been shown that particular cell, long ago she had seen a picture of a woman awaiting execution, and she had been haunted by the drab horror of the starkly furnished little room.

In her dream the Governor and the Chaplain were there, with her, but instead of being, as they ever had been, kind, considerate, and even courteous, they were gazing at her with the hatred and contempt men show to one they believe has foully deceived them. Suddenly she heard the Governor's voice: "Have you anything to say, Laura Dousland?" And she cried out: "You surely know that I am innocent?" and with that word "innocent" on her lips, she awoke in the dark night, shaking all over, and with scalding tears streaming down her face.

V

When Laura awoke the next morning, she looked about her with a sensation of complete bewilderment, and then—she remembered everything.

Closing her eyes again she visualised the Assize Court at Silchester, and lived once more through the final scenes of her trial.

At this same time yesterday she had still been in her prison cell, and unknowing as to what was to be her fate. Although yesterday morning seemed years, instead of hours, ago, a physical tremor ran through her delicate body as she recalled what had happened then. She also recalled the fearful dream which had been like a page torn from pulsing life, rather than the projection of a fevered imagination. How strange that the vision of what might have happened had come to her here, in the King's Room at Loverslea, instead of in her cell at the New Prison!

As to the hour spent by her at No. 2, Kingsley Terrace, she only remembered her short colloquy with Angelo Terugi. She felt glad that she had compelled him to admit that he had told a lie as to the Chianti flask—and that though she did not mean ever to make use of his admission, for she hoped never to utter either of those two hateful words again.

Could the long drawn-out agony of shame and misery she had endured with what had seemed to those about her such stoic courage be really at an end, and for ever? She found it almost impossible to believe that the answer to that question was "yes." She alone knew that it had not been courage, but apathy, which had caused her to face with fortitude what had appeared not only to her friends and supporters, but to her official accusers, the most agonising ordeal to which a human being can be subjected. During most of the time she had been in the dock she had not only felt, she had known herself to be, alike to an automaton.

True, now and again she had felt a surge of pain and even of anger sweep over her, especially when what she knew to be quite untrue had been asserted, either in the speeches of the Counsel for the Crown, or by some witness. Especially had she resented—she recalled that now—the evidence tendered by Dr. Grant. He had said, with some heat, that his first suspicion had been roused by her callous demeanour when he had entered the house on the morning of Fordish Dousland's death.

"The widow on such an occasion is nearly always in tears," he had observed sententiously. "I noticed that Mrs. Dousland was quite composed, less affected indeed than the Italian manservant; he was in tears, in fact crying bitterly."

The prisoner, listening to that statement, had remembered the state of stupefied misery in which the old man had found her; and particularly had she recalled his inquisitive, at the time she had felt them to be indecent, questions, as to the relations which had existed between her husband

and herself. He had shown exaggerated surprise when he had learnt that they had not been sharing the same room the night before; and the resentment she had betrayed during that interrogation had been probably one of the reasons why he had shown such animosity against her throughout the inquest, and, in as far as he was allowed to do so, at her trial.

Again, when Angelo Terugi had sworn positively as to the Chianti flask having been placed on the tray prepared by him on the crucial evening, something, some entity maybe, outside herself, had impelled her to make what she had immediately felt to have been a most unseemly interruption. But it had seemed to her unendurably monstrous that this Italian—to whom she had always been kind—should go far to destroy all the efforts her good friends were making on her behalf, by asserting what he must know to be a lie. She had believed then, and she knew now she had been right, that the lie had appeared to Terugi when he had at first told it, an unimportant lie. But having told that lie and learnt, no doubt with distress, of its importance in the case, he had not had the courage to retract.

She had not dreaded going into the witness-box, and she had not even been conscious, when there, of the hundreds of eyes turned on her. In as far as she had felt afraid, she had feared the benign yet probing examination of Sir Joseph Molloy, for she had been nervously afraid of disappointing him. But during the formidable cross-examination, she had felt none of the hideous terror she knew the poor wretches who had gone through what she was enduring almost invariably do feel. Yet she had not been able to restrain a storm of tears when a question had recalled her husband's coarse and cruel complaint that she was not even good for bearing a child.

Mrs. Hayward's outburst on her behalf had taken her entirely by surprise. But then, deep in Laura Dousland's heart, Mrs. Hayward—to herself she still could not call her "Alice"—had been ever since her arrest a continuous surprise. From being a kindly, but a patronising and not altogether an approving, older friend, this woman had suddenly become her passionately protective and enthusiastic defender.

Of the summing-up by the Judge, Laura remembered nothing. No single passage had reached the recording part of her brain, and when had come the moment for her to be taken below to wait for the verdict, she had been awakened as if from a trance. Indeed she now only vaguely recalled the time—it was exactly forty minutes—of waiting, when the officials detailed to be with her had tried to show her both pity and sympathy.

When she had been brought back to the dock to watch the return of the jury, she had been the calmest and least moved person in Court. And not till the full meaning of the word "Not Guilty" had penetrated her brain, did she realise that, after all, she had never believed there could be any other verdict.

And now she was face to face with normal life once more—free, also, as she had never been free since she had been a gentle dreamy schoolgirl who only lived for the times, called in her little world "the holidays," when she would be with the father who was all she had to love, and who was the only human being she had ever loved.

But though she knew she was now free in a sense she had never yet been in her thirty-two years of life, real freedom would not be hers till she had left Loverslea, and had attained what she had now long ardently desired, that is solitude. She was, however, aware that even the preparation of her simple defence had cost a good deal of money; and she was determined that every penny of that money should be repaid, as soon as she had realised Fordish Dousland's meagre estate. With what would then remain she intended to buy a measure of peace before taking up again the burden of a working life. Meanwhile, with the help of that clever understanding young doctor, Mark Scrutton, she must get sufficiently well to be allowed by her almost over-solicitous friends to go away and find the short respite for which she craved.

It took her a little while to decide that to-day was the tenth day of June, and a Saturday. What made her feel sure of the date and day was that the prison wardress had said she hoped the trial would not go on until to-day, as Friday was an unlucky day.

She wondered what time it was? The bright, hot-looking shaft of sunlight now piercing through the cleft between the heavy damask curtains drawn across the half-moon window, made her feel it must be late. But she was too bodily weary even to put out her hand and look at her watch.

Uncomfortably aware that soon Mrs. Hayward would be coming to see how she was, she knew it would be well for her if, before that happened, she had had a cup of tea. So she rang the bell, but before it could be answered there came a sharp, imperative knock on the door, and her hostess swept into the room with what appeared to be every newspaper published in the country piled up in her arms.

"Still in the dark, Laura? Really it was too bad of Rose not to have come in and drawn your curtains! Oh, I remember, now—Dr. Scrutton said you were to sleep on till you woke. I'm afraid I did wake you, but it's after ten."

She waited a moment, then said kindly: "I may as well draw the curtains, hadn't I?" And, after she had done so: "I ordered every paper that had anything about you or the trial to be sent here this morning, for I knew you'd like to see them. Just look at this pile! I should think that hateful man, the Coroner, must be feeling very cheap this morning," and she laid the mass of newspapers down on the end of the bed.

As Laura remained silent, she went on: "I'm really sorry Dr. Scrutton wouldn't allow you to have come down last night. I don't believe it would have done you a bit of harm, and Lady Molloy was very disappointed at not seeing you. She has had to leave this morning. She said she had never attended such an exciting trial for murder! Yet she's been to about a dozen affairs of the kind at the Old Bailey, though Sir Joseph doesn't like her to be there when he's in a case."

The woman lying in bed shut her eyes, she had not become accustomed, yet, to bright sunlight. "I'm sorry I couldn't come down, but I did feel really ill last evening," she said in a low voice.

"No one can expect you to feel really yourself yet awhile. Still, you might look worse, Laura—and by the way, Dr. Scrutton said he would be out here early this morning. But I wonder what he calls early? John has to go up to London this afternoon, for he has got a business dinner engagement, and I know he wants to see you."

"I want to see him too, very much," Laura roused herself, for she had remembered, all at once, her promise to Angelo Terugi.

"I'll bring John up as soon as you've had a proper breakfast. Now what would you like? Eggs, fish, or some cold meat?"

The speaker was remembering something the doctor had said yesterday, which had rather startled her. "We must not forget, Mrs. Hayward, that Mrs. Dousland was seriously under-nourished at the time of her husband's death," was what Mark Scrutton had said in his quiet voice.

Somehow she, Alice Hayward, had never thought of anyone of her own class as being under-nourished, and the word had remained in her mind. She knew that the Douslands had lived in what to herself she called "a poor way," and the fact had always puzzled her. All the same, she had felt sure that in Laura's place she would have soon found an excellent cook-general who would have stayed with her. As for the Italian's cooking, she for her part enjoyed eating foreign dishes when spending a few days in Paris, though she realised that constant macaroni and tomatoes, however well prepared, might become monotonous, after a while. Still, Laura Dousland, as mistress of the house, could surely have ordered anything she chose for herself?

The young maid had now come into the room, and the invalid was drinking her nice cup of tea, and eating some thin bread-and-butter, while feeling slightly ashamed of the pleasure that both the tea and the bread-and-butter afforded her, after the kind of breakfast which had been sent in each morning to the prison from an hotel near-by.

After a while: "This is all I shall want," she observed in a low voice. "Perhaps I could see Mr. Hayward now?"

"I'll go and fetch him, my dear; but I feel you ought to have a proper breakfast, for you look thin, and we must fatten you up."

There came a rush of tears to the eyes of the woman who was sitting up in bed. How grateful she ought to be to this kind soul who had done so much for her!

She longed to say: "May I see Mr. Hayward alone?" But she lacked the courage to do that, and there she was wise, for Mrs. Hayward would have been surprised at such a request. Surprised, and just a little hurt. It was she who was Laura Dousland's friend, not John.

And it was true that as he walked into the room, the master of the house thought it rather absurd that their ex-governess should have been given this magnificent apartment. But when he gazed down into her face, his heart was stirred to deep pity, for she looked what to himself he called "terrible" this morning; wan, exhausted and, in the dark eyes which secretly he had always regarded as beautiful, there was now a tragic and bewildered expression.

"I don't think it can be pleasant, looking out on to the bright sunlight!" he exclaimed. And then: "Why don't you have the bed made up the other way? *I* should."

His wife intervened, quite sharply for her.

"Really, John, you are a freak! Why, it's one of the loveliest views in southern England."

"One can't see much of the view from the bed. In fact, all one can see is the glare. Now am I right, or am I not, Laura?"

He was talking in a hearty, jovial way, and poor Laura liked the sound of his kind voice.

"I think you're right," and there came the quiver of a smile over her face.

"D'you mean you'd be more comfortable with your head lying the other way, staring at the wall?" asked Alice Hayward.

"Well, yes, I think I should," came the hesitating answer. "My eyes are aching a good deal."

"Very well, my dear, when you've finished talking to John, we'll have the bed made up in any way you like."

But there was a ruffled note in the kind voice. The mistress of Loverslea liked to have everything done properly, and in order.

If Dr. Scrutton had really meant what he had said, namely that Laura Dousland ought to remain in bed for some days, then no doubt she would be receiving, up here, in the King's Room, a certain number of the Silchester ladies who had taken so strong an interest in her case. It would look indeed ridiculous, if she insisted on seeing them with the bed in which she was lying made up the wrong way.

"Now then, John—do sit down! Laura won't keep you many minutes, but you may as well begin by telling her what you think about her house."

He fetched from the wall on which hung a fine piece of tapestry, one of the Carolean chairs and, leaning rather forward, gazed again at the woman of whom he still thought as standing in the dock waiting to hear whether she was to die or live.

He had been told, and the fact had impressed him, that no intermediate verdict would have been possible.

He wondered uneasily if his wife realised how completely broken up was this unfortunate creature? Laura Dousland had never looked as if she would make old bones, and perhaps it was not very much to be wished that she should. After all, in a way, her life was at an end. Wherever she was, whatever she did, unless she went to some entirely different part of the world and changed her name, her personality would be for ever associated with the cruel thing which had just happened to her.

Already, this morning, although he had not told his wife so, a reporter had arrived at Loverslea, asking if he could see Mrs. Dousland. He had come, it seemed, to make her an offer for what he called her "life story," on behalf of the editor of the paper which claimed the largest circulation in England, and it had been quite a job to get rid of the man, the more difficult as he had been quite a decent young fellow.

"Now then, John? Do tell Laura what you think ought to be done about 2, Kingsley Terrace."

"It isn't what *I* think, it's what your lawyers suggest should be done."

And then Mrs. Hayward chipped in: "Mr. Malefield said last evening that there are a few fairly good antiques in the house, to say nothing of the Italian statuary in the garden, and that if you would consent to having a sale there in the next few weeks, some big prices might be realised."

John Hayward jumped to his feet. "Here! Give her something, Alice—I think she's going to faint."

Laura made a supreme effort over herself. "No, no," she cried. "I'm not going to faint. I only turned over rather queer, and when that happens to me I always go white."

She appealed to the woman who now stood by the bedside staring down at her with a concerned expression. "Don't you remember that time at a picnic, years and years ago?"

"Of course I remember it. But you'd been working all night finishing a fancy dress for Polly, and it was a frightfully hot day."

Laura was now looking straight at the husband and wife, "I would hate to have a sale in the house."

She uttered her fiat with difficulty, and yet it was a fiat.

She had been a slave for so long! For five years slave to this kind, determined woman, and then, for four years, slave to a cantankerous, eccentric man. Since his death she had become the slave of circumstance, having been taken up as a feather is taken up and tossed by a mighty wind this way and that. But she was now, and it was with surprise rather than pleasure she knew it was so, mistress of herself, with the right to do as she wished, and the power of preventing others doing what she desired they should not do.

"I should like to wait before selling the house till—till everything is forgotten," she murmured.

Mrs. Hayward felt what she seldom allowed herself to feel, irritated. After all, they knew what it was best for poor Laura Dousland to do. She said dryly: "If you do that, you'll have to wait a long time, my dear."

But Laura took no notice of the tart remark. She said with a touch of eagerness: "What I want to know, Mr. Hayward—" somehow she had never found it easy to call him "John"—"—is about any money I have a right to? Shall I get it soon?"

"I'll find out all about that within the next few days," he said kindly. "Meanwhile, of course I can advance you any money you require."

"I require fifty pounds," she said falteringly.

"Fifty pounds," echoed Mrs. Hayward. "What do you want that for?"

"I want it for Angelo Terugi."

"D'you mean that man pretends you owe him fifty pounds? Why, his wages have been paid every week, and not only his wages, but his board wages, too! Isn't that so, John?"

"Well, yes, it is. You see, Laura—" he looked at her uncomfortably, "—all that absurd fuss about the Chianti flask made the position a rather difficult one with regard to this Italian. There was a discussion with your lawyers about the matter some time ago," he did not like to say "Just after your arrest." "Mr. Malefield thought the Crown ought to pay for his keep, as he was their witness; but your husband had made some kind of contract with Terugi, or so the man asserted, and finally I agreed, on your behalf, that he should receive his wages weekly till the trial."

"He is going back to Italy, and I told him yesterday I would give him fifty pounds. You see, Mr. Hayward—"

She was now betraying both agitation and distress, and his voice suddenly became very gentle and soothing: "Yes, Laura?"

"Fordish," she brought out the name with an effort, "promised Angelo Terugi should have his fare back to Venice."

"Though the journey is expensive, it doesn't cost fifty pounds to travel second-class to Italy," said Mrs. Hayward in what was for her a most unusually sharp, aggressive tone. "I never heard of such a thing! It would look very bad if it came out that you had given that man fifty pounds within a day or two of your being acquitted. Why, he did his best to hang you, Laura! No one doubts but that he lied deliberately and, as I told you yesterday, most people say he ought to have been arrested for perjury the moment he left the witness-box."

John Hayward looked deprecatingly at his wife. "Now, Alice, my dear—"

"There's no 'Now, Alice,' about it! I think it will be a monstrous thing if Laura gives Angelo Terugi anything."

"I *must* give it him, Alice. I promised I would. Besides, it isn't very much more than he's entitled to have."

Laura Dousland's voice had become firm, even defiant. Then with a cry she added: "I'm so thankful that he's going back to his own country, and that I shall never see him again!"

"She's right there, Alice. Quite right. It would have been

a very disagreeable thing for Laura if that man had stayed on in England, and if the Press had got hold of him."

John Hayward was telling himself how unpleasant it would be if the young man he had seen this morning, and whom he had persuaded to go away, had made for Angelo Terugi, and got, maybe, a new story out of him? That would mean more worry for them all.

"If you think it right, John, to encourage perjury, I've nothing more to say."

"I don't believe the man did commit perjury," said her husband stoutly. "I think he was telling what he believed to be the truth about that Chianti flask."

"I think he was too," said Laura dully.

Then she felt shocked at herself for telling such a lie.

"I don't agree with either of you! I think that Terugi has a grudge against you, Laura—" exclaimed Alice Hayward.

"He was very kind to me yesterday," said the other in an almost inaudible voice.

"Kind? How d'you mean—kind?"

There came a knock at the door, and then it opened.

"Mr. Allan asks if you can see him for a minute or so, ma'am. It's about the new fountain in the rose-garden. He says it's very important," and to the relief of the two others, the lady addressed left the room.

"Now, Laura, tell me exactly what it is you want me to do with regard to this Italian chap?"

The words came quickly, urgently, and the answer was equally eager and urgent.

"I should be most grateful if you could send him fifty pounds to-day, Mr. Hayward. I said I'd telephone, and that he could come out here and get the money. But I don't want him to come now, for it would upset Alice."

Alice's husband gave a chuckle. "It would indeed!" Then he felt ashamed, for he was always loyal to his wife.

"I'll start now, at once, for Silchester, draw the fifty pounds from the bank, find your man, give him the money, and tell him to scoot. In fact, I don't mind giving him a lift into London. Will that set your mind at rest, my dear?"

He put out his great big hand and gripped her fragile fingers. Poor little thing! He told himself he wouldn't be a bit surprised if she didn't leave the King's Room alive.

"Now that's settled, isn't it?"

"I'm more grateful, Mr. Hayward, than I can say. You and Alice have been angels to me. I did not know there could be such kindness in the world."

He felt as moved as it was in him to be.

"I only wish we could do more for you, my dear girl. For look here, Laura? I've always felt grateful to you, though I never said so till now, over my Polly and Emma. You had a lot to do with making them the dear good girls they are. No one knows that better than I do, though I don't say Alice would agree. She probably thinks they were just born well-behaved and good!" And he laughed his loud jovial laugh, filling the great room with the sound.

"They have always been angels to me, too."

But there came a pained look in her face, for the elder of her ex-pupils, the Haywards' married daughter, Emma, had had to write to her on the sly, because her husband, a pig-headed fellow, did not share his parents'-in-law belief in Mrs. Dousland's innocence. The fact had become known to Laura, and it had hurt her very much.

"I'll be buzzing off now. Don't say a word about this business to Alice. She never changes her opinion about anybody, as you know. But you're right! That chap believed every word he said about the wine. There's no real Chianti flask mystery at all. Terugi just mixed up the two occasions; that was it, wasn't it?"

"Yes," she repeated, "that was it."

"And what he said about the elephant and the fly was the exact truth, too. It was all a mighty fuss about nothing."

When he reached the door he heard her voice calling out feebly: "Mr. Hayward?"

He turned round: "Now then? My name's 'John,'" and he shook his finger at her.

"I mean John—"

He came back to the side of the bed. She looked better now, and she had lost what he described to himself as "that dying look."

"You won't let Mr. Malefield do anything about the house, will you?"

Quickly he acquiesced. "Of course I won't! You leave everything to me, Laura, and don't worry about your money. When everything is settled up, I hope and believe you'll have a clear hundred pounds a year. It isn't very much, but still it will prevent your having to take any job that offers."

And then, lowering his voice, he asked: "You haven't thought of going right away, I suppose?"

She looked surprised: "Right away? Where do you mean?"

"If you'd like to make a real fresh start, I might hear of something in Canada. I'm in touch with business folk out there, as you know."

Half jokingly he added: "I don't suppose 'the Chianti flask mystery' has gone as far as that. All the same, I'm afraid you'd have to change your name."

"I wouldn't mind doing that," she whispered.

"You just think it over, Laura. And if I were you," he lowered his voice too, "I wouldn't discuss it with anyone, or ask any other person's advice. It's a question you should decide for yourself."

He knew his wife would strongly demur to Laura doing anything of that kind. For one thing Alice would undoubtedly take the view that Laura should live her past down, and so prove an example to every innocent woman who had ever been accused unjustly, or ever would be.

"I won't tell anyone, and I'll think it over very seriously," she said in a grateful tone.

"I'll see that someone tells the housemaid to remake your bed the other way," and then he took himself off.

He had been somewhat surprised at the way she had taken his suggestion. That Laura Dalberton, as he still sometimes thought of her, was a far cleverer young woman than his wife supposed her to be, he had always known, but he had doubted if she realised how difficult it would be for her to obtain a suitable post in England.

If she took his advice and went to Canada, it might be her duty to tell any prospective employer the truth about herself. But after all she had been acquitted, and so had a clean slate. One had only to look at to-day's papers to see how shamefully she had been treated by the Coroner, and how badly had been managed the preliminary enquiry. He, John Hayward, hadn't a doubt but that his eccentric old schoolfellow, Fordish Dousland, had committed suicide. Like the Judge who had presided over the trial, he had been greatly impressed by that exchange of words between Fordish Dousland and Dr. Scrutton when the question of the poison, and of its effect on a human being, had come up between them.

On leaving the King's Room, he saw the head-housemaid, "Trimley? Will you see that when Mrs. Dousland's bed is next made, it is turned round?"

"Turned round, sir? I don't understand. It's a great big heavy bed; we'll have to have four men come upstairs to move it."

"I don't mean that the four-poster is to be moved. I want the bed made up so that Mrs. Dousland won't be facing the light."

The woman looked both surprised and cross. "Very good, sir, but I'd better tell Mrs. Hayward before I do that, for if I don't she'll feel surprised when she sees it's been done."

"Of course Mrs. Hayward knows all about it," he said sharply.

He had seen an expression on the stolid face which had annoyed him. Trimley looked as if she had caught her master coming out of a bedroom where he had no business to be.

Now in a way that was true. Trimley had seen her mistress go downstairs, and to her mind Mr. Hayward had stayed over long in the King's Room. After all, Mrs. Dousland was still a young woman. But there! Trimley was aware that queer goings-on went on among those she called in her own mind "gentlefolk."

Not the least queer, to her mind, had been the acquittal of the young lady to whom such honour was now being paid in Loverslea. But, she knew her place, and always carried out her orders well and quickly. That was what naturally made her highly valued by Mrs. Hayward. So calling her underling, Rose, the head-housemaid proceeded with what she had been ordered to do.

After they had got Laura back to bed, and were once more outside the room, Rose whispered: "Poor thing! She do look bad, don't she?"

"You'd look bad if you'd done what she did, and gone through all she has. She must 'a' seen herself dangling from the gallows many a time in her dreams, and I expect she always will, to her dying day."

"What a 'orrible idea! D'you still think she did it?"

"I'm not one that alters her opinion," replied Trimley in a malignant tone.

"Now, Laura, here's Dr. Scrutton. I think he'll agree that you look wonderfully better, and I hope he'll allow you to come down. You'd be far better out in the garden, than lying here and staring at the wall as you are doing now. John gets such absurd ideas in his head sometimes!"

"I was just thinking," said the young doctor, smiling, "what a very good idea it was. In fact I credited *you* with that idea, Mrs. Hayward. For my part I hate lying in bed opposite a window, and it's bad for the eyes."

"I should have thought it strengthened them."

There was a pause.

"I suppose you wish to be alone with your patient?"

"Well, yes, for just a few minutes, if you don't mind."

As soon as the door had closed behind this woman whom he was beginning, irrationally, to hate, Mark Scrutton became quiet, impersonal, in a word professional, in his manner.

"How do you feel to-day?" and he looked at Laura keenly.

"I have had a business talk with Mr. Hayward, and that has made me feel much better."

It was curious how something within her seemed to compel her to tell the truth to this man.

He felt her pulse. "You are better, Mrs. Dousland, and in a way Mrs. Hayward is right. It would do you far more good to be lying out on the terrace in the open air than staying in bed up here. But if I allow you to do that, can I rely on it that you won't be disturbed by tiresome chattering visitors? You have gone through a terrible ordeal, and it will take you a long time to get completely over it."

"I shall never get completely over it," she said in an almost inaudible voice.

"I hope you will, and I think you will," he said feelingly. "But only if you and those about you behave with common sense. If you allow anyone to tyrannise over you, even with the best intention in the world, you will go through what you have avoided, up to now, by sheer strength of character."

"What do you mean?"

"I mean a bad breakdown. Now can you trust yourself to defy Mrs. Hayward? She has no idea how serious, for the moment, is your physical condition."

"I know that."

"What do you feel yourself?"

She hesitated, "I should like to be downstairs, but perhaps I had better wait for a day or two. I know that several people telephoned from Silchester this morning to know if they could come and see me. If I get up I shall be expected to see them, for some of them were very kind to me."

"They are not kind now," he said grimly. "They are full of stupid, vulgar curiosity."

"I'm afraid Mrs. Hayward will expect me to see two or three of her friends up here," and she looked at him pleadingly.

He got up. "That's out of the question, of course. But I mean to tell Mrs. Hayward you can come down to-morrow afternoon, if she will undertake to allow no one to see you for a full week." He waited a moment, "And I should like to tell her something else—if you'll allow me to do so. I don't wish any allusion to be made in your presence to the events of the last few months."

Her look of gratitude and deep relief was the only answer he craved, and he received that in full measure.

VI

THE WEEK OF COMPLETE SECLUSION WHICH HAD BEEN ordered by Mark Scrutton had been reduced, at Laura Dousland's own request, to four days. She was of too reserved a nature, and also too loyal, to have given the doctor the real reason. This was that Mrs. Hayward spent hours of each day talking to her, both when she was lying in the King's Room, with her face to the bright light, for she had been persuaded that it was really foolish to have a bed made up the wrong way—and even more when she lay out of doors on the comfortable garden couch on the terrace.

Loverslea was a hospitable house, with, as a rule, a great many visitors coming and going, so Laura's hostess found time hang heavy, and that though during those dull days she paid many calls to neighbouring houses where she was to talk her fill concerning the extraordinary affair which had just come to so happy a conclusion.

But by now the central figure—old-fashioned people would have said the heroine—of the *cause célèbre*, had just granted what Alice Hayward had playfully called "audiences" to several ladies who had taken a kind and active interest in her late terrible plight. Two of them, the wife and the sister of the Dean of Silchester, had been asked to-day to lunch, and though Laura had not joined the party in the dining-room, she had been able to see them from where she lay, and the sound of their voices had floated out to where she was having her tray meal. Then had followed a long talk with them both, and when they had at last risen to leave her, a group of other visitors had arrived, and stayed on till the lawyer, Mr. Malefield, had been announced.

How surprised they would all have felt had they learnt that Mrs. Dousland had lain awake most of the night before feeling nervously miserable at the thought of being again brought into contact with ordinary people in an ordinary way! Although those about her were unaware of it, it was years since she had been in any kind of society.

What is now called being "poor" among educated people does not mean the breaking of natural ties. But a penurious way of life, if followed by a married couple who are supposed to enjoy a certain level of cultivation and intelligence, does mean solitude to any woman who is either herself unnaturally careful about money, or who is in the power of a husband, brother, or son, who happens to be so.

During the four years her married life had lasted, Fordish Dousland's wife had rarely met, to talk to, either a man or woman of her own kind.

Mrs. Hayward at last left the lawyer alone with his client, though she could have enjoyed playing a part in the discussion she knew was about to take place.

"You don't look well even now," said Mr. Malefield, and he appeared really sorry.

"I'm only tired from seeing a good many people."

And then she asked him certain questions all dealing with what, after all, is the most important thing in life apart from life itself, that is money.

He was surprised to hear his client's determination that everything that had been spent on her behalf should be paid, as soon as possible, out of the few hundreds of pounds that would remain at her disposal when everything had been settled.

"Now with regard to 2, Kingsley Terrace? It is always better to sell that sort of property in the summer than in the winter, so I am anxious for your leave to put it up for sale at once. I don't suggest a board, which would only attract, just now, the morbid sort of sightseer. All I ask you to do is allow me to say the house is for sale to the chief house-agent in Silchester."

"I would rather not do anything yet about the house," and there came such an expression of pain into Laura Dousland's face that he felt sorry he had raised the question.

Still, he told himself that eight hundred pounds well invested brings in some forty pounds a year, and he felt certain that the fragile-looking young lady lying on a luxurious couch on this delightful terrace was quite unaware of what life would be really like if she tried to live, for even a very short time, on the minute income which would be produced by the wise investment of the little money Fordish Dousland had left. It was a fact that his unfortunate young widow's Defence would absorb about a fifth part of her capital.

"If for any reason you don't care to part with the house, why not let it?" he suggested.

"I would far rather do nothing for the present," she said wearily. "I hope to get right away for a little while; when I'm back, I'll go into the whole matter."

"How long do you think you will be away?"

She put her hand to her forehead, her mind, for the moment, a blank. Then he came to her help. "We are now just in the middle of June, and of course every day that goes by would make a difference to the public interest, if you ultimately decide to hold a sale there. On the other hand, you will probably find it easier to sell the house to an ordinary buyer once all the excitement has died down. Would September be too soon for you to consider disposing of the house?"

"I will certainly be back by September," she murmured. "I promise you that."

Mr. Malefield put his hand on hers. Though she was not a pretty woman, there was certainly something attaching, to himself he even used the word alluring, about the poor creature life had used so hardly.

"Don't promise anything," he said kindly. "I want you to do what is best for yourself. But from now on, Mrs. Dousland, especially as you are going to be so extremely honest, most people would say so over-generous, with regard to the expenditure which has been incurred on your behalf, you will have very little money, and house property isn't like stocks and shares. I suppose you will leave a caretaker in charge? Before the war one could get a woman to live in a furnished house for almost nothing, for she was glad of a roof over her head. But that's not the case now."

"I am not proposing to have anyone living in the house," said Laura quietly. "I shall just leave it empty. There is nothing in it worth stealing."

"That's true, of course. Also I noticed as I passed by, that Number 1, Kingsley Terrace, has been either let or sold, for there was a furniture-van outside the door. You must have found it cheerless living in a house with no neighbours."

"It was cheerless, and I used to think sometimes that I heard strange noises in the empty houses on either side."

She smiled, "Mrs. Hayward believes in ghosts, for there are two quite important ghosts here at Loverslea—but I never saw either of them."

He smiled back at her as he exclaimed: "I was glad to see that furniture-van! The fact that next door is inhabited will make it easier for you to sell the house when you have made up your mind about it."

He stood up. "And now I'm going to give you a piece of advice which has nothing to do with property or the law."

She wondered what he was going to say. So much advice had been given to her in the last few days—mostly advice that she did not mean to follow.

"I think you should use a couple of hundred pounds of your capital in having a real holiday, and in your place I'd go abroad, as soon as you feel up to leaving Loverslea. I'd willingly advance you the money—I mean as a friend of course."

She felt truly moved by this kind man's thought for her.

"I'll think over what you say, and I want to tell you again, Mr. Malefield, how deeply grateful I am to you for all you did for me."

"I hope I'd have done as much for anyone who had been as wickedly and wantonly falsely accused! Also, to do anything for *you,* Mrs. Dousland, has been a real pleasure."

He had not been gone three minutes before Laura was joined by her hostess.

"Now that we're alone and that you're beginning to look yourself again, you and I can settle down to what I've been longing to have with you, my dear, that is a good heart-to-heart talk. I don't suppose you guessed that while you were having what I can only call your rest-cure, Dr. Scrutton didn't want you to talk, or be talked to about anything except—well, I suppose one might say 'Shakespeare and the musical glasses'! However, you're all right again now, aren't you?"

Alice Hayward had come out of the house with her embroidery frame. She was working at an elaborate fire-screen, a copy of one she had seen at a loan collection. It was said to have stood in the sitting-room of Catherine of Braganza, Charles the Second's Queen, and so appeared, to her mind, singularly appropriate for the drawing-room at Loverslea.

"I noticed you ate nothing with your tea, Laura. I mean while that tiresome woman was going on and on about prison discipline—enough to make a saint swear! Now what is there that you would really like? There must be something with which I can tempt you?"

And then her guest made what seemed to the hostess a most astonishing request.

"I think I should like a little brandy," muttered Laura Dousland.

Mrs. Hayward pushed her embroidery frame aside and got up. "Certainly you shall have some brandy, if, that is, I find the key where John generally puts it. When we first married we left everything out, but we very soon left off doing that!"

How often had her listener heard that last sentence uttered, with just the same intonation, and the same little laugh at the end. She even remembered, the first time they had been said in her presence. She had been a forlorn girl, taking up her third situation, and she had been surprised when Mrs. Hayward had made that remark, for her own father had always left everything out, in the generous foolish way which was characteristic of his nature.

Alice Hayward was generally better than her word, and she was soon back on the terrace with a liqueur-glass full of brandy in her hand.

Laura sipped the brandy, and it did take away the strange giddy feeling which had come over her just now. She longed to go upstairs to bed; not to sleep, just to be alone. But she knew there was no chance of her being allowed to do that till half-past seven. At that hour Mr. Hayward would arrive from London, and his wife would have something else to think of than Laura Dousland and her future.

Alice Hayward sat down, and bending again over her work, she enquired: "Well, my dear, was your talk satisfactory? Has Mr. Malefield been able to tell you exactly how much you will have left, when everything has been settled up?"

As regarding money the speaker was not as generous as her husband. She considered it only honest that her friend should refuse to accept as a gift any of the help the lawyers engaged in the legal proceedings had lavished on her. After all, Fordish Dousland's widow was still young, and she had been an excellent governess of the old-fashioned kind. It should not be difficult to find Laura a good position with, say, a well-to-do widower, who didn't quite know what to do with two or three young daughters. True, Laura was not a good housekeeper; but it is always a mistake for a governess to do anything in a house, apart from her own work. That work should consist in causing her pupils to become what Mrs. Hayward prided herself her own two daughters had been taught to be. That was really nice old-fashioned girls of a kind that really nice, old-fashioned young men hope to find with a view to marriage, in a world now full of the kind of girls who make selfish, even sometimes naughty, wives.

She came back from these cogitations to hear Laura's answer to her question. "Mr. Malefield is sending me a statement in two or three days, and then I shall know exactly where I stand."

"And did he say anything about disposing of the house?"

"Yes, he did," said Laura in a low voice.

"I'm glad of that, for I'm sure you will never want to go back and live, even for a very little while, at Silchester."

"I don't suppose I shall," and then she roused herself to add: "Mr. Malefield thinks I ought to spend a little of my capital in getting a thorough change—he said abroad."

"Of course you could do that; but it would seem to me so very much better for you to look for a post as soon as you feel up to it. After all the life of a governess—I mean with nice people, and in a nice house—is not a hard one, is it?" She waited a moment, "We shouldn't dream of letting you go anywhere but to a really good post, and to people about whom we could find out everything. Also, Laura, I hope I need hardly tell you that you are always to regard Loverslea as your home. We shall always look forward to having you here during your holidays."

The speaker of those kind and feeling words looked up from her embroidery frame, and gazed thoughtfully at the prone figure before her. Every word she had just said was true; all the same, she felt it would be a comfort to see poor Laura normal again, and so fit to start her new life.

She couldn't help feeling puzzled, as well as disappointed, at the younger woman's present condition. Laura had been so brave, so—gallant was the word some man had used—at a time she might well have been excused, had she betrayed fear and despondency. So it was really very odd that she should have so completely given way after her fearful ordeal had come to a triumphant conclusion. And then a singular suspicion came into Mrs. Hayward's mind.

Could it be that in a way Laura Dousland, now that she had time to do so, was fretting after her husband? After all, the two had been married four years, and though he might not have gone on adoring his wife as he had done at first she, Alice Hayward, had known more than one widow who had sincerely mourned the death of a husband everyone about her had regarded as a good riddance. Laura, under that reserved manner of hers, undoubtedly had an affectionate nature. She had been truly attached to her pupils, and she had actually cried on Emma's wedding-day, a thing Emma's own mother had not felt the slightest inclination to do.

"I suppose you are sometimes haunted by the thought of poor Fordish; had it ever occurred to you that he might commit suicide?" she observed.

Laura shook her head.

"It was very fortunate he had said that to me, wasn't it?"

And this time Laura answered the question, but in so low a voice that the listener could scarcely hear the murmured: "I suppose it was."

"It certainly was! Lady Molloy thinks my having remembered it impressed the Judge more than anything said by any other witness."

She waited a moment, and the other forced herself to say: "I expect it did."

"I suppose Fordish was a rather peculiar man?"

Laura said nothing in answer to that remark.

This was the first time, since the conclusion of her trial, that anyone, excepting Mr. Hayward when discussing Angelo Terugi, had mentioned Fordish Dousland to his widow.

Since listening to one or two things which had been

asserted in the course of Laura's trial by the Prosecution, Mrs. Hayward had felt extremely curious concerning a side of Laura's married life the two had never discussed, or even touched upon. Now, she felt, was her chance of finding out what she desired to know. But she was ashamed of her curiosity, and she intended to be both decent and delicate in her examination and cross-examination of her friend.

"No doubt your husband couldn't bear your not loving him in a certain way—you know what I mean, Laura?"

"Yes."

"Men are so strange about that."

Alice Hayward uttered this observation in an impressive tone. It was as if she were giving voice to a great discovery of her own.

As the other said nothing in answer, she went on: "Perhaps I wasn't plain enough with you, Laura; I mean the day before your wedding?"

The woman lying there on the garden chair moved restlessly, as she forced herself to answer: "The trouble was—" and then she stopped.

"Yes, Laura? Tell me—what was the trouble?"

"Fordish had felt sure that once we were married, I shouldn't be able to help falling in love with him."

"You mean in the way I mentioned just now?"

"Yes."

"But you got on fairly well at first—even in that way—or didn't you?"

Laura sat up suddenly. This interrogation was a thousand times worse than what she had had to endure in the witness-box. Yet if Alice Hayward wished to know the truth as to Fordish Dousland, she should now be told all that Laura felt she could bring herself to tell.

"We never got on—never, never, never! Either in that way or in any other way! Oh! what a fool I was to lack the courage to say 'no' at the last minute. Yet I had a warning the week before we were married."

Mrs. Hayward pushed aside her embroidery frame, and stared at Laura in dismay. This was a young woman she did not know—an unrestrained, violent young woman. Also, what had she meant by that mysterious allusion to a "warning"?

"I don't remember anything happening a week before your wedding," she said rather coldly.

She was trying to recall the days just before the then governess's marriage. But nearly five years had gone by, and nothing came back to her.

"Don't you remember we went for the day to Amberley? If I'd had the pluck to tell you that evening I couldn't go on with it—oh! what shouldn't I have been spared."

"Do you mean the day you and Fordish went to see a pageant together?"

"Yes, that is the day I mean."

Laura was gazing as if into space, her face so convulsed with feeling that she did, in very truth, look like another human being.

"But what can have happened that day? I don't understand. Surely he was not unkind to you on that day? The one thing I do remember clearly about that time was his dotty love of you."

"He let me pay—in fact, he made me pay, for everything—*everything* that day!"

"My dear Laura, what a funny thing for you to remember. Perhaps the poor man forgot to bring any money?"

She was looking at the woman whom she believed to be

her close friend with astonishment and discomfort. She had always thought—they had all always thought in that opulent house—the Laura Dalberton of that far-off time far too indifferent to money. She might have saved double what she had saved out of her good salary, if her nature had been different.

"I have often, often thought of that day, of his horrible meanness, and cursed myself for a fool," went on Laura in a strangled tone.

There came across Alice Hayward a feeling of slight disgust. She was distressed, as well as dismayed, at hearing that admission, phrased, too, in such a brutally frank way. She was now becoming acquainted with a side of Laura she had never suspected was there, even during the years they had known one another as she had thought, so intimately. This Laura had about her something that was primitive and even—to herself she uttered the horrid word "coarse."

"You were astonished when I first told you, Alice—I mean in the prison—that I had nothing left of my savings. I didn't tell you then that I had spent the whole of that money the first eighteen months of my married life in buying food."

"Food? But how extraordinary!"

"It's the truth."

"Why did you do such a thing? It was stupid, apart from everything else."

The question, and the words which followed the question, were uttered in a censorious tone.

"Fordish was very particular about what he ate," said Fordish's widow in a bitter tone.

"I know he was. John and I thought him very greedy."

Alice Hayward was shocked with herself at making this admission, now that the poor man was dead. But this, after all, was a very frank kind of conversation, wasn't it?

"He would never give me enough money to pay for decent food," followed after a moment's pause. "He thought me a bad manager, and I suppose I was."

"You weren't exactly a good manager, Laura. I remember how the bills went up that time I left you in charge, when I was nursing poor mother. But you were very young, and cook likes to be extravagant. Of course I allowed for that."

Laura was still staring before her in a queer absorbed way and, oddly enough, she gave no sign of having heard what had just been said to her. So it was in a rather louder tone that the older woman exclaimed: "Still, you ought not to have spent your own money on the housekeeping! I wish you had asked *me* what to do, for I would have said a word myself to Fordish Dousland. A good many men expect to be made comfortable on nothing."

Laura shook her head. How to explain to a woman who had just made that remark the sort of man Fordish Dousland had been? She suddenly decided that it was no use attempting to do so, and that she must try and bring this hateful discussion to an end.

"Things got better after a while," she said, speaking quietly now, "for I turned myself into a fair cook. All the same, after my own money had all gone, I had a wretched time till Angelo Terugi was engaged as houseman, for Fordish would never pay enough wages for us to have a good maid."

"Let me see? You had saved just over two hundred pounds, and it would have been more, if you'd been careful. John and I used to be quite distressed at your spending your own money over the girls. You were far too generous, my dear," and she looked at the other with puzzled, considering, eyes.

There followed a pause, and again, oddly enough, Mrs.

Hayward felt as if her guest had not heard what had just been said to her.

"Oh, how glad I was the first day Angelo Terugi was there, and when Fordish said, 'I'm going to do the housekeeping now with the help of this Italian'!"

It was as if Laura was speaking to herself.

"But you got awfully tired of the macaroni and the onion stews, didn't you? It was the only complaint I ever knew you make."

"It was stupid of me to mind that," said Laura listlessly. She felt very much ashamed of the passion she had shown just now.

"It was curious, wasn't it, that your husband was so fond of that Italian wine?"

"It reminded him of Italy; also—"

"Also what?" came the eager question.

So many, many people had spoken to her of that Chianti flask! She longed to question Laura about the one mysterious factor in the otherwise simple story. And now had come her chance.

"Were you going to say something about the Chianti flask, Laura?"

"No, not about the flask. Only that Chianti happens to be the cheapest wine of the sort Fordish liked."

Alice Hayward felt pleased that Laura was now talking in a quiet sensible manner. Till this afternoon she had obeyed Dr. Scrutton, and had not spoken of the past to his patient. But now she felt that unnatural silence might well come to an end. Indeed, according to the latest theories regarding the health of mind and body, it did an ailing person good to talk freely of anything peculiar or painful; it rid him or her of what is called an inhibition.

So she asked, with some eagerness in her calm voice, a question to which she longed to have a true answer.

"What exactly happened the first time your husband hid the flask? Where did he hide it? I can't remember what you said—"

"He put it in the dress cupboard in my bedroom."

"Did he tell you he had done it?"

"Yes."

"What happened then?"

"Angelo Terugi guessed what had happened, and was very much offended."

"And then you persuaded them to make it up?"

"Yes."

"In a way it was odd that Angelo Terugi should have been so positive that he did put a flask of that wine on the tray that night—I mean the evening before Fordish died, wasn't it?"

Laura did not answer at once. But at last she said slowly: "I am sure the police forced him to say that, and then he was afraid to eat his words."

"My dear Laura—I don't think our police would ever *force* a witness to say anything! They leave that sort of thing to the police of other countries."

"They tried to force *me* to swear to things that weren't true." But the assertion was made in a listless tone.

"When d'you mean?"

"I mean just before the inquest, when they already knew what Dr. Grant was going to say about me."

Now Mrs. Hayward would have liked to challenge that statement, for she liked and indeed admired, all she knew of the police, but she was intent on the mystery of the Chianti flask.

"Something must have happened to that flask, even if it was empty," and she looked expectantly at Laura.

But Laura said nothing.

"Of course I've never doubted—neither has John—that Terugi had drunk up the remainder of the wine before he left for London that evening. But the point is what did he *do* with the flask after having finished the wine. Haven't you any theory?"

"I haven't any theory."

"Even now it's an important point, Laura."

"Why?"

"Because," said Alice Hayward firmly, "as long as what happened to that Chianti flask remains a mystery, a certain number of people will believe you did poison your husband."

"I can't help that."

Laura Dousland's voice was hard, and her face, naturally white, became suffused with colour as she added: "I think I had better go upstairs now, and, if you don't mind, I'd rather not come down again this evening, Alice. I feel stupid with tiredness."

"I'm afraid John will be very disappointed! He was going to have brought a man back with him to dinner, and I told him he mustn't do that, as you were going to dine downstairs for the first time."

"It won't hurt Mr. Hayward to dine alone with you for once."

The woman to whom that remark was addressed felt so surprised at the tone in which it was made, as well as at the remark itself, that she remained silent.

What had come over Laura Dousland this afternoon? It was as if the quiet, sweet-natured young woman she had known so long had become, in the course of an hour, another person, and, what was so disturbing, such an extraordinarily unpleasant, rude kind of person.

Mrs. Hayward felt the more, not the less, annoyed and puzzled, when Laura, slipping off the couch, exclaimed in a choking voice: "I was a beast to say that! But have mercy on me, Alice; I'm so dreadfully unhappy—"

Without waiting for an answer, she then tottered quickly across the flagged terrace, and disappeared into the house.

"Dreadfully unhappy?" What could Laura Dousland mean by saying such a thing as that? She ought to be, in fact she must be, even if she didn't realise it yet, extremely happy—now. A week ago a hideous fate had still been hanging over Laura's head, suspended, as Sir Joseph Molloy had well put it in his final speech to that stolid jury, like the Sword of Damocles. She, Alice Hayward, had been very much impressed by that simile. In a way it had added to the dreadful anxiety from which she had suffered during the last couple of days of Laura's trial.

How strange, as well as how unfortunate, that the poor thing should suddenly have become—hysterical was the only word which described the state in which she had just shown herself to be, both when speaking of her late husband and his oddities, and also when she had said that rude queer thing about its not hurting her kind host to dine alone with his wife for once. Why it would please John—of course it would—for them to dine together, and it would remind them both of their honeymoon.

When Laura reached the King's Room, she took the ornate key out of the door on the corridor side, and locked herself in.

She was shaking all over, hardly able, indeed, to stand. In

how short a time could she decently leave Loverslea? Not for some days certainly—and that whatever befell her further in the way of inquisitive, torturing cross-examination, as to a past she was making an intense effort to forget and put behind her for ever.

Slowly she undressed, and then she unlocked the door. Alice Hayward had not known she was being hideously cruel. Indeed she was, in actual fact, a truly kind woman. But she, Laura Dousland, in that unreasonable, as those who have been flayed alive are no doubt apt to be, felt that she would give years of the life she had long valued but lightly, never to see that kind woman again.

VII

A further week went by, and Mark Scrutton stood outside the great front door of Loverslea. It was close on noon, and he had had a long morning's work.

His face was set and stern, for his last call had been on a rich retired London tradesman, who had declared it to be his belief that Mrs. Dousland had been certainly guilty. When asked the reason for that belief by his pretty nurse (whom Scrutton to himself described as "an impudent hussy"), the old man had observed, with a chuckle, that he shouldn't be a bit surprised if it came out some day that the standoffish fine lady, for so he designated her, had been fond of the Italian fellow! Hadn't she taken Angelo Terugi's part when in the witness-box, and that though his evidence concerning the disappearance of the Chianti flask had gone some way towards hanging her? To that the nurse had observed, with a smile at the good-looking doctor, that it must be trying for a young woman to be married to a man nearly thirty years older than herself "and dotty for love of her."

"'Amorous' was the word the judge used in his

summing-up," had added the patient, and Mark Scrutton had listened to that interchange of words in a turmoil of anger and of disgust, too.

Was that sort of base insinuation always made when a woman—however noble-minded and innocent—became the central figure of a *cause célèbre*? He had seen a good deal of the ugly side of humanity in his thirty-three years of life, but he was primarily a scientist, and between his first experiment in private practice, and the few months he had just spent at Silchester, what to himself appeared a lifetime had elapsed. With all his soul he pitied the general practitioner who has to endure the sort of vapid, vulgar and, as he had experienced to-day, grossly libellous talk from patients he must not, or dare not, offend.

It was with a certain grim satisfaction that he remembered, now, how he had put the fear of God into that old beast. He had done it very quietly, and suavely too, by simply observing to the nurse, in her patient's presence, that she must be most careful not to repeat what had just been said, even if only in joke, as Mrs. Dousland could obtain enormous damages against any man, or woman, too, if it came to that, who in the presence of a third party had expressed disbelief in the justice of the verdict which had exonerated her. This especially would be the case if the remark were coupled with any doubt as to her moral character. "It would be," he had concluded with what he hoped had appeared to be a smile, "a case of paying up and looking pleasant, for no lawyer would advise his client to go to court if threatened with such an action for libel and slander." And at once the old man had adjured both the doctor and his nurse to forget what had been said.

The trifling episode had the more sickened and

distressed Mark Scrutton because since he had been seeing her here, at Loverslea, the admiration he had felt for Laura Dousland during the time he had been able to spend in the Court House, had increased a hundredfold.

He had never felt such instinctive sympathy for any human being as he now felt for this fragile, yet indomitably brave, young woman. And to that admiration was now joined considerable anxiety, for he was distressed, as well as puzzled, to find that she was making so little progress; in some ways she seemed to be more listless, and physically less well, than she had been since he had pulled her through the first collapse, which had followed immediately after the conclusion of her trial. And now, kind and generous though he knew the Haywards to be, he strongly desired to get her away from Loverslea; and when Mark Scrutton strongly desired anything, it generally came to pass.

So it was with much inward satisfaction that he learnt Mrs. Hayward had had to go to London for the day, and so would not be present, as she generally chose to be, at his interview with Mrs. Dousland.

Alice Hayward, too, had observed that Laura was not making much progress, and the fact disturbed her, partly because, though she would have denied that such was the case, she and her husband longed to begin once more their pleasant placid round of entertaining and of being entertained. With Laura Dousland becoming more, instead of less, an invalid, it was difficult to ask people to the house, and it would have been against Mrs. Hayward's code of good manners to leave any guest alone while she went off, as she so much desired to do, on a round of visits among friends of hers who had all taken an excited interest in the mysterious case with which the owner of Loverslea and his wife had been so closely associated.

Mark Scrutton found his patient lying out on the lawn, under a cedar tree, and he was glad to find her there, for had she been on the terrace, all he was about to say to her could be overheard from certain rooms in the house.

As his tall figure advanced over the grass, Laura turned and looked at him with an unconsciously welcoming glance, for he was the only person she had seen, since her acquittal, who never jarred on her nerves, or made her feel on the defensive.

As he came close up to her: "You're not so well as you were yesterday morning," he said abruptly. "Why is that?"

"A lot of people came to tea, and I had to see them all; but no one is coming to-day."

"You haven't a hope of pulling round till you get away from this place," he observed.

Then he sat down, and looked into her white face intently.

God! How she had suffered, and how plucky she had been.

"I know that's true," she said quietly, "and I'm going to tell Mrs. Hayward this evening that after next Monday I need no longer presume on her kindness. I heard from an old schoolfellow yesterday, with whom I hadn't been in touch for years, and she asks me to come and stay with her for a while. She has a job in Newcastle, and I feel I could be her paying guest, and so really independent. That's impossible here."

"It's queer these good people can't understand that all you want is to be left alone."

"I was foolish to come here. I had no idea it would be like this. You see in Newcastle—" and then she stopped suddenly.

"Yes, Mrs. Dousland?"

"There, at any rate, no one will want to see me, or talk to me. Oh! if you knew how I dread being talked to—even by the kindest people. So if you can patch me up enough to get off next Monday, I shall be very grateful. In fact, I wondered if you would have the kindness to telegraph for me to my friend? I can't post a letter here without someone telling Mrs. Hayward, and then come endless questions and discussions. I do so long to be away from everything and everybody in the neighbourhood of Silchester."

Mark Scrutton exclaimed: "I have a better plan for you than this Newcastle plan!"

She looked at him apprehensively. Already she was beginning to lean on him, and to feel she must do as he wished, and she was afraid he was going to suggest she should go into a nursing home for a while. He had asked her more than once if she would consent to do this, but she shrank from the thought, for she had suffered far more than she now cared to remember from the well-meaning prison wardress who had had charge of her. That wardress had begun life as a trained nurse, and she had both the virtues and the faults of her profession. She had been an enthusiastic believer in her prisoner's innocence, and had always predicted she would be vindicated; but often Laura had felt she would have preferred cold indifference.

"I ask you to listen to my plan," said her new friend earnestly, "because I do believe that it would be the wisest thing you could do for a while. But don't feel I shall be offended if you make up your mind to reject it in favour of going to Newcastle."

She felt greatly relieved. What he had just said could not be a preamble to his former suggestion of a nursing home.

For a moment she forgot herself, and wondered with a flicker of interest and curiosity as to what sort of a man was Mark Scrutton, underneath his cool, matter-of-fact manner? He was so unlike any of the few men she had known in her life, especially in the days when she had lived here, in beautiful Loverslea, as governess to Emma and Mary Hayward. They had all been men of business, absorbed in various forms of money-making. Mark Scrutton had nothing about him of such men. His face was that of the intellectual worker who is never wholly able to throw his work aside. Money, except as a means of carrying on the kind of medical research to which she knew by now he meant to devote his future life, meant nothing to him.

"Listen, Mrs. Dousland!"

He looked at her with a touch of boyish eagerness in his face, and she smiled as she answered, "I will listen, Dr. Scrutton."

"My parents live in Devonshire, where my father inherited a small estate some years ago called Mellcombe. It includes a stretch of seashore, and practically on the beach is a small one-storeyed house, built before the days of bungalows. In fact, it's called Beach Cottage. There are three rooms, a tiny kitchen, and a bathroom, and when I was twenty-one my father gave me the little place as a birthday present. Now and again I lend it to a friend. My suggestion is that you go there, now, for a thorough rest and change. Of course, it's lonely, but I don't think you'd mind that, just now."

He stopped speaking, though he was looking at her intently.

She murmured: "I don't know how to thank you for having thought of this for me. It sounds too good to be true—" and her voice broke.

"There is a village girl who would be delighted to sleep there, and look after you. She was a maid in our house for a while, and my mother says she is quite a fair cook."

"Do your parents know you are thinking of lending me your cottage?"

"No, and I shall simply tell them, after you are there, that I have lent the place to one of my patients."

She said hesitatingly: "The other day Mr. Hayward told me I can change my name without paying much for the right to do so. I am thinking of taking my mother's maiden name; she was Laura Ordeley. Mr. Hayward thinks I should be wise to change my name; do you agree with him?"

"Indeed I do," said Mark Scrutton emphatically. "I will find out how you can do it with the least trouble and, which I think is important, the least publicity, possible."

For a while they both remained silent. To-day had been Laura's worst day, up to now. She had been feeling unutterably miserable. Though she was longing to leave Loverslea, she had felt, between the lines of her one-time schoolfellow's letter, an inquisitive desire to meet again one whose name had been on thousands of lips as the centre of an exciting mystery. But now, the knowledge that she was going far away from where she had suffered so acutely and, further, to enjoy a spell of real solitude, seemed to give her anew what she had lost, the will to live.

"May I suggest that you say as little as possible of this plan to Mr. and Mrs. Hayward? Leave it to me to tell them I know of a place where you will be comfortable, and where you can have the kind of rest and change your present condition demands, if you are to be restored to health and strength."

Again she said falteringly: "I don't know how to thank you."

"Don't think of thanking me! I'm glad to have the little place occupied. In a way it's too near my home for me to feel I can live in it myself, and more than once when I have lent it to a patient, he or she expected my people to provide some kind of entertainment. As you can imagine, that made difficulties, for my father and mother only care to be together, with now and then some old friend, who when staying with them respects their love of quietude."

He leaned forward and gripped her hand. It was piteously small and thin, like a child's hand. Somehow the touch of that fragile hand, cold, too, on this hot day, made him feel more vividly than he had ever done before, the long drawn-out agony she had gone through.

He asked, as he released her hand: "Could you be ready by Saturday? I'm going home for the week-end, and so I could settle you in on that day. I would go down Friday, meet you at the nearest station, eight miles from Mellcombe, and arrange to have everything ready at the cottage. Of course I'll tell my mother that Mrs. Ordeley doesn't wish to be called on—at any rate for a time."

He smiled, and it transformed the character of his face.

When she thought of Mark Scrutton, and lately Laura had often thought of him, for he paid an almost daily visit to Loverslea, she saw him as he had looked during the half-hour he had stood in the witness-box, being first examined, and then cross-examined, as to his slight acquaintance with Fordish Dousland.

She was aware that his clear, passionless account of the discussion which had taken place between himself and her husband concerning the effects of the poison which had undoubtedly caused Fordish Dousland's death, had played a crucial part in her acquittal.

Though he was looking at her, now, with a softened and most kindly expression, there came back to her the sound of his voice when he had been sworn. It had been a firm resonant voice and she, the poor soul standing in the dock, had felt suddenly fearfully afraid. She had known that on his testimony much would depend, and that all those who had her interests at heart were intensely anxious to hear exactly what he was prepared to say, concerning the last visit he had made to the then owner of 2, Kingsley Terrace.

She suddenly came back to the present to hear him exclaim, with a touch of eagerness: "Later on I should like you to know my parents! They are wonderful people, though I say so. I'm their only child, and, of course, my father would have liked me to be a soldier like himself, but he never said a word when I told him what I really wanted to be, and it was the more splendid of him as I was still only a boy, and might not have been supposed to know my own mind."

As if half ashamed of having said as much, he leapt to his feet. "I'll come over to-morrow and speak to Mrs. Hayward. And you must back me up, Mrs. Dousland. I think she's quite likely to make difficulties."

"I'm sure she won't," and he saw a singular expression cross her face. "Since I've been here, she hasn't liked to ask anyone to stay, and I'm afraid she and Mr. Hayward have found me a trying visitor. I'm sure it will be a relief to them both, when I leave Loverslea."

He felt surprised. "I can't believe that of Mrs. Hayward. She's so devoted to you."

"She doesn't care for the real me—she never has." And then she sighed convulsively. It was as if she couldn't help saying what she believed to be the truth to this man. She went on: "I haven't been able to pretend as I used to do, when I was governess here. So, since they took me in the day my trial ended, Mr. and Mrs. Hayward have found me, I'm afraid, a sad disappointment."

There was a world of bitterness in her low voice, and her listener felt she was stripping her soul to his gaze.

Mark Scrutton was too honest a man to say nay to that confession. He told himself that no doubt it was true that the husband and wife, who had been living at high pressure during the many days Laura Dousland's trial had lasted, were now, though doubtless unconsciously, longing to settle down to the pleasant existence they had led before this tragedy had come athwart them. The presence of this poor scarred woman in their delightful country home had become that of the skeleton at their feast of life.

VIII

It was a fair summer evening, and a golden stillness brooded over land and sea. Laura Dousland was moving quickly about the old one-storeyed little house which lay above the stretch of shingle and of sand, and now appeared, in her imagination, her own domain, and that though she had only been at Mellcombe for just over four weeks.

She had finished her fruit and bread-and-butter supper, and she had just washed up, for the village girl who had slept at Beach Cottage, and waited on her for the first ten days of her stay there, had been called away to a married sister who was ill. Since then Mrs. Ordeley, as Laura now called herself, and had come almost to feel herself to be, had done with ease, and even something like pleasure, the few household chores there were to do. It was heavenly to be alone, quite alone, in this now dear little homestead, where such peace and strength had come to her as she had not known for years.

She not only felt, she was, a different woman to the

broken, haunted, still most miserable creature Mark Scrutton had settled into the cottage a month ago.

When he had left her, then, she had known he had been full of doubt and anxiety as to whether he was doing wisely in giving her what she had so earnestly said was the only thing she wanted in life, that is utter solitude.

He knew, now, that he need not have doubted, and that her instinct had been right; but he was still unaware that she lived here quite alone. She had concealed the fact from him, afraid that he would try and persuade her to have a substitute for the village girl who had possessed what is a rare gift in English village folk, the gift of silence.

With every day, Laura might have said with truth with every hour, that slipped by, the past had receded, and grown dim in her mind. This in a sense was the stranger, as Mark Scrutton himself, who had been so closely associated with the last terrible lap of her life, had remained in constant touch with her.

Each had discovered the other was a reader, and that had become a bond even in the short time they had known one another. Not content with sending her books and magazines, he had written her longish letters, and every evening the telephone, which formed her only link with the world, had rung, and they two had had a talk. But never had he written, or uttered even an accidental word, touching on the event which had brought about their singular, and to her now most comforting, and comfortable, friendship.

It was the physician questioning his patient who got through just for a few moments of kind advice each evening. The telephone ring would sometimes come at eight, sometimes at nine, sometimes even at ten, but never had he failed her; and since, some ten days ago, he had arrived at

Mellcombe Court to spend his yearly holiday with his parents, and he and Laura had met every day, she found herself missing each evening the tinkle of the bell, and the deep measured voice asking, "Is that Mrs. Ordeley?"

She wondered, sometimes, a little sorely, why he had seemed nearer to her when he had been far away than now, when he was living close by, and when he would come down most mornings, and always every afternoon when he had had tea with his mother. Yet so it was. She knew that after all her good friend, when at home, must be leading a life full of divers interests in which she could have no share or part at all; and maybe it was that which sometimes made her feel forlorn, and very lonely as well, in spite of those daily meetings.

Laura longed to know Mrs. Scrutton, but she was afraid to suggest a meeting, for she still felt like one who has been flayed alive and flinches from the lightest touch, even after the healing process has begun. Also, so far, Mark Scrutton had not suggested she should meet his parents.

It seemed strange to her, now, that she could form no inward picture of his home, though she knew, with a familiar knowledge, what the outside shell of his dwelling-place was like. She had but to walk for a very few minutes up the path which indeed actually began at what was now her own front door, to see the low white building, standing high on a plateau, called Mellcombe Court, though it was a good quarter of a mile from the shore.

Laura had looked forward to Mark Scrutton's arrival for his holiday as to something which would be very pleasant, indeed, delightful. And then, well? everything had been different to what she had expected, and she had felt less, rather than more, intimately acquainted with him, than during those solitary days when his letters, and the brief telephone call each evening, had been the only thing which bound her to the world of living men and women. For one thing she now felt increasingly ashamed that he should go on believing that the village girl slept at Beach Cottage. But it was after all entirely her own affair whether she chose to live alone, and do her own housework. All the same, she could not help knowing that he would be both dismayed and uneasy, at her sleeping in an unguarded house on one of the loneliest stretches of shore in western England.

Laura Dalberton had been born impulsive and singularly truthful, but she had become, with time, increasingly secretive, and, to herself, she used the ugly word, "sly." Early in her life she had learnt the lesson that any girl or woman who earns her living in subjection to another human being is bound to learn, that of curbing her impulses, and bridling her tongue. Especially had she found this to be the case when she had come as governess to Loverslea, for with such an employer as Alice Hayward she had had to batten down almost all her natural impulses and emotions. But with Mark Scrutton she had known from their first real meeting—that which had taken place on the evening of the day her trial had ended—that she need not now stop to ask herself if she was about to say what would shock or surprise her listener.

Yet, on this very day the two had had a talk which had left her, for the first time since she had been living at Mellcombe, restless, and even troubled in her mind. It had been in a sense her fault, for in answer to a question as to whether she was now sleeping without the aid of what she called "dope," she had exclaimed: "I have not slept for years as I am sleeping now. This place has made me feel young again, and I would like to go on living here for ever and ever!"

He had looked at her gravely: "Do you mean that?"

"Why of course I do!"

"Then there is no reason in the world why you shouldn't stay here during the rest of your life. If it would make you feel comfortable, I will make over the little place to you by deed of gift."

As, astonished, she had shaken her head, he had gone on quietly, "If you won't take it as a gift, we can arrange for you to buy this cottage from me, and then it won't matter if I die within three years."

There had come a cold feeling round her heart. "Die within three years?" she had repeated, and her dark eyes had become full of questioning fear and pain.

He had got up suddenly: "Don't look like that! I'm perfectly well. But if you make a deed of gift to a person, and the giver dies within three years, he or she must pay legacy duty. That's all I meant! I'll see about your buying Beach Cottage next time I'm in London, but you must let me fix the price."

It was as if she could still hear his voice, thoughtful, measured, calm. And then, without saying good-bye, he had left her. She had thought he would surely come again in the late afternoon, but he had not done so, and so she had had plenty of time to go over these few sentences again and again. If he had really meant what he had just said, had he been offended when she had shaken her head in answer to that matter-of-fact offer to give her the house which had been, as she had suddenly remembered, his own father's gift on his twenty-first birthday?

Could it be true that she need never give a thought to her future any more, and that she could live here for the rest of her life, her only contact with human kind remaining that with her friend Mark Scrutton? Already he spent all his spare time here, at Mellcombe, and some day the delightful place would be his entirely, and he would spend his old age—though she could not imagine him any older than he was now—in the house where he was living to-day. He would be an old man then, and she would be an old woman. But they would still be friends—even better friends maybe than they were now, for there would have been long years when they would have had time to grow closer to one another—time, too, during which she would have time to forget—everything.

At last she undressed and went to bed in the room next to the one living-room. There, also, a door opened on to the solitary shining stretches of shingle and of sand beyond which lay the placid sea.

Laura suddenly got out of bed and opened wide the door. She often slept like this, for she was a fearless woman, and no stranger had ever appeared anywhere near this remote and indeed hidden corner of the Mellcombe estate.

Colonel Scrutton possessed a long stretch of shore, and as there were shifting shallows near the land, and dangerous currents a little way out, fishing boats kept well away from the beach.

All day there had been a haze over the sea, but now the mist had lifted, and the moon riding high in the sky shed splashes of pearly light on the dark waters. And as Laura lay awake, from the flower garden Mark Scrutton had been at pains to make on two sides of the little house, there drifted delicate scents which mingled with the more pungent odours of the shore.

In obedience to what she knew to be his strong wish, she was trying to break herself from the habit of taking some form of narcotic. She had had nothing of the kind to-night, and so her brain was unnaturally alive.

For two full years before her husband's death she had read very little, though for as long as her savings had lasted, books, both old and new, had been her solace and refuge in what had often seemed an intolerable existence. But when she had been obliged to ask Fordish Dousland for the money which would enable her to renew her subscription to a circulating library, he had refused to give it to her, saying the hours she spent in reading were a waste of time, and likely, also, seriously to affect her eyesight, and therefore her appearance.

After her arrest, while she was awaiting her trial, an effort had been made, by those concerned with her welfare, to persuade her to take out books from the prison library. But she had found it impossible to concentrate her mind on any printed page; and on one occasion her talkative wardress had told her that both the governor and the doctor felt very much surprised that Mrs. Dousland was not a reader. She had been too numbed and bemused during those weeks of waiting for her trial, to do anything but sit and knit during the long hours she had to be alone.

After the end of her trial, there had come over her, at Loverslea, a sudden longing to read a novel of which all the world was then talking. She had had a secret hope that this story might take her mind off the fearful events which, try as she would, remained hideously alive. But Alice Hayward had decreed that reading an exciting novel would be bad for her nerves.

Within three or four days of her arrival at Beach Cottage, she had taken to books again. At first it had been only to please the man who was sending her something to read almost every day; and then because she found that yes, a good book did take her out of herself, as the saying is. So it was that she had fallen into the way of reading herself to sleep.

But to-night she had put her book down, and turned off the lamp, almost as soon as she had got into bed.

At last she told herself that if she lay thus awake through the night, she would look ill and, what she now feared to appear for the first time in her life, worn and old looking, in the morning. So she sprang again out of bed, shut out the moonlight and, as far as was possible, the sounds made by the waves lapping the stony beach.

Then she pushed the bolt into the heavy old door. Mark Scrutton, on the first evening he had left her here, had been insistent that she do this always, although he still believed that a strong village lass slept in the second bedroom of the little house each night.

What would he feel if he learnt that for a long time now, his patient had been quite alone, both day and night, and with every window open to the light and air, for Laura exulted in the wild sea winds which sometimes swept the coast even in summer weather? No doubt he would be dismayed, but those winds brought with them a message that she was free, and only belonged to herself.

So new and wonderful, still, was the knowledge that she no longer owed allegiance and obedience to any human being, that sometimes Laura Dousland felt afraid—for it was as if she had slipped into another woman's life and might, should the fates so decide, slip back again into a servitude which had become unendurable.

It was since the girl had left Beach Cottage that her nerves had quieted, and that she had felt health, and even a measure of youth, returning to her. Also, not once had she felt afraid of being alone.

And yet to-night she was restless and ill at ease. So restless and wide awake that at last, ashamed of her lack of courage, she poured out a full measure of the sleeping-draught she had half promised to abjure; and soon she was sleeping heavily, and dreaming the dreams which are induced by even a few drops of morphia added to any other form of narcotic.

One of the dreams she dreamt to-night took her back to Silchester.

She had had a letter from her lawyer telling her that as a number of houses had been broken into and furniture injured, she would be wise to have a caretaker living in Number 2, Kingsley Terrace, till she either sold or let the house. He had even told her he knew a respectable woman who would be willing to sleep there for a trifling weekly payment. This letter had disturbed her, the more so that she was not going to follow his advice. There was nothing of real value in the house, and she had remembered, with a quivering sensation of pain and disgust, hearing something which had revealed to her while she was at Loverslea the fact that certain ghoul-like curiosity-mongers had tried to get in to see the kitchen from whence the Chianti flask was said to have vanished, and even the meagrely-furnished bedroom where Fordish Dousland had been found dead.

But she had not yet answered the lawyer's kindly-meant letter. And doubtless because its contents lay there, in her inner consciousness, had come a dream-return to that dreary dwelling-place, or rather to the strip of garden which had been transformed by its late owner into what had recalled to him a paved pleasance in Venice.

Dreams being such unpredictable experiences, Laura was actually transported to Silchester in the company of her father, of whom she had only dreamt before on one occasion, since his death.

"Quaint, certainly, but rather absurd, my dear!" he now exclaimed. And she, vexed at the criticism, though it was only what she had often, nay always, said to herself, when in that stone and marble-filled garden, answered, "It is mine now, Father, and no one can come in here to laugh and jeer at anything, unless I allow it."

She was again in a sound and dreamless sleep when she was suddenly awakened by the sound of footsteps close to a window which overlooked the path leading to Mellcombe Court. Instinctively she glanced at her luminous clock, and saw that it was half-past three. Who could have wandered on to the enclosed stretch of manor-land situated so far away from any known highway as to be outside even the hardiest hiker's beat?

And then she saw the dim figure of a tall man pass the window of the room where she lay in bed, and knew he must be making for the shore, for the path stopped at her front door.

Flinging a dressing-gown round her, she went through into the sitting-room, and called out boldly: "Who is out there?"

If the wanderer was seeking a place to lie down and sleep, she could tell him of a cave hard by, above the sea-level, where was a heap of dried bracken. Then, in the morning, she would offer him breakfast in her kitchen.

Suddenly she heard Mark Scrutton's voice: "I'm so sorry I waked you! I'm a clumsy fool not to have kept further away."

She unbolted the door, and the voice was kind and happy

which reached him from the dark living-room, "What's the matter—Mark?"

It was less than a week ago that they had become "Mark" and "Laura" to one another, and each was still chary of calling the other by his or her name.

"The matter is that you're sleeping here alone! My mother was told it in the village yesterday."

"D'you mean you've come here now because of that?"

"Of course I have."

"If you think I ought to have someone sleeping here I'll find another girl. But honestly, I'm happiest alone! You see, it's so peaceful—" Her voice altered: "I've felt at times as if with the coming of night I was in quite another world," and he told himself that this world had been indeed a cruel world to her.

She came through the door, and stood near to him. He could only just see her, and he thought she was wearing the frock she generally wore in the afternoon. So he took her hand and asked, "But why didn't you go to bed, if you're really not afraid of being alone?"

"I've been to bed—of course I have! I only got up when I heard footsteps, but even then I was not afraid."

He still held her hand clasped in his, and she felt a sensation of constraint and shyness. They were speaking in low tones, as if fearing to be overheard, though each knew that the nearest possible eavesdroppers were indeed far away from this solitary stretch of seashore.

"I feel grieved that I have kept you from your rest," she whispered.

Mark, ever since he had come to know her well, delighted in her careful old-fashioned diction. It was so other from the way the younger women with whom his present work brought him in contact expressed their thoughts. From his austere father this man had inherited a strong dislike of slang.

Laura now made as if to draw the hand he held in his away, but he held it all the closer, as he muttered, "I couldn't sleep, and so I got up and went out of doors. I've been lying on the heather under the stars, about fifty yards away from here, thinking of you—"

And then he added, in a matter-of-fact tone: "Surely you know, Laura, that I love you?"

He dropped her hand, and caught her to him. For a moment she seemed to be all his. Then suddenly she gave a stifled cry and, averting her head, she moaned, "You mustn't say you love me, Mark. Never speak to me of love. I thought, I hoped, you meant us to be friends—just friends—always."

He put her from him gently, and she, retreating into the cottage living-room, fell on to the couch where they had of late often sat side by side talking eagerly and happily, it had seemed to him, of everything in the world which might interest and draw together in mental communion a man and woman who are—just friends.

"May I come in?" he asked, in an ill-assured voice.

"Oh yes—yes!"

As he came close up to her the wan glimmer of dawn showed him her pale face, and he felt agonisingly sorry that he had yielded to the impulse which had mastered him when his arms had closed round her, and he had thirsted for her lips.

But it seemed a lifetime, to him, since she had become part of himself, flesh of his flesh, bone of his bone. Again and again he had asked himself during the last few days how it was that he had not known her for his own the first time he had met her, in that sinister house where she had been prisoned for so long? By now he had persuaded himself that, hidden in the depths of his consciousness, the eternal element in Laura's entity he believed to be present in every man and woman, had taken up its dwelling-place—for ever. But now he would, because he must, banish from his thoughts and physical being, the desires and demands for which she had just shown such shrinking fear and repugnance. Still, he felt her his wholly and for ever, and that he must win her assent to this indestructible tie, even if it took years to do so.

Neither knew how long a time they stayed silent thus together. She sitting on the couch, her face cupped in her hands, and he standing by her. But at last he broke the pregnant stillness which seemed to envelop them as if it was a sentient thing in the little room, "I'll never speak of love again, my dear. To be your friend will quite content me."

As she made no reply to the assertion he actually believed he could make true, he exclaimed: "I'll go away now! By the time we meet again you must not only have forgiven me, you must have forgotten what I said."

She stood up suddenly, and threw herself upon his breast.

"Speak to me of love again," she cried wildly. And then, "Say that you love me, Mark—"

She was looking up into his face with an at once piteous, and could it be a beckoning, expression, in her eyes.

His arms closed round her loosely. It would be such agony were she to shrink from him, and avert her head again.

There swept over him, not, alas! for the first time during those days when Laura had become the core of his life, a primitive, savage hatred of Fordish Dousland.

Making a fearful inward effort he now banished that foul

wraith. Then he said slowly: "I adore you, Laura, and with all my soul I ask you to be my wife. If you say yes, I shall only want from you what you feel you can give."

She whispered, "I will give everything—"

She closed her eyes, feeling she could not meet his probing ardent questioning look, for she had been not only unknowing but even quite unsuspecting, of that pure passion of love between a man and woman which is the antithesis of lust. But he, bewildered by her sudden surrender, was afraid.

"Kiss me," she breathed, and their lips met and clung together, while for them both the past became as nought, and their fusion of soul and body the only thing on the earth which mattered, and which would ever matter, to them both.

Yet there was a puritan strain in Mark Scrutton. Reverence for this woman he now knew loved him shielded them both, as she lay, defenceless, cradled in his arms.

He began talking of their future, and she listened, entranced, while he told her of a voyage they would take by way of honeymoon before he settled down to the work to which he was longing to devote his life. Laura said little more than "Yes" and "No," and indeed she could not have repeated much of what it was she heard in that golden dawn. That she was making him happy simply by being herself, gave her such a sensation of bliss that she felt she could not be the same creature she had been yesterday, and would be again to-morrow—the Laura Dousland whose name had echoed and would echo long after she was dead, as that of a woman who had gone through the degradation of a trial for murder.

At last he kissed her tenderly and gently good-bye, for his

was the intelligent and selfless tenderness that is ever seeking to promote the comfort and well-being of the beloved.

"Try and get a little sleep, my precious darling. I want you to look well and bonny when you meet my people."

To that she made no answer, and he saw a look of fear come into her face. His people? The father and mother of whom he was so proud and fond, and to whom—she did not need to be told it—he was their life? How strange that he could be so confident they would not only care for her, but welcome her as a daughter.

After he had gone she found she could not obey him. Instead, she bathed and dressed; and then she sat outside the door gazing at the sea as the sun rose in the heavens, and thinking, thinking, thinking.

At eight the village postman brought her a letter. It was from John Hayward, and she felt, as she read it, that it opened the way, albeit a hard and thorny way, she was bound to follow.

So after waiting a little while, she put a telephone call through to Loverslea, and had a three minutes' conversation with the man who had always shown her not only kindness, but a measure of understanding his wife had never shown.

She believed what had happened early this morning could be forgotten or, if not ever forgotten by her, wiped out in time to come for this man she had come to love, save, maybe, as a fragrant memory.

So it was that when Mark came leaping down the path, he found her with a look on her face which frightened him.

"Darling—what's the matter?"

To that she made no answer, and she allowed him to take her in his arms. But though she did not repulse him, there came no response, and he felt as if he were holding a dead woman.

He put her back into the chair where she had been sitting, and throwing himself at her feet looked up into her desolate eyes. He was trying to tell himself that he had been too rapid in his wooing, and that he ought to have given her longer to become what he believed, nay knew, he had the power to make her, a normal woman who loves and is beloved.

"Laura—what is wrong?"

"Nothing is wrong, but we must forget last night."

"Do you believe that I can ever forget—?" He stopped, for he was hearing again her whispered "Kiss me," and feeling once more the savour of her lips when they had first clung to his. She had not had to tell him that it was the first time she had shared the bliss of an embrace.

She so far saw into his mind that she ended the sentence for him, "—that I love you? No, I don't want you to forget that."

Then, with a sigh: "And yet? Yes, I do want you to forget it, and I mean to do so, too," she ended resolutely.

"Does that mean that we are no longer to meet—even as friends?"

"I am going to Canada."

She spoke in a strange lifeless way as she went on: "It was nearly settled before I came here. Mr. Hayward knows of a rich man in Montreal whose wife is dead, and who is seeking a lady housekeeper to look after his children. He met me years ago, at Loverslea, and lately he wrote and asked if the Haywards could find someone like 'Miss Dalberton.'"

She waited a moment and then, "I had a letter from Mr. Hayward this morning, pressing for a quick answer, and I telephoned accepting, just now."

"But what has changed you since last night?" he asked in despair.

"I only know that I was mad last night."

She turned, and going into the house shut the door.

To Mark Scrutton the closing of that door was symbolic of her determination to banish him from her life. Always it had been left widely open to welcome him the sooner to her side.

With his head bent he walked away, and as he breasted the steep path he stumbled more than once, for he felt as if he were blind, and were now being driven by the furies he knew not whither.

When on the moorland he flung himself down on the heather in a stupor of anguish and revolt. Without this woman he felt he could not go on living. Once she was gone there would be nothing for him to do but kill himself. He thought in his selfish misery that his mother, at least, would understand, and make his father believe in what would be a cleverly-staged "accident."

He had been lying sunk in misery some time when he lifted his head suddenly, for he had heard Laura's voice.

"Mark? Come back! Come back!" came the insistent call.

God! So she had followed him? How could he have doubted that she loved him?

He rose to his feet. But there was no slight figure standing on the path to his right, and all he could see, apart from the sky, the sea, and the solitary moorland, was the shingled roof of the little house from which she had shut him out.

Slowly he began walking on, towards the place where his parents would be waiting for him.

And then, again it was as if he heard her voice calling him from afar off.

"Mark, come back—"

Though he knew it must be an hallucination, he turned

and began running down the steep stony path till he came to the beach. Slowly, then, he walked round the house and listening, through the window he heard the sound of bitter weeping.

He burst open the door; Laura was lying across the couch, her whole body shaken with sobs.

He threw himself on his knees. "Did you call me, my darling?"

She whispered, "Yes. I called out 'Mark, come back—' but I did not think you would hear. Have you been outside all this time?" and then she put out a hand and stroked his face.

He stood up, and then he gathered her, as if she had been a child, to his breast.

"Will you swear never to be so unkind to me again?" he muttered, as he kissed her hair, her eyes, her lips. And once more she whispered, "Yes."

"I wonder if you know how cruel you were?"

"More cruel to myself than I was to you," and she sighed.

A flood of ecstasy filled his heart. Yet even so, "I shan't feel sure of you till we're safely married!" he exclaimed, and it was the truth.

"But Mark," he felt the fear in her voice, "we can't be married for a long time, surely?"

"Why not?"

In a low suffering tone she answered, "It's too soon after—"

And then she disengaged herself from his clinging possessive arms. "Are you sure you will never regret you joined your life to a woman many still believe a murderess?"

He felt as if he had been struck between the eyes. She had never before uttered the vile word.

"If you wish to be happy, Laura, never speak of that again!"

She trembled inwardly, for there was on his face a look of mingled horror and contempt. It was such a look as she had never seen there. She felt suddenly as if this man had become a stranger.

She made no answer to his plea, only stared before her woefully, out at the sea and the sky.

He felt he had hurt her, and putting his arm round her shoulder he said remorsefully, "I was wrong to say that, my darling. Of course you can speak to me of anything. It would make me wretched if I thought you were even tempted to keep anything from me that troubles your dear heart. But oh! I do implore you to try and put the past from you. I thought you had done so, by something you said to me the other day."

"So I had, Mark," she spoke in a strangled tone of pain. "Almost at once after you brought me here I began to feel as if all the horrible things that had ever happened to me had been—" she waited a moment; and ended with the words, "—a long drawn-out nightmare."

"Thank God for that," he said reverently. And then, in an almost inaudible tone, "I have prayed that might come to pass."

A look to which he had no clue came into her face. It hurt Laura that this man she loved believed in God. She now wondered painfully if he remembered her admission of entire unbelief.

But she put that knowledge away from her, "And then when we became friends—"

"Dear friends?" he murmured in her ear.

"Yes—dear dear friends! Then it was just as if a new life began for me."

He could not help asking a question he knew would have been well left unasked. "What made you go back this morning to the past—for you did go back, my darling?"

She turned and looked at him strangely. "I felt how terrible it would be for us both if ever you had reason to be sorry that you had married a woman—"

And once more Mark Scrutton stopped the words Laura Dousland was about to utter. But this time it was with a kiss by which everything in the past, ay, and in the future, sank away in an ecstasy which to the man made up for all the agony which Laura had just inflicted on him.

"I'll leave you now," he said at last. "It's time I told my people of my wonderful good fortune."

He smiled, "They long for me to be married, though they're wise enough never to tell me so."

"Do you want me to see them to-day?"

"You can put off seeing them as long as you like. My mother is the sort that understands *everything*."

As Laura stood looking after him, she asked herself piteously whether there was any hope that even his mother would understand what it was about her which had made her cherished only son fall in love with, and desire to marry, a woman who had had to stand her trial for murder? How could she hope that his parents would understand what was still so incredible a thing to herself? True, she now loved Mark Scrutton with an intensity which frightened her. At any moment willingly she would have died for him. Indeed just now she felt it would be easier to die than live for this man who had all her heart—a heart which till so lately had been atrophied, and cold, cold.

She put through a call to Loverslea, only to be told that Mr. Hayward had gone to London; and after a moment's thought she said: "Will you telephone a message he will get on arriving at his office? It's simply that what I told him this morning is cancelled."

With intelligent precision the butler repeated the words of the message, and she felt at peace.

The man was an excellent servant. But she, Laura, did not like him, for she knew what neither his master nor mistress suspected, that he was very fond of money. She was convinced that it was he who had given a Sunday paper certain titbits of gossip concerning the courtship of Fordish Dousland, that no one else was in a position to supply.

IX

When he reached the house, Mark learnt that his parents had gone out together for a stroll. They were seldom parted even for as long as an hour, and sometimes their son would smilingly complain that he found it difficult to see either his father or mother alone!

He walked through into what was called the long parlour of Mellcombe Court. It was a singular looking apartment, though a most comfortable and charming living-room, with noble views of the sea and coast-line. The walls were closely covered with paintings, engravings, miniatures, and even photographs, connected with the Scrutton family. Everything there, even to the chairs, of which the covers in *petit point* had been worked by a great-aunt, ministered to that feeling of ancestor worship which seems inherent in human, and more especially in British, nature. Even Mark, though he would not have liked to admit it to himself, was quite as proud as was his old soldier father, that he came of a stock which had served King, Queen, and Country, for what seemed to him countless generations. Often he gazed with inward pleasure at the portrait, hanging over the fireplace in this long parlour, of the Scrutton who had been among the west countrymen who had sailed with Raleigh from Plymouth Hoe. He couldn't help being glad that the woman who would in days to come reign here as his cherished wife was, by birth, a Dalberton of Dalberton, of ancient Yorkshire stock. In the pedigree which hung in his father's own room were many other well-known English and Scotch names.

Now, for the first time since his love, nay his absorbing passion, for Laura had filled his being, he forced himself to consider his parents in relation to this woman who had become all his life. He was sorry, indeed, that he had not begun by telling them the truth concerning the patient to whom he had lent his cottage. But he had been determined that Laura Dousland should begin what he had intended should be an entirely new life, amid new surroundings, and with even a new name to shelter her from cruel prying curiosity. He had come to know, though with many an inward feeling of revolt, that it is impossible for a man and woman to wipe out the past. Neither of them would ever forget the events which, awful as they had been, he yet now had cause to bless, for those awful events had brought them together.

He walked about the long familiar room with quick, restless footsteps, as he tried to put himself in his father's place.

How would he feel had he a son, and were such a revelation made to him as was about to be made to Colonel Scrutton? He was far too honest a man to try and pretend that the revelation of Laura's identity would be of small moment. He knew that even to such a modern thinker as himself the marriage of an only son would appear a matter of paramount importance. As for his own relations with his parents, they had always been as nearly perfect as is possible in an imperfect world.

Mark had been the child of Colonel and Mrs. Scrutton's middle age, for they had had one of those faithful attachments lasting over years, of which the world to-day seems to know nothing, and which had indeed been more usual a full generation before their own young days. During their long engagement years had been spent by the then Captain Scrutton in India and in Africa; and an accident had made their son aware that in his mother's bedroom was an old chest of drawers containing thousands, rather than hundreds, of the love-letters they had written the one to the other.

And then, as after all sometimes happens in this curious world where life is for so many a balanced ration, fortune had been prodigal in her gifts, and Colonel Scrutton had come into this delightful property. Here he had been happy to live, both before and since the Great War, during the course of which he had escaped, as by a miracle, with nothing to remind him of four terrible years, excepting a wound which occasionally gave him a twinge of pain. While high among the gifts Providence had lavished on him had been the crowning mercy that his son had been born just too late to be joined to the holocaust.

It had been assumed that the boy would become a sailor or a soldier. But from the very first Mark's bent had been towards medical research, and soon among those competent to judge, he had been noted as likely to make a name for himself. It was by his own wish that he had gone twice for a while into general practice. But, as he had told Laura, that experiment, for so it had been on his part, was now coming to an end, and there were two or three posts open to him in connection with his special branch.

Suddenly he stopped in his restless pacing, for he had caught a glimpse of his father and mother coming up one of the steep paths which led to this side of the house. And, for the first time in his life when confronted with those he called "his people," there came over him a feeling of anxiety and discomfort.

Stepping out of the French window, he waved to them, and his father waved back, as they quickened their footsteps.

They had both noticed, especially during the last few days, how often Mark went to see his patient at Beach Cottage, and in Mrs. Scrutton's mind there had come an uneasy stir of curiosity concerning the widowed Mrs. Ordeley, on whom her son had asked her not to call for a while.

He did not walk forward to meet them; he stayed where he was till they came up to him.

"Have you been waiting for us, Mark? I'm afraid we've delayed your starting for Hartling Point," said his mother.

"I've put off going there till to-morrow."

He spoke more abruptly than usual, and at once she saw that something was troubling him.

As they all stepped up into the long parlour, his father observed: "I'll go and put my hat and stick in the hall," to be countered quickly with: "Let me take them, Father. I—I want to speak to you and Mum."

"Mum?" The childish name for his mother he now seldom used.

Since her son had grown up Mrs. Scrutton had always had one secret dread. She greatly feared he would wish to spend some years in a tropical country. She was aware that the light would then go out of her life, and that she would have to keep that shadowing from the knowledge of her husband. Yet the thought of trying to stop Mark doing so would never have entered her mind. To Colonel Scrutton the world is a young Englishman's parish; he himself had left England when he was nineteen, and for near on twenty-five years, he had only been back and forward at rare intervals on leave. Besides, fond and proud as he was of Mark, it was his wife who held all his heart.

The time of waiting for her son's return from the hall seemed long to Mrs. Scrutton, though it was hardly more than three minutes. And as she sat down with her back to the wonderful views of sea, land, and sky, she told herself the while that nothing here, in the home she dearly loved, would ever again seem the same.

As for Colonel Scrutton, when Mark came back into the room, shutting the door behind him, he looked enquiringly, maybe a little searchingly, at his son. But the fear which gripped his wife did not touch him. He always, like the wise man a hard life had made him, allowed trouble to come to him, instead of hastening to meet it, as is a woman's way.

"I am going to be married, Father."

"My dear boy, my dear Mark—this *is* good news," the older man took a step forward, and grasped the younger man's hand. He felt not only moved, but very, very glad. Mark was thirty-three, and he had never betrayed the slightest wish to marry. Like most young men of his age and standing he was fairly often thrown in the company of girls both here, in Devonshire, where the Scruttons knew what is called "everybody," and wherever his work took him.

Once or twice his mother had thought him attracted, but she was a reserved woman, and she had never questioned him. She was aware that among the people he had liked at Silchester were the Dean's wife and the Dean's daughters.

She now supposed, and indeed she hoped, that she was going to be told that one of these three girls was to be her son's wife. But what his words had actually brought to her was a sense of measureless relief.

She got up and kissed him, and then, stepping back, she glanced fondly into her son's face, and then she was struck, painfully struck, by the expression on that face.

It was a stern, even a suffering expression, and there flashed athwart her heart a feeling of sharp foreboding. That look of strong emotion meant that he cared, and cared desperately, for the woman he was to marry, and she wondered if there was any obstacle barring the way of his passion.

But she knew she was given to what her husband called building a bridge for trouble. So she gathered up her courage: "What is my dear daughter-to-be like, Mark?"

His face softened, "Not a bit pretty, mum! She's a little creature—about five foot two, I should think. She has beautiful eyes, and what you'll like, long dark soft hair. She's rather my idea of a mermaid, and she's so little vain that she's never had herself photographed, a fact which was most fortunate—" and then he stopped abruptly.

His father smiled: "We ought to begin at the beginning, my boy. What is the young lady's name, and how long have you known her?"

"I have known her—"

And then Mark Scrutton stopped dead again. In one sense he had known Laura nearly a year, but in actual truth only a few weeks; so he evaded the question.

"She is a widow, Father, and I knew her slightly before her husband's death. But circumstances, as I will explain to you in a moment, have thrown me very closely with her since she became a widow."

And then his mother asked a question: "Is it Mrs. Ordeley, Mark?"

He looked relieved, and rather surprised. "Yes, it is. I wonder what made you guess that? She's been ill; that's why I didn't want her to see anybody, not even you," and he looked deprecatingly into the face of the one other woman he loved, or would ever love.

Meanwhile Colonel Scrutton was speaking, more or less to himself.

"I stayed in Yorkshire during my first leave home from India, and I met some people called Ordeley. There was a charming girl called Laura Ordeley—"

His son cut across him harshly: "Ordeley is not her real name."

Into the mind of Mark's father there stole unease, and he exclaimed: "Why does she call herself so?"

"Ordeley was her mother's maiden name, and it was on my advice she called herself by it when she came here. She has been very unhappy, for a terrible thing befell her, and I was anxious that as far as possible she should cast the past behind her."

Colonel Scrutton felt disturbed, and that though he had complete trust in his son. The word "past" had struck upon his ear unpleasantly. He told himself quickly that this Mrs. Ordeley, he could not think of her by any other name, was probably what is called an innocent divorcée.

Mark said in a firm, rather loud tone: "Mrs. Ordeley's real name is Laura Dousland."

"Laura Dousland?" repeated Mrs. Scrutton. In a sense the name seemed familiar, yet she could not recall in what connection.

"Yes, mother; that is still her legal name."

There came into her mind a disquieting suspicion, "Do you mean—" and her son saw the look of deep dismay which flashed across her face, and that though her face was in shadow.

His heart contracted. For the first time in his thirty-three years of life he felt angry with his mother.

He said coldly: "I think you know now who she is. You will remember that I was one of the witnesses called on her behalf."

Colonel Scrutton threw a questioning glance at his son, and then he looked at his wife's pale face. "D'you mean the woman—" quickly he corrected himself, "—the lady who was tried for murder the other day?"

As Mark remained silent, he went on: "Everything turned—didn't it—on a bottle of that Italian wine which is sold in a queerly shaped bottle?"

He was endeavouring to speak in a matter-of-fact, even a cheerful, voice. But he failed, and knew that he failed. Still he went on gamely: "D'you mean that Mrs. Ordeley is really Mrs. Dousland, Mark?"

"He has just said so, my dear," and Mrs. Scrutton touched her husband on the arm.

"So he has, Mary," and then he tried, as he put it to himself, to gather his wits together.

"I remember that you wrote and told your mother you felt very sorry for her, and I suppose that pity became akin to love, eh, my boy?"

He was making an effort, a painful, even an agonising effort, to remember the details of what even he knew had been called "The Chianti Flask Mystery." True, the trial had been fully reported even in the old-fashioned daily paper which arrived each afternoon by the second post, but apart from the passage in which his son's evidence had been printed, he had not read the accounts of the case. He felt no interest in murder, and he had been surprised as well as disgusted at the interest some of their neighbours had shown in what had seemed to him a sordid story. But now, faced with this astounding revelation as to the identity of the woman his son intended to marry, he did remember having read a leading article in which it was made clear that the writer regarded the Coroner who had conducted the preliminary enquiry as having been greatly at fault.

The story had remained far more clearly in Mrs. Scrutton's mind, partly because one of her neighbours, a Mrs. Stevens, had talked about it whenever they had met last winter and spring. This lady had expressed a passionate belief in Mrs. Dousland's innocence, and had rejoiced at her acquittal.

Mark's mother now recalled, while looking into her son's sombre face, how that eager, enthusiastic woman had actually telephoned late one evening: "We have just been listening to the news, and I know you will be glad to hear that Mrs. Dousland has been acquitted!" And, in a way she had been glad, for she had followed the case more closely than had her husband because her son had played a part, albeit what had seemed to her a small part, in Mrs. Dousland's trial for murder.

She now heard herself say: "I'm longing to meet your fiancée, my darling; I know that I shall love her, if she loves you."

"Thank you, Mother."

Then he, too, sat down. "I should like to tell you just a few things about Laura before you meet her."

"Tell us everything you feel you can tell us," said his father kindly.

Excepting that his mouth had become set and stern, no one seeing Colonel Scrutton, or even hearing his voice, could have told how this astounding news had affected him.

"I feel I can tell you everything," and Mark slightly stressed the "you." Then he began, speaking slowly and, or so thought his mother, choosing his words with care.

"Laura's father was the last Dalberton of Dalberton, in Yorkshire, and he ran through his estate and what money he had by the time he was thirty. Her mother who, I expect, Father, was the girl you met when you were a young man, died when Laura was five. Captain Dalberton must have had a clever side to him, for he went into the city, and at times made money, but when he died he left only debts, and Laura, who was then eighteen, became a governess. She had been sent to an old-fashioned school—you know the sort of thing, 'for the daughters of gentlemen.' So she had had no kind of training."

He addressed his mother: "If you read the reports of the trial, you will remember what was said about—" he hesitated, then said firmly, "—about my darling, by a certain Mrs. Hayward."

"Yes, I remember how very warmly Mrs. Hayward spoke of Mrs. Dousland, and how absurd she thought it was that anyone should suspect Mrs. Dousland of—" and then Mrs. Scrutton also hesitated. She could not bring herself to utter the word "murder."

"As you will readily understand when you have met her, Mother," Mark now spoke in a hard, matter-of-fact voice: "Laura gave every satisfaction to her various employers. Though she is not highly educated, she has a good deal of natural culture, and when she was about twenty-three she had the luck to go to the Haywards, who have a beautiful place near Silchester called Loverslea. She was a governess there to two girls, and the whole family became devoted to her."

"Mrs. Hayward spoke of Mrs. Dousland in a really wonderful way when in the witness-box," and Mrs. Scrutton looked deprecatingly at her husband.

Her son began speaking again, and as he did so, his voice again hardened: "Miss Dalberton, as she was then, had been at Loverslea five years, and would naturally have been seeking a new post, for her pupils were now grown up, when an old schoolfellow of Mr. Hayward's, named Fordish Dousland, came there on a visit. He had retired with an income which was to die with him, of six hundred a year, and was looking for a place where he could settle down. He fell in love with Laura, but he was nearer thirty than twenty-five years older than herself, and she refused him three times. But he was very persistent, and at last Mrs. Hayward persuaded her to marry him. He bought a house in Silchester, and they were still living there when—well, you know what happened?"

He was still looking at his mother, but it was his father who answered: "Well, no, Mark, I don't know what happened, beyond the bare fact that Mrs. Dousland was tried for murder, and acquitted."

"Then I'll tell you, father, as shortly as I can, what did happen."

He waited a moment. Then went on: "Fordish Dousland was eccentric, and selfish. His grandfather had committed suicide as a result of a love-affair when he was already elderly. As for this man, he told Mrs. Hayward, before the engagement, that if Laura finally refused to marry him he would do away with himself." He added: "As you read Mrs. Hayward's evidence, Mother, you will remember that she stated this on oath in the witness-box."

"I do remember that, my dear."

"After his marriage, Dousland grew odder and odder, spending most of his time at auctions; in fact, he furnished his house entirely with things bought at sales. To show you how queer he was, there were only a few sticks of furniture in the house when he and Laura married. Oh! and by the way, he had a passion for Italy, and had always spent his holidays there during his working life."

Colonel Scrutton looked at his son, "And did you become their doctor, Mark?"

"Oh no, Father! I occasionally met Fordish Dousland at the golf club, and one day, as he felt rather ill on the course, I went home with him."

Again he waited a moment before going on.

"That was the first time I saw Laura, and I remember thinking she looked ill, and not over happy. The place looked very odd to me. There were all sorts of Italian things, both inside and outside the house, for whenever he could get it cheap, Dousland bought any object which reminded him of Italy."

"And they had an Italian manservant," interposed his mother.

"Yes, a man called Angelo Terugi."

He stopped speaking, and stared out of the window against which Mrs. Scrutton's head was silhouetted, longing for this, to him intolerable, interview, to be over.

"The Judge summed up in the sense that Fordish Dousland committed suicide—at least so I seem to remember," interjected Colonel Scrutton.

"There's no doubt he took poison, though that was not suspected for some time. Laura found her husband dead in bed one morning, and as they had no regular medical attendant she telephoned for me. Unfortunately, I had gone up to London for a couple of nights, and the man who answered her was Dr. Grant. Grant was puzzled as to the cause of death, but instead of saying so, he signed the death certificate, and Dousland was duly buried. Laura went to Loverslea to stay with the Haywards, and at last Grant made up his mind to speak to the Silchester Coroner of his half suspicion. Fordish Dousland was exhumed, and it was found that he had died from the administration of a considerable dose of rat poison. That, you may remember, was where I came in."

Colonel Scrutton bent his head. Even so, there was a puzzled and an anxious look in his eyes, and he listened intently to his son's next words.

"I unfortunately had recommended Mr. Dousland to get some new stuff which is supposed to kill any animal which takes it painlessly, and he showed what I thought at the time was an unusual and indeed a morbid interest in the effects of the poison."

"I now recall your giving evidence to that effect."

"It was quoted in the summing-up," said Mark quickly.

The Colonel was beginning to remember more concerning the Dousland case. He said hesitatingly: "The Italian manservant gave evidence which told against Mrs. Dousland—or am I mistaken?"

"No, Father, you're right; but as to that I blamed the police, rather than Angelo Terugi."

"What exactly did he say, Mark?" asked his mother.

"The police made up their minds that Dousland had absorbed the poison in this Chianti which he took at every meal; and the Italian signed a statement declaring that he was positive that on the crucial afternoon, before leaving for his evening out, he had put a partly filled flask of the wine on the tray he had prepared for his master's evening meal. He further declared that by the next morning the flask had disappeared. All the efforts made by the police, and by everybody concerned, to find this Chianti flask failed, and that is the only touch of mystery in the whole story."

"What do you think happened to the flask?"

"I don't know what to think, and I don't much care. Laura is convinced that there wasn't a flask on the tray that night. One theory is that Terugi had drunk the wine, was afraid to admit it, and threw the flask away. That's what the Haywards believe, and it may have happened. However, making great play of Terugi's story of the disappearance of the Chianti flask, the Coroner practically directed his jury to send Mrs. Dousland for trial. But almost at once it was realised that her arrest on a charge of murder was a shameful miscarriage of justice. I never had the slightest doubt but that she would be acquitted, but there were a few people who even against the evidence believed her guilty. I hope and indeed I feel sure that no one does now, for everything that came out at the trial showed the kind of woman she is. Noble, selfless, kindness itself, loved and respected by everyone who had ever had an opportunity of knowing her—all that and more was proved during those awful days."

His face was working now, and his mother's lips quivered.

"I doubt if even I know how much she suffered! She was marvellously brave, Father. I didn't know there could be a woman left in the world of such heroic stuff. I haven't had much luck, you know, with girls."

Both his parents looked at him in surprise.

"Oh, well, I oughtn't to have said that! Of course I know

there are nice girls in the world, but unluckily for me I never felt in the least attracted by any nice girl."

"Did you like the other sort, Mark?" asked Mrs. Scrutton.

"Well, yes, I did, Mother, in a way. Most men do. However, I've never got to look at a girl or a woman again, thank God. I shall only look at, dream of, live for, Laura, my cherished darling, my heart's love," and his voice died away.

"May we go and see her now?" asked Colonel Scrutton.

The young man looked deprecatingly at his father. "I'd rather my mother saw her first. All this has shaken her to bits. She kept up till the end, and then she collapsed, utterly."

"How well I can understand that," cried Mrs. Scrutton feelingly.

"She didn't think she ought ever to marry, or be happy, again; in fact, she refused me definitely, but it has all come right, now. I suppose I ought to have waited a bit longer, but well? she's become all my life."

"And when are you going to be married?" asked his father.

Mrs. Scrutton looked at her husband, and then she turned to her son, "The trial only ended—some time in June, wasn't it, my dear?"

The young man made no answer to that question. It was true that the trial had ended a bare nine weeks ago, and he had only known he loved Laura less than half that time, but he felt as if he had always known her—and always loved her.

"She thinks we ought not to marry till Fordish Dousland has been dead a year. That would make it next January. This seems to me utterly unreasonable, and perhaps you'll be able to make her see it, Mother? After all," he waited a moment, "they hadn't been anything to one another for a long time. The man was over sixty when they married five years ago. Also he was prematurely old in every way."

"Yet I think she's right, Mark. I mean about not being married until about a year has gone by. It's hard on you, I know, but everything seems to me to point to its being the only decent thing to do."

It was his father who said that, and in a very decided voice. And then he asked a question: "Sir Joseph Molloy was in the case, wasn't he?"

"Yes, he defended Laura."

"I used to meet him years and years ago. Did you like him, my boy?"

"I think so; all the same, I was rather sorry Laura's lawyers briefed him, as his nickname is 'the murderer's friend.' However, Mrs. Hayward was determined to secure him. He didn't take any real trouble; he just walked through the case, and demanded an acquittal as a right."

In the early morning of the night that followed her son's confidences, Mrs. Scrutton, who had lain wide awake ever since she had got into bed, whispered: "George?"

"Yes, Mary?"

"Have you thought of trying to see Sir Joseph Molloy when you go up to London to-morrow?"

"I hadn't thought of doing so. But of course I will, if it will afford you any comfort, dearest."

"I should like to know what he really thinks of her."

"I don't suppose he'll tell me if he thinks ill of her."

"I believe you could make him tell you the truth," said Mark Scrutton's mother, "especially if he has a son of his own."

X

Mrs. Scrutton had spent a long afternoon and night alone, and her son had left early to fulfil an old engagement some forty miles away.

It had been arranged that she should go down to Beach Cottage at twelve o'clock, and till then there were all sorts of things she had planned to do on this free morning. But she found it impossible to settle down to anything.

That Mark should be engaged to be married was in itself to her one of the most important events that had ever happened in her long life; and now that all-important event was fearfully affected by the identity of the woman he loved and was to marry.

Like every mother of an only son she had sometimes wondered, and anxiously, as to what sort of woman would become his wife. She had been afraid that he might be attracted by the type of modern girl she felt convinced cannot make a success of marriage, for Mark's odd confession with regard to himself, and the kind of woman who attracted him, had not surprised her as much as it had done Mark's father. One London girl who had been staying in the neighbourhood two years before, had made a dead set at him. But whether with a view to marriage or—well, the other thing, the mother had not been able to make up her mind. Still she had become aware that her son had been both amused and excited at being the object of this shameless chase, and for a short time she, Mary Scrutton, had felt painfully afraid. She now asked herself miserably whether any possible marriage might not have held the promise of more normal happiness than this marriage was likely to do.

At last she decided to while away the time by writing some letters, and so she went into her husband's study. Then, as she went through the door, there suddenly came back to her something which had happened about a fortnight ago. She had lifted a heavy book which stood on a rosewood-inlaid table, and under the book someone, no doubt her careful old-fashioned housemaid, had placed a sheet of newspaper to save the delicate inlay. She remembered, now, how that sheet of the picture paper taken in by her cook had been illustrated.

For the first time in her life the mistress of Mellcombe Court went across the room and locked the door. Not for the world, in view of what would soon have to be told the servants, who had all been in her service for years, would she have been caught doing what she was now going to do.

Quickly she walked to the window where stood the table on which lay the heavy book. She lifted the book; and then she felt a tremor of pain and yes, of disgust, for the whole of the sheet of paper lying there contained but one illustration. It was that of a flask, or bulbous-looking bottle, and on the round, bowl-like part was the portrait, obviously reproduced from a photograph taken some years before, of an elderly man. Underneath ran the caption:—

"One of the twenty-three flasks of Chianti which were returned to the wine-dealer in Soho the very day following the death of Fordish Dousland. Twenty-four had been actually supplied, but the twenty-fourth mysteriously disappeared, and has never been found. The portrait is that of Fordish Dousland, whose wife is being tried on the charge of having murdered him. For Angelo Terugi's evidence concerning the missing Chianti flask, see page 2."

Mark Scrutton's mother took up and stared fearfully down at the curious-looking picture. Then she went across to the fireplace, and setting a light to the sheet she watched it burn.

It seemed to her incredible that her brilliant, good-looking, and still young, son, should be going to marry the widow of that—to herself she used the words—mean, common-looking old man. And her sense of misery, and yes, shame, was increased by the knowledge that though he had not said a word, her husband had been stricken to the soul by Mark's confession of love for a woman who had stood her trial for murder.

She was still standing by the fireplace, staring at the ashes of the sheet of paper she had just burnt, when there came a knock at the door, followed by someone attempting to enter the room. The handle was turned, but of course the door remained fast, and Mrs. Scrutton felt annoyed and mortified. How foolish of her to have locked the door! After all she had a perfect right to look at, and burn anything she liked, in her husband's study.

She called out: "Wait a moment, Benning." Then she turned the key and opened the door to meet the surprised gaze of a woman who had never found a door locked against her in that house before.

"It's Mrs. Stevens, ma'am. She says she hopes you will excuse her calling so early. She says she has come about something that is urgent and important, or she'd have telephoned. I have shown her into the long parlour."

"I wish you had first come and asked me whether I would see her. I do so dislike seeing anyone at this time of the morning."

Benning looked what she felt, injured. Not in six months was a cross word said to her either by the master or the mistress. What could be happening to make Mrs. Scrutton behave to-day in a way so unlike herself?

"She walked right in, ma'am, as the front door was open. Shall I go and say you can't see her?"

"As she's here, of course I must see her. The truth is I'm tired this morning."

"You don't look well, ma'am."

Mrs. Stevens was the woman who had been so passionate an upholder of Laura Dousland's innocence, and whose son was on the staff of a popular Sunday newspaper.

As Mark's mother walked across the spacious lobby of the old house, she told herself that Mrs. Stevens would certainly prove a good friend to Mark's wife, should Mrs. Mark Scrutton ever want a friend in the neighbourhood. All the same she shrank, unreasonably, from the thought of seeing just now the woman who had been so eager a believer in Laura Dousland's innocence.

"Please forgive me for coming over in the morning like this, dear Mrs. Scrutton—but I've a *great* favour to ask of you!"

It was plain that the visitor, who always talked in italics, was now what she seldom was, ill at ease, and even nervous. Mrs. Scrutton felt sorry for her. Perhaps Bob Stevens, who was a reckless lad, had committed a serious motoring offence. If so it would not be the first time, and Colonel Scrutton was a magistrate.

"Why, what's the matter?"

"It's in your power to do my boy, I mean Bob of course, a *great* kindness, Mrs. Scrutton."

And then the visitor looked at the hostess pleadingly.

"I heard yesterday Bob had come home. I hope he's all right?"

"Quite all right, thank you, dear Mrs. Scrutton. The truth is—I want to be quite frank with you—it's come to my boy's knowledge that the lady now living in Beach Cottage on the shore, though she calls herself by some other name, is *really* Mrs. Dousland—of the Chianti Flask Mystery!"

To that unexpected statement Mrs. Scrutton made no answer.

"If it's true, and my son says there's no *doubt* about it at all, I've been wondering whether you could persuade Mrs. Dousland to see Bob? The paper is willing to pay quite a *large sum* if she'll write something which can be published under the title of 'The Story of My Life,' or something of that sort. I believe she is very poor, and so it would be a great thing for her to get, say, a thousand pounds! Bob went to a place called Loverslea just after the end of the trial. But Mrs. Dousland wasn't in a fit state to see *anyone* just then; and naturally, being a gentleman, he did not insist. But his editor was very much put out, for he seemed to think that Bob at any rate could have written her a note, explaining how *very much* to her advantage it would have been for her to see him even for a few minutes. You see, Mrs. Scrutton, as a matter of fact Bob would write 'the story,' as I believe they call that sort of thing in the press world, if she would sign it. He's already done that on two occasions—but of course I tell you that *in confidence*."

Mrs. Scrutton still remained silent. She desired to say something, but her throat had gone dry, and she felt as if no words would come.

"I *hope* I have made myself clear? I suppose poor Mrs. Dousland is a friend of yours? I know she has some very influential friends, and of course your son's evidence helped to get her off. It would be *greatly* to her advantage to tell her side of the story. There is still great interest felt in the case, so it would be worth her while from every point of view—it really *would*," and she looked expectantly at the woman who up to now had not said a word in answer to her eager words.

Surely she had been quite clear? Though the mistress of Mellcombe Court was becoming an old lady, by now, and though no one had ever thought Mrs. Scrutton a *clever* woman, still she held her own in a quiet way, and was still active in local affairs. Perhaps she was afraid to do anything in the absence of her husband? Colonel Scrutton was a great martinet. Also he had once much offended Mrs. Stevens by speaking with contempt and dislike of the popular press.

Sure enough: "I think I shall have to consult my husband," said Mrs. Scrutton hesitatingly. "Colonel Scrutton is in town, when he is back I will ask him to send Bob a note."

"But the matter is so *very* urgent. If Mrs. Dousland would be willing to see Bob *to-day*, he and she could prepare a rough outline, as most luckily he knows shorthand, and so could take *copious* notes. That would make it all so easy, wouldn't it?"

"I suppose it would."

Mrs. Stevens smiled, more at her ease, now. "I hope you will tell Mrs. Dousland how tremendously we all believed in her innocence! I mean before it was *proved*. From the very beginning I felt *convinced* that that horrid man—I mean her husband, Fordish Dousland—had committed suicide."

"I wonder how your son discovered that she was staying here?"

"He didn't *discover* it exactly. The news really came through someone belonging to a place called Loverslea, where Mrs. Dousland was once governess."

Bob Stevens' devoted mother looked rather embarrassed. "There was quite a *hue and cry* after Mrs. Dousland left that place Loverslea, for her friends, Mr. and Mrs. Hayward, had promised not to tell anybody where she had gone. But yesterday morning, before coming home for a *well*-earned holiday, Bob telephoned to make one last attempt to get in touch with her. As Mr. Hayward was out, the butler took the message, and the long and short of it is that Bob did quite a little bit of *detective* work over the telephone. But as to that of course I'm supposed to know *nothing;* he is simply acting on 'information received,' as they call it."

There was a pause, an uncomfortably long pause for the visitor. But at last she broke silence again.

"Think of it, Mrs. Scrutton—a thousand pounds! That's a lot of money, isn't it? It came out in the trial that Mrs. Dousland was going to be very, very poor. That was *one* reason why she got off, for she was *much* better off when her husband was alive."

And then Mrs. Scrutton spoke again, and this time with a strength which surprised herself: "Millions would not tempt me to do such a thing," was what she said in a firm voice.

"Ah! but *you* have always been well off. If you would allow *me* to go down to Beach Cottage, I'm sure *I* could persuade Mrs. Dousland to see Bob. You know what good manners he has? In fact, though *I* say so, he's a charming lad. All women like him!"

"I'm afraid I can't ask you to see Mrs. Dousland, or rather, for she is changing her name by deed poll, Mrs. Ordeley."

"Yes, *that's* the name! I couldn't remember it. Stupid how my memory is going. But then that happens to us *all,* as we grow older, doesn't it? I'm sure she'd see *me,* if only you'd tell her how very, *very* strongly I believed in her. I converted quite a lot of people in the neighbourhood who were convinced she *had* poisoned her husband."

"She's still very far from well. In fact, no one is allowed to see her without my son's permission." And then Mark's mother felt suddenly sorry she had said that.

"D'you mean Dr. Scrutton?" There was great surprise in the voice which asked the already answered question.

"Yes, I do, Mrs. Stevens. Mrs. Ordeley is his patient."

"That simplifies it. Bob shall ask *him*. We heard he had come home for a short holiday. I suppose he's out just now?"

"Yes."

"I thought Mrs. Dousland was a friend of *yours*."

"So she is; but my son is looking after her and it was because he thought her in need of absolute rest and quiet, that we lent her the cottage."

The visitor got up. "Bob will be *very* disappointed if he can't see Mrs. Dousland to-day. I do *hope* he won't think I've bungled things! But I always think it's best to put one's cards on the table at once."

She waited a moment. "In a *little while* the Chianti Flask Mystery, as they called it, will be more or less forgotten, and then of course that offer—I mean the offer of *the thousand pounds*—won't hold good any more."

Mrs. Scrutton felt a great lightening of the spirit. Oh! what a mercy it would be if in a little while people would really forget that miserable story.

"I'll tell my son as soon as I see him," she said quietly.

"I think Mrs. Dousland ought to know of that offer at once, don't you?"

"I think Mark will certainly tell her of it."

"Mind you—I don't want you to feel that the offer wouldn't hold good for, say, *a few more days*, Mrs. Scrutton, for I'm *sure* it would."

The speaker looked flustered, undecided, and worried. "Do you think it would be a good thing if Bob could come and see Dr. Scrutton *after lunch to-day*? He could be here by two o'clock."

"Mark has gone away for the day. He may not be back till to-morrow."

"*Away*? Where you can't get at him? What an unfortunate thing!"

Mrs. Stevens got up, and walked across to one of the windows.

"One doesn't even see the shore from here, does one? I've *never* been down to Beach Cottage, but I've heard it's a *delightful* little house."

To that observation Mrs. Scrutton made no answer.

"One couldn't have found a better place to hide oneself, *could one*?"

"I suppose not."

"Poor woman! How *wise* of her to change her name. My son understands that she is going away—I think to Canada." Her voice became instinctively lower, as she went on: "That was *really* how Bob found out where she was. She telephoned yesterday *morning* to Loverslea about going to Canada, and though of course the butler at Loverslea had no business to give her away, the promise of a fiver, as Bob calls it, unlocked his lips. It was such *luck* her being near to where I live, wasn't it?"

Mrs. Scrutton accompanied her visitor to the front door and saw her into her car. Then she stood watching the car till it became a speck on the road which ran along the cliffs beyond the gates of Mellcombe Court. For the first time she felt consciously glad that the whole of the ribbon-like carriage-way through the park could be seen from where she stood.

Then she turned back and went into the long parlour, feeling glad indeed that neither her husband nor her son had been at home. Had they been here this morning, one or the other, maybe both of them, would have made an enemy of Mrs. Stevens. For the first time in her life—there had been many first times for Mary Scrutton since yesterday—she felt it would be a serious thing for them all were they to raise enemies now that Mark was going to marry a woman who had been the central figure of a *cause célèbre.*

XI

Colonel Scrutton was shown into the large cool apartment which was Sir Joseph Molloy's own room in his London house.

As a humble scholar of Trinity College, Dublin, the young Joe had told himself that one day he would have just such a study of his own as was this room, and he had achieved his ambition. But he would willingly, now, have given everything he possessed in exchange for his vanished youth.

Two high green marble columns bore busts of Edmund Burke, and O'Connell the Liberator, and between the columns were two deep easy-chairs, and a broad brass-inlaid writing-table. Everything, here, breathed quiet, security, and peace, and the windows gave on to a lawn surrounded by high trees which hid the neighbouring houses.

But the man now waiting for the famous advocate took no note of what was round him, as he began pacing up and down the room. He was feeling very unhappy because, for the first time in his long life, he had the sensation of being embarked on what was according to his code a dishonourable enterprise. What would Mark feel, were he ever to discover that his father had sought out an almost stranger to discover from that stranger the character of the woman whom Mark worshipped, and intended to marry as soon as she was willing to do so? The answer to that wordless question was plain. Mark would feel as deep a sense of offence as a man can feel, and never wholly would he forgive his father.

But Mark's mother, when urging her husband to do what he was doing now, had said with a sob in her voice: "He need never know, unless you feel, which God forbid, that after your talk with that lawyer it is your duty to dissuade him from this strange marriage."

All the same, the old soldier who was waiting for Sir Joseph Molloy's arrival from the country felt as if he were about to commit an act of treachery against his only son. Ever since Mark had told him this bewildering news, he had felt sorry he had lived on to old age to be confronted with such a problem.

He felt the more wretched because, inasmuch as he had ever thought of the man for whom he was waiting so anxiously, since the far-away days when they had been thrown together in a casual way, he had felt a prejudice against the Irishman. So it had been bitter to have to ask Sir Joseph such a favour as that of granting him an interview regarding a private matter which was only of moment to himself.

The door of the room was flung open, and the atmosphere became charged as if with electricity, so buoyant and vital was the great lawyer's personality. Sir Joseph was wearing rough country clothes, yet he looked as if he were full of business, for he was one of those men who never allow themselves a real holiday.

"Forgive my being late! I had a breakdown! The first time it has ever happened—"

"It was kind of you to come up from the country specially to see me," said Colonel Scrutton stiffly.

"I'm delighted to see you again—after all these years. Besides your name, which is a peculiar name, has lately been familiar to me, though I can't think in what connection."

"My son, Mark Scrutton, gave evidence in the course of a trial for murder last June, in which you had been retained for the Defence."

Sir Joseph looked puzzled, even ruffled. He hated to think that he was growing—not old, that he would never admit—but older, yes, and that his memory was not as good as it had been, say, thirty years ago.

"You were defending a lady called Mrs. Dousland. The trial took place at the Silchester Assizes."

"Why of course, I remember all about it, now! Your son's evidence was most valuable to that poor little lady. In fact, it made a great impression on the Judge, and affected his summing-up."

Only stopping to take breath he went on: "Your son made it clear that Fordish Dousland, the man whose death we were investigating, had long had the thought of suicide in his mind. Dousland showed a morbid interest in the action of a certain poison, not only on the vermin which it is sold to destroy, but on human beings, too."

Colonel Scrutton drew a long breath. He felt as if the question he had come to ask was answered already.

He said, in a tone of relief: "My son has fallen deeply in love with Mrs. Dousland, and hopes to marry her some time early next year. He is our only son, and his mother and I were deeply troubled when he told us the news. It was owing to my wife's insistence that I ventured to telephone to you. If you have sons yourself, you will forgive me for seeking you out."

The other looked exceedingly surprised: "God bless my soul! What a strange thing—"

He stopped short, trying to remember how Mark Scrutton had impressed him in the witness-box; and gradually he recalled the tall dark still young-looking man whose evidence had been of such vital moment to Laura Dousland. Had the two been friends before Fordish Dousland's death?

And then unconsciously he shook his head. No, no! Laura Dousland was a virtuous woman. He had felt convinced of the fact during that interview he had had with her on the eve of the trial, in the Silchester prison. All the same, it was certainly curious that the one man who had ever been a visitor during the lifetime of Fordish Dousland to the drab, oddly furnished house, he himself had taken the trouble to go over, should now be going to marry his widow. Colonel Scrutton who, under a stiff, cold manner, possessed a considerable knowledge of human nature, as must have any man who has ever commanded a regiment, guessed something of what was passing in Sir Joseph Molloy's mind.

"I should like to assure you," he said earnestly, "that my son was practically unacquainted with Mrs. Dousland till after the conclusion of her trial. It was when she was staying with some good friends of hers, the Haywards, that Mrs. Hayward asked my son to see Mrs. Dousland. She was really ill, as a result of all she had gone through. That was how their real acquaintance began."

"Pity no doubt was akin to love; that often happens," observed Sir Joseph.

"Then I may tell my boy's mother that in your view there

was a grave miscarriage of justice, and that this lady ought never to have been brought to trial?"

The answer was longer in coming than Colonel Scrutton had thought it would be; but it came at last.

"Most certainly tell your wife that! Though, mind you, I'm not one of those who consider that in a case of suspected murder there should be no arrest unless there is certainty. The police are too fond of not advising an arrest unless they feel sure of a conviction. Oddly enough, they do seem to have felt sure this time; but that was the fault of the Coroner. By the way, may I ask if you followed the case?"

"Neither my wife nor I take what seems to be an almost universal interest in crime; but of course when we realised that our son was to give evidence, we read the report of that day's proceedings."

"I should like to tell you that I have never had a better witness than Mrs. Dousland. I put her in the box because nowadays if a prisoner does not give evidence on his or her own behalf, it is regarded as a bad mark. I regretted having to do so in this case, for I thought it would be very hard on her. She is a delicate, sensitive woman. But she emerged from the ordeal with flying colours."

"Was any reason suggested why this man, Fordish Dousland, should have committed suicide?" asked Colonel Scrutton.

"If I remember rightly the only reason suggested was that he was tired of life. Mind you, it's clear the marriage was not a happy marriage. Dousland had had one of those curious late—between ourselves I think I might call it senile—passions, which sometimes seize on an old bachelor. The girl refused him again and again; then she was persuaded to say 'yes' by Mrs. Hayward, the determined lady who was at once her friend and her employer. Of course Mrs. Hayward did as she thought for the best, but it was a cruel thing to do by such a young woman as was my future client. But there! I need not tell you that—as, of course, you know her."

"I have not seen her yet," was to Sir Joseph the surprising reply, "I hope to do so within the next day or two."

"I think you will like her! Indeed, I don't see how anyone can help liking Laura Dousland—"

As Colonel Scrutton remained silent, Sir Joseph went on: "Of course from the worldly point of view, your son could do much better, for I remember being told that he was an exceptionally clever, indeed able, man."

Mark's father said briefly: "He is all that."

"Still, if he loves her, and she loves him—well? they will no doubt face life bravely together. I don't say it will always be pleasant, for whatever people may say, it is uncommonly difficult to bury one's past. I presume Dr. Scrutton will not go on practising at Silchester?"

"He intends to take up a certain branch of medical research after his marriage. This may mean going abroad for a while."

"I think that will be a good thing."

"I should like to ask you one more question." The Colonel waited a moment, then he said: "How would you feel if your own son came to you and said he wished to marry a woman situated as Mrs. Dousland is now situated?"

Sir Joseph hesitated. "Frankly I should regret it very much. I am sufficiently old-fashioned, may I say Irish? to hate anything like notoriety in connection with a woman. I'm afraid it will be impossible for Mrs. Dousland, however happy in her second marriage she may be, to get right away from that story. Now and again she will be bound to come across someone who will recognise her. But mind you, Colonel Scrutton, I would far rather my son married a lady situated as poor Laura Dousland is now, than he took to wife one of those girls who have neither manners or morals. By the way, when are they thinking of getting married?"

"I don't think any time has been settled. Have you any special reason for asking?"

"My only reason is that though the young lady has crowded the happenings of many lives in the last few months, it would not look well if it should come out that she had married again within a comparatively short time of her husband's death. And, further, that she had married a man who had been a witness on her behalf at her trial for murder."

Sir Joseph Molloy spoke very gravely indeed, and Colonel Scrutton's face altered. He looked, and indeed felt, suddenly deeply troubled.

"Had you any doubt in your own mind as to the relations between my son and Mrs. Dousland while he was giving evidence on her behalf?"

He spoke in a low voice, but with an almost terrible intensity.

Sir Joseph was moved in a sense he had not yet been during his interview with this cold, stiff-mannered soldier. How would he feel if one of his own cherished boys both, he thanked God, still at school, were about to do so unwise a thing as to marry a woman who, however innocent, had been written about, talked about, and thought about, as had been the case with ill-fated Laura Dousland? Well he knew in his heart that he would go to almost any length to prevent such a marriage.

He put his hand on the older man's shoulder. "I give you

my word of honour," he exclaimed, "that while your son was in the witness-box such a thought never crossed my mind! I am convinced Dr. Scrutton only saw Mrs. Dousland on two occasions before the death of her husband. The first time when he accompanied Dousland home from the golf club because the old chap felt ill on the course, and the second time when your son went to the house to bring Dousland some bulbs. It came out during the case that Mrs. Dousland took no interest in the garden, but that her husband was always pottering about out there. Though singularly penurious he did spend money, oddly enough, on what are called garden ornaments. I went myself to the house in Kingsley Terrace, and I was astonished at the look of what was after all only what most people would call a cat-run. The little garden was almost entirely paved over, and there was a lot of statuary."

"It was on his second visit to that house that the discussion on poison took place."

"Yes, and your son's evidence made easy my task of convincing the jury that Dousland had committed suicide. Your son, oddly enough, wasn't called at the inquest."

"I believe he was absent from Silchester at the time."

"Ay, but they ought to have got him. Had he given then the evidence he gave at the trial, not even the malignant stupidity of the Silchester Coroner, and the animosity of a certain Dr. Grant the poor woman had sent for when she first discovered her husband was dead, could have prevented a *felo de se* verdict."

"I only realised yesterday the part that flask of Italian wine played in the case. What was your theory about that?"

Sir Joseph waited a few moments, then he answered: "I think the police, as is sometimes their way, made a mountain out of a mole-hill—the mole-hill being a casual remark made by the Dousland's servant, an Italian named Terugi."

"Yet it seems almost certain the poison was taken in the wine—by the little I do remember of the case."

"That, allow me to say, is pure supposition."

He again waited a moment. "Mind you, Colonel, I'm sorry that the disappearance of that Chianti flask was never cleared up. It is the one mysterious point in the story. But I fear it will always remain a mystery, unless the flask is found by chance some day, wherever it was thrown away, or hidden either by Dousland himself, or by the Italian Terugi."

Reflectively he added: "I do think it probable that Fordish Dousland did poison himself with the help of that wine if, that is, the Chianti hadn't already been all drunk by the servant. For one thing, Dousland seems to have been one of those curious men who have a dislike for plain water. He either drank coffee, or this wine. I watched the Italian closely when I was conducting his cross-examination, and I formed the impression that he was lying most of the time. Also, I entirely believed Mrs. Dousland to be in good faith when she stated that to the best of her belief there had been no flask placed by Terugi on her husband's tray that evening."

"Dousland must have been an odd man."

"Odd indeed! For one thing he had peculiar nocturnal habits. Now and again he would wander about the house, even in cold weather, for no reason that can be suggested, save that he felt restless. I think it likely that he went downstairs in the course of that night to the basement, and that while there, acting on a sudden impulse, he put a spoonful of the powder into what remained of the wine in that flask of Chianti. Then, having drunk some of it—the flask is said to have been a quarter full—that he threw away, or hid in some secret place, the flask which contained the rest of the poisoned wine. The only other reasonable theory is that the Italian, Terugi, drank the wine, and took the empty flask away with him, disposing of it on his way to London. But I incline, and always shall incline, to the theory I put to you just now, though I should be obliged if you would keep it to yourself. In my speech for the Defence I avoided mentioning the Chianti flask, and I regard the way in which Terugi was handled by the police as having been highly discreditable."

"I will leave you now," said Colonel Scrutton, "and I am deeply obliged for all you have told me, and for your kindness in seeing me. I take it that I may tell my wife that you advise, in Mrs. Dousland's own interest, that the marriage shall not take place till, say, her husband has been dead a year?"

"I don't go quite as far as that! But I would say that it might be as well for them to wait till the late autumn. Also, if I were your son I should be married in Paris, for in that way may be avoided any mention of the wedding in the English papers."

The speaker accompanied his visitor to the front door, and then, as he grasped Colonel Scrutton's hand he exclaimed: "I would like to beg you to do what I begged Mrs. Dousland to do just after she had been acquitted on what had been a wicked, and should have appeared an incredible, charge. That is, put right behind you this painful and cruel story! Think of this poor soul only as a sweet-natured and, I should say, a truly good, woman, who deserves the happiness I believe she is going to enjoy with Dr. Scrutton. I am of course assuming that his love is not one of those short-lived passions which sometimes turn into indifference."

"My son deeply loves this woman," said Colonel

Scrutton, and for the second time his face showed deep emotion. "But for that, I should move heaven and earth to stop the marriage. Still, as to this matter, deeply though he loves his mother and me, I might as well try to make an impression on marble. He worships Mrs. Dousland. By the way, I have not told you that she began by refusing him. But when he went to bid her a final farewell, his distress broke down all pretence, and she acknowledged that she loved him. Though even then she told him again and again that he ought to pause, and ask himself if he was prepared to face life with a woman whose name had rung through the world."

"That is just what I should have expected of her! Unlike most of the people concerned in her story, I consider Laura Dousland a remarkable woman. I don't know if you are aware that her husband's death left her almost penniless? In fact, as the Coroner ought at once to have realised and told his jury, it was all to her interest to keep him alive. Yet, poor though she be, she insists on paying every penny of the costs connected with her defence. So your son is going to marry a singularly honest and upright woman, Colonel Scrutton."

XII

Mark's mother knew, by now, that he had already built up the whole of his house of life on this to her still unknown woman. And, as she walked down towards the place where she was to see her future daughter-in-law for the first time, she grew more and more despondent and afraid. The interview with Mrs. Stevens had filled her with a sense of degradation, as well as of disgust. It had shown her, as nothing else could have done, what Laura Dousland had had to endure and—must still endure. To Mrs. Scrutton it was now a frightful calamity that this poor woman should have come here and, while actually living on part of Mark's noble inheritance, stolen his heart and so proposed to smirch his honoured name.

Some time had gone by since she had come down to Beach Cottage, and she felt enchanted, even in the midst of her distress, by the beauty of the stretch of shore, and the charm of the small one-storey house which stood just above the shore. Partially covering the weathered stone walls were delicate flowering creepers, for Mark Scrutton, in his spare time, was a clever and a keen gardener. When she had been stronger and younger, Mrs. Scrutton had sometimes felt it would be very pleasant to give up the responsibilities of the large house and live down here by the sea, with the husband who was all her life, apart that is from that portion of herself which was absorbed in her son.

It was with a slow, hesitating tread that she walked round to the front door, and saw it was wide open to the sea and sky. Even so she knocked on the door with her stick, and Laura Dousland came out of the inner room, and stood face to face with the frail figure she knew to be that of Mark's mother.

She said in a clear, toneless voice: "Do come in, Mrs. Scrutton."

As the other obeyed she felt inexpressibly relieved, for this slight pale woman her son loved looked entirely different to what she had feared to find her.

Laura shut the door, and for a moment the pretty room seemed strangely dark, for the only light now there came in from a side window which gave on the steep path leading up to the heath which formed the upland between the shore and Mellcombe Court.

"I think I ought to tell you at once, Mrs. Scrutton, that I have just written to Mark saying I cannot marry him. I am going away to-day, and I hope he will never know where I have gone."

Her eyes were bent on Mark's mother with an intent, questioning gaze. And indeed she wished to learn that worn face, so that she might remember it when she was far away, and thought of her heart's love, and of his loneliness.

"Why do you feel you must do this cruel thing by him?" asked Mrs. Scrutton, and she, too, spoke in a muted voice.

"Surely you and his father don't wish Mark to marry me?"

The older woman waited for a moment; then she felt she must answer truth with truth, sincerity with sincerity.

"Mark loves you with all his soul, and you ought to weigh that fact deeply before you decide to break with him. And I would still say that to you, even if you did not care, as I can't help believing you do care for him."

And as Laura only looked at her in dumb misery, she added desperately: "The only thing that matters to me and to his father is his happiness."

"It's because I know that if I marry Mark it must lead to his unhappiness if not at first, then later on, that I have made up my mind to give him up."

Laura was not now looking at the mother of the man she loved; there had risen before her some inner vision of the soul which filled her with doubt and foreboding.

"Why should you think your marriage would lead to unhappiness? Mark cares nothing for public opinion; besides, you have public opinion on your side."

"I'll try and tell you why I feel as I do." She waited a moment, then said slowly: "Mark believes that all that happened to me last winter and spring will fade into nothingness after a while. But he is wrong! Even now, though I love him with all my heart," and for the first time her face quivered with feeling, "what remains real, what I dream about and what I wake remembering, are not the weary weeks I spent in prison and the awful days of my trial—no, what I cannot forget is what happened after my acquittal. Till I came here I felt as if I were being burnt alive by a curiosity that wrapped me round like a sheet of flame. More than once—" she turned her sunken eyes full on Mrs. Scrutton, "—I was frightfully tempted to kill myself. But if

I had done that it would have been letting all the people who had been so good to me down, down, down." She sank on the couch and began rocking herself backwards and forwards, giving way as she had not yet given way before any human being.

Mrs. Scrutton was filled with dismay, and, yes, sudden acute fear. Perhaps this woman was right, and however awful the wrench, parting might be the best and wisest solution for both her and Mark.

"You ought not to have lived alone down here; how could Mark have thought of letting you do it, my poor child?"

"Mark did right, for I have felt if not happy, at least sheltered and at peace since I came here. Now and again, not often, I even forgot all that had happened to me. Also—" a flood of colour rose to her face, "—since his holiday Mark has often been with me, and when we were together all seemed well—for the time."

"But if you marry Mark, he will be with you always."

Laura shook her head. "He would have his work, Mrs. Scrutton, and that would mean more and more to him, as I meant less and less." The colour receded from her face and there came into her eyes a dark gleam of sombre despair.

Mrs. Scrutton remembered Mark's expression, she seemed to hear the very sound of his voice, as he had said: "I didn't know there could be in the world a woman of such heroic stuff." And, all at once, she felt she must give battle for Mark. Even if it were for ill, and not for good, he loved Laura Dousland in a way which would mean that the loss of her would leave him maimed.

"If you can forget yourself, my dear, you will find that Mark will love you more and more, not less and less. You're a hundred times more attractive than I ever was, and though

I'm an old woman now, Colonel Scrutton can hardly bear me out of his sight, when he's at home."

"Ah, but that's different."

"Why different?"

"Because Mark is in love with me; he hasn't known me long enough to love me," and she sighed a woeful sigh.

"He says," said Mrs. Scrutton slowly, "that he fell in love with you the very first time he saw you."

The effect of those words, half playful in intention and indeed in fact, had a strange effect on the woman to whom they were addressed.

She leapt to her feet. "No, no, no!" she cried violently. "I couldn't bear to think that. Oh, say that isn't true, Mrs. Scrutton! Why, he only saw me for a moment—"

"He had time to see you were very unhappy."

Laura sank back on the couch, "I was unhappy—more unhappy than anyone will ever know."

"Why not wait six months, even a year, before you really decide to give up the greatest thing in the world to a woman—the love of a man like my son Mark? You and he would be such true comrades. I have seen so many marriages wrecked because the woman could not be her husband's comrade. Wait awhile, my dear, and for God's sake"—she uttered the three words very solemnly—"I implore you to wait."

Laura put her hand on Mrs. Scrutton's arm, and she grasped it with unconsciously painful strength. "I can't wait. If I did, I should give in. How could I help it, loving him as I do? If I have the strength to give him up now, it will be for his sake. What I long to do is to go out of life—but I couldn't do that without Mark knowing I had done it. Also, if I killed myself then perhaps he would believe—" she stopped, and again she began rocking herself backwards and forwards.

Mrs. Scrutton looked down on the swaying figure with pitiful eyes. "Nothing would make my son believe that you had done the awful thing of which you were accused. Never think that," she said firmly. "He'd sooner believe himself capable of doing that of which you were accused than that you did it."

She spoke with passionate conviction.

Laura stood up. "I think that's true," she said as if to herself.

There came the distant sound of a bell floating from the land to the shore.

"That's to tell me my husband is back from town," said Mrs. Scrutton, and her face which had been sad flushed with joy.

And then she felt startled, and pained, too, for, "I suppose," said Laura musingly, "that Colonel Scrutton has been to London to see what he could find out about me?" And as there came no reply to the half question: "There isn't much to find out, Mrs. Scrutton. Only that I am a fearfully unhappy woman, and that the fates have been terribly cruel in their dealings with me."

Colonel Scrutton drew his wife into the smoking-room. He was in haste to unburden himself, and too absorbed in all he had to say, to notice how deeply troubled and unlike her usual self she looked.

"I feel very much happier," he exclaimed. "It would have done your heart good, Mary, to have heard the way Sir Joseph Molloy spoke of that poor girl yesterday. He has a high opinion of her. He said she faced up nobly to that horrible accusation, and made me feel that she is a real heroine."

"I think she is a noble woman, George."

"And then I went to the club, and read up the reports of the trial! The Judge's summing-up was given almost in full, and I felt no human being was ever more ill-treated than was Mrs. Dousland by the Silchester Coroner. He must be stupid, as well as malicious, and had a real animus against her. It is monstrous that she should ever have been brought to trial. Why, that man Dousland's grandfather actually killed himself because some woman, much of his own age, wouldn't marry him after he became a widower! What's more, he had always been a queer eccentric chap. He had threatened on one occasion to commit suicide, and it's plain he was bitterly disappointed in his marriage. This poor woman admitted she had never liked him. He just bullied her into marrying him."

He stopped, and for the first time he looked at his wife, and what he saw frightened him.

"Is anything the matter?"

"I have just been with Mrs. Dousland, and I don't believe she will ever marry Mark."

Colonel Scrutton looked exceedingly surprised, and as was his way when surprised, he remained silent.

"She is convinced that the shame and dishonour surrounding a trial for murder will always stick to her, and she thinks that if Mark marries her, it will ruin his life."

"She may be right as to that. But he is mad about her. Nothing will make him give her up, Mary."

"I did my best, for oh! George, I do like her, and I don't wonder that Mark loves her. There's something about her that's curiously appealing. Apart from this dreadful affair, she is the kind of woman I'd have chosen for Mark. There is something so—"

"I know—womanly," Colonel Scrutton said quickly.

She nodded and smiled for the first time that day. To be womanly was all, or nearly all George Scrutton demanded from any woman. And with reference to this instinctive demand his wife often had reason to feel that he had been born out of due time.

He went on, now, eagerly for him: "That's the impression I got both from Sir Joseph, and on reading the reports of her trial. Yet she's a good plucked one! That interruption she made when that Italian was swearing away her life must have asked for a good bit of courage—"

"Yes, she must have hated doing that," and Mrs. Scrutton sighed, as there rose before her Laura's sensitive face and fragile appearance.

"It was the more plucky of her to do it as she didn't seem to care which way the case went. The papers said she was as if stunned for most of the time, though now and again she would rouse herself, especially after she had seen Mrs. Hayward. I'm sorry Mark doesn't like Mrs. Hayward. She was a splendid and most loyal friend, and her evidence went a long way towards clearing Mrs. Dousland."

Mrs. Scrutton was now lying back in an easy chair; she looked both ill and unhappy.

"Mary?"

"Yes, George?"

"Perhaps she's doing the best thing for our son, after all." He waited a moment. Then he said reluctantly: "In fact, I'm sure she's right, my dear."

"But I thought," she murmured, "I understood, George—"

"I was trying to make the best of a bad business, Mary. I do think the poor young woman has been most evilly treated and deeply do I pity her. But Mark is a proud man. It would be a fearful thing for him if he and his wife were dogged, wherever they went, by this dreadful story."

And then Colonel Scrutton asked his wife a certain question: "If we had had a daughter, would you have liked her to have married Captain Mayfield?"

A Captain Mayfield in the Colonel's regiment had been caught, according to two eye-witnesses, cheating at cards. He had brought a libel case, and he had won it, but shortly after he had shot himself.

And now Mrs. Scrutton said uncertainly: "I should have hated any girl to have married him. And yet if we had had a daughter, and if she had loved him as I loved you, George, could we have had the heart to try and stop her?"

"I don't suppose we should have tried to stop her, but I'm not at all sure that we'd have been right." And then he sighed, for he would have liked to have had a daughter, and so would his Mary. They had both had dream children, though neither had ever said so to the other.

"She is giving him up for his sake, not for her own, George. I'm afraid she loves him almost as much as he loves her. And it seems to me so awful a thing that he should lose that love."

"Men get over such affairs more quickly than they do anything else," said Colonel Scrutton grimly. "Not one man in a million remains faithful to his first love."

And then he came and bent over his wife, adding, with a twinkle in his eye: "You must think me a damned vain chap, my dear?"

There came a quivering smile over her white face. "For all you know Mark may be like you—the one man in a million."

"He hasn't known her very long, has he?"

"Long enough, I'm afraid, to feel that she has become flesh of his flesh and bone of his bone."

This was a curious expression for Mark's mother to use, and Mark's father felt suddenly doubtful if he was being hard and mean in feeling the relief he undoubtedly did feel.

"At any rate we have time to think it over," he observed, "Mark won't be back till late to-night."

And then they heard their son's voice in the hall: "Is the Colonel back from town?"

His father called out: "I'm here, Mark."

"Ought I to say anything to him?" whispered Mrs. Scrutton.

"I'm afraid you ought to tell him before he sees her," and he walked out of the open window.

"Mother—have you seen her?"

"Yes, my darling; I went down to Beach Cottage this morning. We had a long talk, and oh! I don't wonder you fell in love with her. I think she is a wonderful creature, I—I—" and then her voice broke. Mark Scrutton supposed her tears had come in pity for a fellow woman who had gone through so fearful an ordeal, and though he felt touched, they did not surprise him.

He patted her hand: "It's such luck finding someone who will fit in here, I mean with you and Father—as I know Laura will!"

"I'm afraid she's still very unhappy, Mark."

There came a fierce questioning look on his face, "Did she say anything about that horrible business?"

"She didn't say much—but oh, Mark, I'm afraid she has made up her mind it would be wrong of her to marry again."

"How d'you mean? I don't understand."

"She feels she would bring disgrace and unhappiness on any man she married."

"She and I have been over all that," he said roughly, "and it was too bad of her to start it again with you."

And then remorsefully under his breath, he exclaimed: "My poor little darling! The wonderful thing isn't that she can't forget all that hateful affair, but that she never says one word against all the cruel stupid people who made her suffer such torture."

"I think she is a very noble being, Mark. In fact, I have never met anyone who impressed me in some ways as much as she did to-day. I felt she was only thinking of you, but I am afraid—"

"Afraid of what, Mother?"

"That she really did mean what she said to me."

"What exactly did she say?"

"She believes a time would certainly come when you would regret having married her."

"Why should she think that?" he asked in a hard tone.

"Because she is quite sure that wherever you and she might be, you would be dogged by the fact that she once had to stand her trial for murder."

"That would be less than nothing to me, who know her to have been innocent. Besides, everybody now knows she was innocent."

He waited a moment. "I suppose I made too great haste. I ought to have waited. I've been a selfish beast. Yet—she does love me, Mother?"

She could not keep from him what she believed to be the truth, so "With all her heart she loves you," she said in a low tone.

"Then nothing else matters! I don't mind how long I wait," he jerked the words out with hard emphasis. "When I used to see her being tormented at Loverslea by that dreadful well-meaning woman, Mrs. Hayward, I used to wonder, Mother, how she could bear it. And it wasn't only Mrs. Hayward! All the busybodies of Silchester who had as they called it 'taken her part,' thought they had a right to see her and cross-examine her about this or that or the other. More than once I felt that in her place I'd be tempted to kill myself to get away from it all."

"She told me she was tempted to do that. But she felt, poor girl—" there came a great tenderness into Mrs. Scrutton's voice, "—that to do that would be letting down the people who had been kind to her."

"Aye, it's true they would have felt let down. They were such fools, all of them! A woman like Mrs. Hayward, if she had been in poor darling's place, would really have enjoyed what she would have called 'her great triumph.' But it was just a blur of red-hot agony to Laura."

He got up. "I'll go and see her now. When we are together I scare away the blue devils! I don't think she'll dare say to me what she said to you."

But twenty minutes later she heard his voice coming in through the window—"Mother?" And before she could answer that loud discordant cry, he stood before her, "She's gone!"

Then he asked, "How long ago was it that you left her?"

"It can't have been more than an hour ago."

"She must have made for the Exeter express. Oh God! why did I leave her—even for a few hours?"

"Has she taken anything with her?"

"As far as I can make out, everything! And now I must go after her at once. You do understand—"

She bent her head.

"I'll telephone this evening, but you mustn't expect to see me until I've found her—I'll follow her to the end of the earth."

After he had gone his father and mother walked down to the shore. The door of the little house had been left open by Mark, and as they walked through it, Mrs. Scrutton felt a chill descend upon her heart, for everything in the sitting-room had been left unnaturally tidy. In the bedroom fireplace was a little heap of ashes.

"Look George? She burnt all his letters before she went away."

"Ay, and her boats as well," observed Colonel Scrutton, and half to himself he said, "I should have liked to see her, Mary, just once."

She came up close to him and putting her hands on his breast said soberly: "You'll see her very often, unless I'm entirely mistaken. Mark will never give her up. He said he would follow her to the ends of the earth. I don't think she will let him go as far as that."

XIII

"WHO IS IT? PLEASE SPEAK MORE CLEARLY... YES, I AM Mrs. Hayward, but who are you?... Why, Dr. Scrutton? How very funny! I didn't know your voice. Aren't you well?"

And then to his relief, before he could answer, came another question, "What can I do for you?"

He called back, in as matter-of-fact a voice as he could manage: "I want to get in touch with Mrs. Dousland."

He was in the call-box of a London hotel, and it was well that the woman at the other end of the line could not see his worn haggard face. Before calling up Loverslea, he had done everything in his power to find Laura. But her lawyers did not know where she was, and her banker, who did know, had refused to tell him. So at last he had decided to speak to Alice Hayward, and much as he disliked her, it was yet a comfort to hear her clear resonant voice. Somehow, though he told himself he was absurd in so feeling, she did seem a little bit of Laura.

"Mrs. Dousland? You mustn't call her that now, Dr. Scrutton! Laura is Mrs. Ordeley *now*. John is taking a lot of trouble over her change of name by deed poll, and we're trying to get used to calling her that."

"Then she's with you now?"

There was a touch of hesitation in Alice Hayward's confident voice as she answered, after a slight pause, "Oh, no, Mrs. Ordeley is not here; I believe she's in London."

"Where is she in London?"

"I can't tell you off hand, Dr. Scrutton. She's staying in a quite small hotel. Where are you speaking from? If you'll give me your address I'll send you a postcard. My husband knows where she is staying."

"I want to get in touch with her at once. An important telegram came for her to Mellcombe, just after she left for London. I've brought it up for her."

"How odd of her not to leave her London address at Mellcombe!"

"I felt sure you would know where she is."

"I'll go and look in John's study, if you'll hold on."

And he did hold on, it seemed to him for an eternity, till he heard an unknown voice exclaim: "You've been cut off, sorry, sir. Did you make the call?"

Then after another intolerable delay came: "We were cut off, Dr. Scrutton; but in a way that was a good thing, for this call is costing you a lot of money!"

"Have you found the address?" he asked in a rasped tone.

"Yes, I found it in a drawer in my husband's study. But, well? I don't know if I ought to give it you, for John wrote on the envelope, 'This address is on no account to be given to anybody.' Funny, isn't it?"

There was a pause.

"Of course you can give it to *me*, Mrs. Hayward. After

all I'm Mrs. Ordeley's physician, apart from anything else. Also, the telegram is really urgent."

The listener felt a touch of surprise, for the voice at the other end had changed; it had become pleasantly cool and professional.

"D'you know what's in the telegram?" she asked.

"Well, yes, for I opened it. As a matter of fact—" He was not good at lying, and he hesitated before he went on: "It contains an exceptionally good offer for the house in Silchester, and there's a time limit. So you see, it *is* urgent, isn't it?"

"Then I had better give you her address. I'm sure she wouldn't mind your having it."

"I hope she wouldn't."

"She's at Smith's Hotel, Bentley Street. The truth is that she's so afraid someone connected with the Press will find out where she is, that John said he would rather not tell even *me*, so that I should be able to say, if I was asked, that I didn't know! We hope, however, that she will come here for a day or two before leaving for Canada."

"For Canada?"

"I do hope you approve of what she is going to do. It's thanks to you, isn't it, that she has had that splendid change and rest?"

"Yes, but why Canada?" He hardly knew what he was saying.

"Surely you know that it was my husband who has found her that splendid post in Montreal? The man is a widower, and met Laura here ages ago, long before she was married. He never forgot her. Isn't that strange? It would be indecent to think *yet* of her marrying again. Still—" she stopped abruptly, for they had been cut off for the second time.

"Smith's Hotel, Bentley Street?"

Mark Scrutton leapt into the car he had hired for the day, and twenty minutes later he was standing in the hall of a small shabby house in a small shabby street.

"Mrs. Ordeley? She's leaving here in a few minutes. She's already paid her bill." And then the slatternly-looking woman turned to a boy: "Didn't she say she'd want a cab?"

"Yes, but she didn't want it called till she came downstairs, ma'am."

"Shall I send up, sir, and tell her a gentleman is asking for her?"

She looked with some curiosity at the tall, good-looking young man. He was breathing quickly, just as if he had been running, instead of driving up in the nice car which stood outside the door of her family hotel.

She and the friend who helped her had made up their minds there was something queer about this Mrs. Ordeley, though there could be no doubt that she was what they called "respectable"; in fact, amusingly old-fashioned, a real country mouse—maybe the widow of a clergyman—and no mistake.

"It isn't necessary to send up if Mrs. Ordeley is just coming down. I'll wait over there," and he stalked off into a recess where stood three or four basket-chairs.

Suddenly he heard her light step on the threadbare carpet of the steep staircase, and he walked back into the hall.

As they came face to face he said quietly: "I have called for you, Laura."

She stared at him as if, so said to herself the woman who was observing the two closely, he were a ghost, instead of a personable gentleman. Also, Mrs. Ordeley had a wild look in her large dark eyes, which were the only pleasing feature in a very ordinary-looking face.

"My mother is expecting you," he went on, "and we haven't long before the west country express. You have paid up, haven't you, my dear?"

She muttered, "Yes, but I was going to get some change."

"You mean for tips?"

She nodded, and he put a pound note on the hotel desk with, "Will you divide this money between your staff?"

And then he took Laura's arm and, guiding her out of the door, settled her into the car next to the driver's seat.

Neither spoke to the other on the way to the station, or while Mark ran the car where it would have to stand till he had telephoned from Devonshire to the garage where he had hired it, to tell them where he had left it. He hadn't time to do that now, for they were only just in time to catch the last express of the day. Neither would he leave Laura alone, even to go into a telephone box.

After he had taken their two tickets, he went down the platform looking for an empty compartment. There was still a good deal of holiday traffic, and a coach had been added to their train, composed of ancient first-class carriages of a kind which have no corridor. Then he stopped.

"Shall we get in here?"

"Yes, if you like," he had to bend to hear the answer.

The guard of the train came forward, smiling. A newly-married couple without doubt? This sort wasn't like the usual young pair who flung their money about the day they were married; but he had known every sort and—you never know your luck! Sure enough: "We don't want to be disturbed. We are going a long way, and this lady feels ill."

The guard looked at Laura. Up to now he had concentrated on the gentleman, but now he saw that maybe he had made a mistake, and that this pale tragic-looking young lady wasn't a bride, but just an ailing woman.

"I'll see that no one gets in here, sir," and he locked the door after they were safely in the carriage.

As at last the train slid out of the station, "You are to lie down now, Laura, and not say a word," said Mark.

After she obeyed him he put the rug he had taken from the hired car over her feet. Then he looked down at her in an impersonal way that somehow hurt her. Was he angry with her? He had the right to be.

Turning away he stared unseeingly out of the window as he observed: "We can talk everything over to-morrow, and if you still want to leave England you shall, of course. But—but"—and now his voice altered as he ended with the words—"decently and in order."

She sat up and held out her arms, "Forgive me, Mark! I'm not worth all the trouble I'm giving you."

"Funny, isn't it, that I think you are?"

And then his good pretence at complete composure broke down, and as he flung himself down on his knees on the floor of the fusty Victorian railway compartment, he cried, "Did you really think you could hide from me, my precious darling? I'd have found you if it had taken years of seeking—"

But very soon he had made her lie down again and close her eyes, and for the rest of the journey he pretended to read a book.

Colonel and Mrs. Scrutton stood in the doorway of their house, waiting to welcome their future daughter-in-law, for Mark had managed to send them a telephone message through a porter during the few moments they had waited at Exeter for a local train.

"I wonder where he found her?" said his father.

"I shall never ask him that," said Mrs. Scrutton quickly. "The thing that matters is that he did find her, and that she has come back to him, George." Glancing at her husband, she exclaimed: "Surely you're glad Mark is going to get his heart's desire?"

"I'll try and be glad if you're glad, dearest. But the poor soul is right, all the same; her past will dog them, always. I trust he has counted the cost."

"I'm sure he has."

"I hope you're right. You may be, for he's your child, and maybe you know him better than I do."

"I simply think, George, that my child, as you call him, takes after his father; and if I'm right, this poor girl will be a lucky woman," and stepping on tiptoe she kissed him. Then she cried happily: "Here they come!"

Mark had left the fine motor-car Colonel Scrutton had given his son as his last birthday-present close to the local station when he had gone up to London three days ago.

As he drew up, his face was illumined with pride and joy.

"Here she is, Father!" and he almost lifted Laura from her seat.

The old man grasped her hand. "Welcome to my house, Mrs. Ordeley," and he looked, if with a kindly, yet with a long measuring glance, into her pale face. "Both my wife and I hope that you will stay with us for a few days before going back to the cottage," he said.

And then Mrs. Scrutton opened wide her arms, so wide indeed that they clasped both the newcomers to her breast.

"Darlings," she whispered, "how very very glad I am to see you for the first time like this, together."

As the rest of the evening wore away Colonel Scrutton began to fall under the quiet charm of the woman for whom his son felt so ardent and absorbing a passion, that it had made of him a different man.

There had always been something cynical, and almost carping, in the way Mark would speak of the other sex when alone with his father; and the older man had long ago made up his mind that the younger would never make what to himself seemed the one thing that mattered supremely in life, a really happy marriage. He felt now that he had been mistaken, and that Mark had met the one human being in the world who would be to him all that a civilised man longs to find in his mate in the way of physical and mental response.

But how ironical was the fate which had ordained that this one woman in the world for Mark should have been the central figure of a great murder mystery! Looking at her, as he did look at her again and again, during their simple dinner, and afterwards when he and Mark joined the two ladies in the long parlour, the Colonel could hardly believe that Mrs. Ordeley could be the Laura Dousland with whose name the world had rung. Yet they all had to face that fact, and he was filled with wrath when he recalled the odious interview to which his wife had been subjected by their neighbour, Mrs. Stevens.

At ten o'clock Mrs. Scrutton took up the visitor to a charming room, which was only given to specially-honoured guests in this old west-country house.

The heart of Mark's mother was very full to-night, and not, as was the case with Mark's father, of conflicting emotions. She was feeling absolutely content with, and every moment more drawn to, her son's future wife.

At the door of the room she said, "Good night, my dear, and God bless you for making my boy so happy."

The other murmured, "I am ashamed of having given Mark so much trouble."

Mrs. Scrutton turned round, and the look on Laura's face—a shadowed, suffering look—made her exclaim: "Are you sorry he found you?"

The woman who had been found gave a cry, "I couldn't have gone through with it—I should have died instead. I feel—"

"Tell me what you do feel," said Mrs. Scrutton gravely. "When my son found that you had gone, without even leaving a note to explain your conduct, his condition alarmed not only me, but his father. He was as if demented."

All the joy which had been rising, as if in a great tide filling her heart during the evening had left her, and fear and sadness suddenly encompassed her.

She walked into the room and turned out the lights which showed Laura's mournful face.

"Let's sit in the moonlight for a while, my dear," and she sat down, feeling old, despondent, almost despairing.

"Come close to me, and let us have this out for the last time."

Laura sat down on the floor at the older woman's feet.

"You love Mark, and Mark worships you. Isn't that enough? Can't you forget what happened to you last winter, and live in the future?"

"What will the future hold for Mark when his wife is

pointed out as having been what is called the heroine of a mystery? Oh, how I have suffered from that word—from those three words."

"What words do you mean?" asked Mark's mother uncertainly.

Laura answered in quick short gasps, "The word *mystery*, the word *Chianti*, the word *flask*."

Though her listener was naturally unaware of the fact, this was the first time she had ever uttered two of those words aloud since the day she had been compelled to utter them again and again in the witness-box. And now, having uttered them, it was as if she must do so yet again.

"All my life long there will be people who will say 'Look at that woman! Don't you remember the Chianti Flask Mystery?' What will Mark feel when he knows that whenever we appear at any social gathering, that sort of thing may be said of his wife?"

She spoke despairingly, and her voice rose to something like a scream.

"Now look here, Laura." Mrs. Scrutton bent over her and stroked her soft curling hair. "You're acting very wrongly. Wrongly to yourself, and, above all, very very wrongly to Mark, by harbouring such imaginings. My son is like my husband."

She waited a few moments before going on, for she was a deeply-reserved woman, and she had never told to any human being what she had made up her mind to tell this still stranger.

"George and I first met and fell in love when I was twenty-one and he twenty-seven. We were not able to marry, owing to various circumstances with which I need not trouble you, *for eighteen years*. So I was thirty-nine, and he was forty-five, when we did marry."

Once more she stopped speaking, and then, with an effort, she began again: "I am convinced, it was not necessary for him ever to say so, that during those years he remained faithful to me in word and in deed. Of course I know he must have been tempted, at times probably greatly tempted. He would not be the man he is had it not been so."

She paused: "And when I was thirty-four I had a serious illness, and what looks I ever had left me. I remember telling myself, indeed, taking a solemn oath before God, that if I saw the slightest change in George Scrutton's feelings for me the next time he came home on leave, I would not only release him, but make him believe that I no longer cared for him. But the first moment I saw him, I knew I need not have felt as I did feel, to my shame, deadly afraid."

Once more she stopped speaking for some moments before she went on: "There are men—I do not say there are many—who can only care, in a deep way, for one woman, and what is more, that fact is not to their credit, for they cannot help it. This was true of my George, and it is true of your Mark. Had you carried through your plan, Mark would probably have married in time, but it would not become a happy marriage. For good or ill you are the only woman in the world for him."

"I think that is true," said Laura in a stifled voice.

With passion Mrs. Scrutton then exclaimed: "What do vulgar curiosity-mongers matter? Think only of this man who loves you, and of a time when you will be able to make all the difference in his life! The work he longs to do is arduous, and from what I understand, often full of disappointment. You will make a home for him and, please God, have children, Laura. Let me think of you from now on as the one human being to whom I shall owe gratitude, as well as love. Some day you will know what a mother feels for her child, and then you will know what I feel about my son."

There came a strange look into Laura's face. "I could never love any child as I love Mark," she said.

She got up: "I won't look back!" she cried passionately. "And I will do what you say, Mrs. Scrutton; I will live in the present, and in the future."

She looked up into the worn moonlit face. "Tell me, do you wish me to marry Mark at once, as he would like me to do?"

Mrs. Scrutton longed to cry: "Yes! Make him happy at once."

But she remembered what her husband had said, so reluctantly she answered, "No, my dear, I think as to that your instinct is the right one. It would look ill, not only for you, but for Mark also, if you married him after so short an acquaintance." She did not add, "And after being widowed in so strange a way," which was indeed the truth.

"I'm glad I asked you," said Laura slowly; and then in an almost inaudible tone she murmured, "I long for him quite as much as he longs for me."

Within a day or two of the end of Mark's holiday his mother said to him: "I want you to persuade Laura to come and live with us till your marriage can take place. It isn't right she should be alone in that little house on the shore."

"I don't know that I can make her do that, Mother. She's rather peculiar, you know." He smiled as he added, "She seems happiest alone, unless she is with me."

Mrs. Scrutton looked at her son, and she wondered if she had been wise in giving that strong advice to Laura as to the postponement of their marriage, for Mark's face looked strained and thin. How would he get through the time of waiting, without Laura's constant presence? "I suppose you will be able to come down here most week-ends?" she observed.

He shook his head. "There isn't a hope of it! I might get away once a month, but I wasn't even able to do that last winter, as you know."

Late that same afternoon Mrs. Scrutton made her way down to the beach. She had become tenderly attached to Laura, and now she was going to do what she had seldom done in her life, that is, interfere with another human being's concern. She was glad her husband and son had gone off together, so that she was not tempted to tell either of them what she was going to do.

Hearing the sound of footsteps, Laura ran out to meet Mark's mother, and with a charming, half-childish gesture, she put her cheek against Mrs. Scrutton's cheek.

"How kind of you to come, *madre mia*," she exclaimed. "I was feeling lonely this afternoon."

"I want to speak to you, my dear."

And then, when they were in the house: "Of course Mark has told you that he feels he ought to go back to Silchester in a very few days from now?"

Laura's face shadowed; the name of the cathedral town had brought back a rush of painful memories.

"It would make us both so happy if you would live with us till you and Mark are married?"

"I think I would rather stay down here," then she added, half to herself: "I wonder how often Mark will be able to come?"

"I'm afraid very seldom, my dear. If it was a question of

money his father would pay anything in reason. But he feels he can't let down his friend. The man only consented to take the year away if Mark would take on the practice."

Laura drew a long breath, and then she said, rather pitifully, "What do you think I ought to do?"

"I know what I would do in your place."

"You would go back to Silchester, I suppose?"

"Do you feel you couldn't bear to do that?"

Laura's pale face crimsoned, "I could bear anything for Mark."

"He wouldn't wish that."

"I will go back—of course I will! After all, it won't be for so very long."

"You will make Mark very happy if you can bring yourself to do it."

Then the speaker's heart misgave her, and she said earnestly: "But if you find, after all, that being again in Silchester intolerable, you have only to come straight back here, to us. There won't be a moment of the night or day when you won't be as welcome as the flowers in May. I think you know that by now, my dear?"

After Mrs. Scrutton had left her, Laura sat on, staring at the sea for a long long time.

Go back and live in the house at Kingsley Terrace, where she had spent four such miserable years and which was now full of tragic and fearsome associations? That was the one sacrifice she could offer on the secret altar of her love for Mark Scrutton, and no one but herself could or would ever know how great that sacrifice would be.

Then a strange look—one of joy mingled with pain—flashed into her face, for she heard her lover's eager footsteps on the stony way.

He walked in through the open door, took possession of her masterfully, sat her on his knee, and pressed her to him.

"My mother has just told me what you're going to do, my darling! How can I thank you for being so good to me?"

"I shall be good to myself, Mark, too." The way she made that admission reassured him. But he was all too ready to be reassured.

"Oh! how happy we shall be. We can phone to one another every morning, and of course I shall often be able to take you out for long runs in my car."

"I don't want anyone to know about us, Mark," and he felt she was trembling.

"No one will ever know, my dearest! They'll only think you're my patient; besides, Kingsley Terrace, thank God, is right away from real Silchester."

"The house next door has been let, now."

He looked slightly surprised. "Who told you that?"

"Mr. Malefield told me, the last time he came out to Loverslea. He'd seen a furniture-van outside the house, and he was quite pleased, because he thought it would enhance the value of Number Two, if Number One were let. But I'd far rather have no neighbours."

"I think you're wrong there—and we must find a decent woman to look after you."

To this she made no answer. She had quite made up her mind she would live alone in that house of sinister memories.

As he kissed his mother good night that evening Mark Scrutton exclaimed: "I can hardly believe that Laura is actually going back to live in Silchester! I suppose she saw how utterly miserable I was at the thought of being away from her—still it was noble of her to have thought of it—"

His mother smiled. "I agree," she said gently. "But then, my dear, I think Laura is a very noble woman."

After their son had gone to bed, Colonel Scrutton turned to his wife. "I'm sorry Mrs. Ordeley is going to do that," he observed.

"Why, George?"

"It is sure to mean talk, however careful they may be."

"I think they will be very careful, and it's very unselfish of her to do this for Mark, for I'm afraid she hates the thought of it. She is a very unselfish woman."

Said Colonel Scrutton, "And she's something else, too, Mary."

"What d'you mean?"

"I mean that she's an exceptionally clever woman."

XIV

THREE WEEKS HAD GONE BY SINCE LAURA'S RETURN TO Silchester, and she was standing by Mark Scrutton's side in the sitting-room of 2, Kingsley Terrace. Strangely incongruous looked a nosegay of autumn roses he had ordered from a London flower-shop, so that it should be in no way associated with the sender.

He had snatched a few minutes out of a long morning and was now about to leave her. Suddenly he exclaimed: "You don't look over well, my precious darling! I do so hate the thought of your living here alone—"

"I'd rather be alone than with a stranger, Mark."

How often had she said this to him—using first one and then another form of words, during those days of mingled agony and bliss, which had gone slowly by since her return to this house of memories.

Mark came as often as he dared—of course he did—for in a way he would not have thought possible, in the days before he had known her, of any sane and intelligent man, Laura had become interwoven with the very texture of his life. But the physical and mental strain they were now enduring was telling on them both. Also, Mark hated to a peculiar degree the kind of deceit he was compelled to practise in connection with those often hasty, and always furtive, calls on his supposed patient.

Laura Dousland's return had soon become known in the town, and she had had a spate of callers. Those who hastened to welcome her home, as several of them expressed it, were mostly women who believed themselves inspired by kindly feeling, but whose real reason was a burning curiosity to see and hear the voice of a human being of their own class who had been the central figure of a trial for murder.

Few days now went by without some allusion being made in Mark Scrutton's presence to the woman who had provided the most exciting and memorable series of weeks the cathedral town had ever known. The majority of these allusions were kindly in tone, but considerable surprise was always expressed that Mrs. Dousland had returned to a house where what was now known to have been a far from happy married life had ended in stark tragedy.

So by now, though neither of them would have admitted it to the other, the position was becoming to them both not only intolerable, but untenable.

Mark whispered something in Laura's ear, and her eyes brimmed over with tears. She put up her face, and they kissed as though they had not already kissed and kissed, since he had come into the house twenty minutes ago.

"I must go now," he said at last. "Sometimes I feel I was a selfish fool to let you come here. When I see you looking as you look now, it breaks my heart. I don't believe you get enough to eat," and though he tried to say those last words in a joking tone, there was such a thread of pain in his voice that she said quickly: "The Haywards are back at Loverslea, and they've asked me to stay there for a week or so. Shall I say 'yes,' dearest? I should get plenty to eat there!"

He looked at her; but there was nothing in her face to tell him what answer she wished him to give to that question. Sometimes he felt that she possessed hidden depths of selflessness he could not hope to probe, and even less to rival, in their close, and ever growing closer, relationship to one another.

Take the matter of her return to Silchester? Had her natural shrinking and distress in doing so outweighed what he could not doubt to be her happiness in those meetings which otherwise would have been impossible, during the time she had ordained must be lived through before they became man and wife?

She had lately given him a latchkey, partly because Fordish Dousland had never replaced the loud bell which dated from when Kingsley Terrace had been built by a mid-Victorian builder. Yesterday he had come in on her before she had known he was there, and he had been startled, more, alarmed, by the expression of tense suffering and even despair on her face. True, when she had seen him, as in a flash delight, nay rapture, had taken the place of that still look of utter misery. But during the hours that had followed his leaving the house, Mark Scrutton had been haunted by what he had espied in that unguarded moment.

He said, now: "Would you like to go there, my darling? Nothing else matters—"

"What you feel about it matters," and she gazed at him with her strangely beautiful dark eyes full of submissive, beckoning love.

"I suppose I could come out there and see you fairly

often," he said hesitatingly. "Especially if you were there a whole week?"

"We should have to be very careful," she murmured.

And then the natural man in Mark cried out in exasperation: "Oh, my dear—do tell the Haywards the truth about ourselves! Why shouldn't you? Though I don't care for Mrs. Hayward, I know she's honestly fond of you. Surely she would understand? Think what it would be to feel able to see one another in peace, now and again!"

"Oh, Mark—I'm sorry but I'd far far rather stay here, and go on as we're doing now, than tell Alice Hayward the truth—yet. She is so exceedingly conventional and inquisitive. She'd want to know when, where, and how, we became engaged. And I should have to pretend it had only just happened—or she'd feel offended and hurt I hadn't told her at once."

He exclaimed in a rasped tone, "What an awful woman—yet she thinks herself your friend!"

"She *is* my friend, Mark. No friend was ever kinder and more loyal than she was to me."

She put her hand on his arm, "D'you remember her in the witness-box? I knew then, and I ought never, never to forget, how she must have hated doing what she did then."

This was the first time Laura had spoken to him of her trial since her return to Silchester, and her listener felt shaken to the soul as the scene to which she had just alluded came back to him, too.

Would all that had happened last winter and spring never fade from Laura's memory? Till a moment ago he had come almost to forget it, in the wonderful thing, the coming of love, which had happened to them both. But now it was as if he heard again Mrs. Hayward's passionate declaration of belief in Laura's innocence, and saw before him the eager, surprised, and in some cases, jeering countenances, of the men who had been surrounding him as those unexpected, explosive sentences had been uttered by the woman standing in the witness-box.

He muttered: "I must be going now," and walked across to the further window of the sitting-room, hardly knowing what he was doing.

Then he made a great effort over himself to appear unconcerned, "I say, dearest? The place on this side of the house does look neglected, doesn't it? An ill-kept garden takes a hundred pounds at least off the price of a house like this. You'll have to let me spend a little time on a Saturday or a Sunday putting it all in order for you."

She came across to where he was standing: "I ought to have seen to it as soon as I came back," she murmured.

"I'll put some small evergreens in the well-head, and along the edge of the wall."

"I've already ordered three dozen plants," she said quickly. "I noticed yesterday how horrid everything looks down there."

She slipped her hand through his arm, and he felt she was trembling. He touched her hand. It was very cold.

He said resolutely: "Look here, Laura?"

"Yes, Mark?"

"I do want you to go to Loverslea for a few days, after all, just to rest for a bit, and have some good food."

As she remained silent, he added: "You'll make me happy by doing that, sweetheart, and I promise not to come and see you too often."

She leant her light weight against him, "I want you to come often," she whispered. "I'm only half alive when you're not there. After all, I shall have to tell Alice Hayward the truth some time, so why not now? I might pretend we're only just engaged."

"I should hate you to do that—I loathe lies!" he exclaimed.

"To tell them even part of the truth would save me from being worried again about that post in Canada."

"They seem to think you're their slave, and must do whatever they think you ought to do," he said sorely.

"Mrs. Hayward was always like that," and she smiled dolorously. "But they are both wonderfully kind, Mark. I've only got to telephone, and Mr. Hayward will send for me at once."

She went with him to the door, and again they clung together as lovers will, and kissed as lovers kiss. And after Mark got into his car, he asked himself how he was going to live through the three months before she would become his wife.

As to the woman he had just left, with the going of Mark Scrutton it was as if darkness—a dark mist of pain enveloping her whole being—descended on her. She longed to stay quietly where she was, but she telephoned at once to Loverslea, and arranged to be called for within two hours. It was Mark's wish she should go there, and perhaps he was right, for as she did her simple packing for this visit to her faithful friends and one-time employers, the air about her seemed filled with threatening echoes of the past.

When she was quite ready to leave the house there came back to her what she had said concerning plants for the garden. It was the first direct lie she had ever told Mark, and she must hasten to make it truth. So she telephoned to a florist and ordered three dozen hardy miniature shrubs in pots:

"Send them next Friday afternoon—as there will be no one to take them in before then," she explained.

There was another thing Laura now told herself she ought to do before leaving this place of sombre and even terrible memories. It was something she ought to have done immediately on her return to Silchester; but she had put it off, day by day, and night by night. For one thing it wasn't an easy or pleasant job, and for another always she had lived, during the last three weeks, from moment to moment and from hour to hour, for the coming of the man she loved. Any evening, just after he had left her, would have been the time for her to do the task that had to be done. But after each of those passion-laden, ecstatic interludes, the doing of anything which recalled the past had seemed beyond her strength. Several times, also, after he had left her saying: "Till to-morrow, dearest," he had come back, mastered by his longing to see her again, even for only a few moments.

Mark was going home, down to Mellcombe, for the following week-end. That would give her three days of solitude, and time alas! to spare. To-day was Saturday. She would come back here Friday morning, and they would spend that evening peacefully together, for all those the matter concerned, his patients, and the doctor's widow with whom he was living as paying guest, would have supposed him to have got well away from Silchester by eight o'clock. His real start for the long drive to Devonshire would be round about eleven, or as much later as his conscience would allow him to keep Laura from her sleep.

It was a quarter to six on Friday morning, and Mark Scrutton was motoring home from a case where he had been all night.

It had been a difficult nay, a dangerous first birth, the mother being a pretty foolish young woman who had slimmed and elastic-banded herself within sight of death. But he had pulled her through, and though he was physically tired, he felt mentally, gloriously well, and happy, too. Also, perhaps because Laura had suddenly given in concerning the date of their marriage, advancing the time by six weeks, he also felt what Scots call "fey."

As he drove through the deserted lanes in the pearly light of this autumnal morning, he thought over certain passages of his emotional life—that secret life which few men ever reveal to their fellows—and he thanked God that he had, as he put it to himself, kept on the whole straight, and so worthy of the crowning glory which was coming to him.

As a young medical student there had been an episode with an alluring nurse, and he had seriously considered marriage with her, after what she had half laughingly, half cryingly, described as "a trial trip." At that time—fool that he had been—he had half believed in the value of such an experiment as a prelude to lawful matrimony. Then a trifling accident had revealed that there had been several such "trial trips" in that alluring nurse's still young life.

That discovery had given him an ugly shock. He had trembled for years at the thought of his escape, and it had left him with at once a fear of, and a contempt for, all women who made efforts to attract him.

So he had lived on, keeping himself apart from emotional disturbances, till Laura Dousland had unconsciously taken possession of all that went to compose his powerful entity. Now he no longer belonged to himself; he was all hers; and exulted in his bondage.

The last few days had made it plain that they two could

not go on for much longer as they had tried to do till now. Mrs. Hayward liked the clever young doctor, who had been so valuable an ally during Laura's trial. And as, in deference to her husband's suggestion, she had invited no other guest during Laura's visit, she felt she had the right to enjoy Mark Scrutton's company when he "dropped in," as he had done several times during that week, on his way back from seeing a patient who lived near to Loverslea. Once their hostess had almost caught her two guests in each other's arms.

That same night Mark had written to and implored Laura to consent to a marriage which should only be known to his parents, and announced to the few that had a right to the knowledge when it seemed well and wise to do so.

She had written back, "It shall be as you wish—" and at their next meeting it had been settled they should be married quietly in Paris before Christmas.

Small wonder that this morning he felt exultantly happy as well as "fey." And, as if to fill his cup of joy to the brim, it had been arranged that he should fetch Laura to-day and bring her home. Indeed, this had been actually suggested by Mrs. Hayward herself, for she had another use for both the Loverslea cars that day, and gravely, he hoped coldly, he had assented to her plan.

In the five minutes he had been alone with Laura, they had arranged to lunch out of doors on their way back to Silchester, and so secure a little longer time together before their separation for the week-end.

After reaching the outskirts of the town, he came to the road where stood Laura's house, just as it struck six from a neighbouring church.

Scarce a creature in Silchester rose before seven, for there were no factories in or near the cathedral city which had flashed into the news for the first time in its thousand years of life owing to the Dousland Case, or the Chianti Flask Mystery, as it was more generally called, and would doubtless so remain in British legal annals.

Mark Scrutton slowed up before the short row which went by the pompous name of Kingsley Terrace. Heavens! How ugly all three houses looked, with their grey painted stucco walls and grimy windows. No wonder two of them had stood empty for a long time. Of the three, that now belonging to Laura looked the least repulsive, for Fordish Dousland had been too shrewd a man not to keep his property in substantial repair. Still, even that house looked dirty and neglected, and he told himself that it would pay to paint and clean the outside ere offering it for sale.

And then he suddenly asked himself why he shouldn't put in two hours' work there, now? He could at least cut the little square of turf in front, and run a hose over the queer back garden which mostly consisted of stone pavement and marble statuary.

He stopped his car, leapt over the gate, and then, with his latchkey, opened the front door. The air in the hall struck dank, and he went quickly along the passage which led to the garden door. He found that it was locked, and what slightly surprised him was that it was not only locked, but bolted, too. In fact, he had quite a job in getting the bolt free from the rust which had eaten into it. It was clear that Laura had never troubled to open that door since her return to Silchester.

When he had gone through it, and found himself in the paved garden, now filled with the early morning sunlight, Mark Scrutton stood still and looked with curiosity about him.

Fordish Dousland, for whom he now felt a strong antipathy, must have spent a good deal of money turning this piece of ground into a paved court! Then he suddenly remembered that the man who had meant so little to him, then, had told him with pride that he had done it all himself, only having in a couple of labourers for one day to help him lay the slabs of stone, and move the marble well-head which stood in the centre of the almost square enclosure. That well-head, brought from Italy in the eighteenth century, had been for a hundred years in an English rose-garden. It had been bought, for a mere song, by its late owner, indeed, Fordish Dousland had boasted it was worth at least fifty times what he had paid for it.

He, Mark Scrutton himself, during his second call at this ill-fated house, had filled up the bottom of the marble well-head with a sackful of cement balls he had brought with him. Then he had put above them a layer of good earth in which he had planted bulbs he had spared as a small gift to his golfing acquaintance. And all that he had done here on that occasion now seemed years, instead of scarcely twelve months, ago.

He turned into the tiny garden shed which had played a part in Laura's trial, for it was there that the tin of poison had been kept. To his disappointment he found no grass cutter in the shed; but there was a hose-pipe, and so if he could do nothing to the little front lawn, he could tidy up the paved garden on this side of the house.

Stepping again into the sunshine he looked with a feeling of disgust at some now dead geraniums within the floreated rim of the well-head. The Venetian manservant, Angelo Terugi, must have put them there, and he had contented himself with simply sticking in the pots on the earth below the rim. Those pots must be lifted out before he started playing with the hose.

Once more he went into the minute shed. As far as he could see there was nothing there but a bucket and, in a corner, the empty sack in which he had brought the cement balls to the house. But there was something under the sack; no doubt whatever gardening things Fordish Dousland had used were there.

He moved the piece of sacking with his foot, and then he was surprised and puzzled to see a small heap composed of some of the round balls, each about the size of an orange, with which he himself had filled up the bottom of the well-head below the sackful of good garden soil he had also provided.

Here was something of an enigma—for he remembered clearly that there had been no cement balls left over, after he had filled up the inside of the well-head. Indeed there had been barely enough of them for the purpose.

Then he saw that the cement balls lying before him on the floor of the shed were discoloured, some more than others—and he realised that they had been extracted from where he had put them. They had obviously become stained by the earth which had fallen in between them from above, during the watering he had told Fordish Dousland must be done now and again.

Feeling really perplexed, he stared down at the small heap of balls. It was plain that someone had gone to the considerable trouble of extracting them from the bottom of the well-head. Why had this been done? The only reason he could think of would have been if a flowering shrub or box tree had been planned to be planted in what to an English gardener's eyes must look like a huge marble tub.

Then he espied lying across the brownish white balls a thin two-pronged trowel with a long handle—the kind of implement which is made to a special order, for the prongs were of fine-tempered steel, and the oak handle was brass-bound. Once more a vivid memory of Fordish Dousland rose to his mind. He, Mark, had noticed that trowel the day he had brought the balls, and he had exclaimed, "I envy you that!" Dousland, with a chuckle which had made his unhealthy-looking pallid face twist itself into a grimace, had answered, "I got it for five shillings! To have it made would cost at least a couple of sovereigns."

Mark Scrutton now stooped and took up the peculiar garden implement, and with it in his right hand he went back into the garden.

Without knowing what prompted him to do so, he glanced up to his right, at the windows of the house next door he knew to be occupied. All the blinds there were still drawn, though two windows were open a few inches from the top.

Laying down the long-handled trowel on the stone pavement, he went close up to the well-head, and lifted out, one after the other, the pots in which were the now withered geranium plants. As he did this, the layer of soil in which they had been wedged crumbled into dust-like flakes of earth, for it had been a dry summer. And then, again he could not have told why, he remembered that on the night of Fordish Dousland's death there had been a great storm of wind and rain, which had gone on for hours; the fact had been mentioned in the course of Laura Dousland's trial.

Slowly, hesitatingly, he took up the trowel, and raising it he thrust the narrow twin-prongs into the centre of the grey-looking crumbling earth which lay in tiny hillocks a few inches below the floreated marble rim of the well-head.

The sharp steel points at once found and slid over a couple, or was it three? of the cement balls which lay beneath the layer of soil, and, as this happened, there issued from Mark Scrutton's hitherto tightly-closed lips an involuntary, almost stuffless, sound, signifying—what did it signify?—something far more significant than mere relief.

Should he rest content with the result of what had been an uncalled for, unnecessary, experiment? No, for a secret deadly suspicion, of which he was agonisingly ashamed, drove him on to do again that he would have been wise to have left undone.

Once more he lifted up the curious long-handled trowel of which he had envied Fordish Dousland the possession, and this time he probed deeper and deeper into the centre of the well-head.

Suddenly the steel prongs came to rest against the curved sides of something far larger than any orange-sized ball.

Mark Scrutton withdrew the trowel. Then he stood quite still, while drops of water exuded from his forehead. Dully his mind noted the phenomenon, for he had done nothing to provoke those drops of acrid sweat.

At last he turned away and fetched the bucket he had seen standing in the shed. Putting it by the well-head, he began scooping out with his fine tapering hands, first the soft earth, and then the layer of balls which lay just beneath the earth.

Having done that he stopped, and again looked up at the house next door. Consciously he thanked God that the blinds were still down, and that he could count on no one seeing what thing it was he was about to lift from the hiding place where it had been safely and snugly concealed for so long.

XV

LAURA WAS WALKING UP AND DOWN UNDER THE ancient brick wall which surrounded Loverslea on the side of the park where ran the high road. She was waiting for Mark Scrutton, and already he was over his time.

The Haywards had both gone to London, and so the slight feeling of unease which had haunted her when in her good friends' presence, had left her. During each day of her visit she had become increasingly afraid Mrs. Hayward would suspect the truth concerning the doctor and her guest, and that when her suspicion was confirmed she would feel hurt as well as surprised she had not been told at once of their engagement. But the mistress of Loverslea accepted Mark Scrutton's almost daily call as a pleasant tribute to herself, quite as much as to the visitor she knew had become Dr. Scrutton's patient. Indeed, now and again she had spoken of the Canadian project as if it were sure to come to pass, once Laura's money matters were settled, and the house in Kingsley Terrace disposed of. "You mustn't wait too long," she had said only yesterday. "That sort of good job might suddenly be filled up."

Laura had felt the position so difficult that she had suddenly made up her mind to marry Mark much sooner than she had first thought would be possible or decent, and this decision had given her a curious feeling of peace. Indeed, during the last two days she had been so happy that it made her feel afraid.

And now there stole a sensation of apprehension into her heart, for this was the first time her lover had ever kept her waiting. He had said he would be here a little before midday, and it was now close on one. It was in vain that she told herself that a dozen occurrences might have forced him to delay. He was a careful driver, but there are motorists on the roads, hundreds of them, who are a danger to everything they come near, and as the minutes went by her vague feeling of fear increased.

And then, just when she had made up her mind to go back to the house and telephone—though that was what they had both agreed she should never do—joy flooded her heart, for his car suddenly appeared at the bend of the road. But was it her fancy that he was driving very slowly? No, for the car seemed to be hardly moving, and she told herself that something was wrong with the engine, and that this accounted for his being late.

But as, at last, he drew up close to her, she uttered an exclamation of concern and alarm, and, "What's the matter, Mark?" she cried.

His face was rigid, and his eyes were full of pain. "Have you had an accident, dearest?"

"Yes—I mean no." He spoke in a hoarse muffled voice. And then: "Will you get in, Laura? Forgive my not getting out. I want to get away from this place."

He was staring straight before him, and he looked so ill and unlike himself that terror filled her heart.

"You're not fit to have come out! You're ill, my darling—"

"I'm not ill. But I've had a gruelling time—all last night—at a difficult case."

Then he added, speaking with an obvious effort, "I've just been there again, and found all well."

"You ought to have telephoned, and said you couldn't come this morning. I could have gone home by the coach which is taking one of the maids and my suitcase late this afternoon."

As he said nothing to that, she said again: "You shouldn't have come out, Mark."

"Perhaps not, but I felt I must see you to-day."

Yet he did not turn and look at her with eyes which, however weary he might be, had always been, even before he knew that he loved her, full of tenderness.

"I'd have come to you, dearest, if you'd sent word you were not well. Nothing matters in the world to me but you! Surely you know that? I have never really cared what people would say or think."

And then it was as if he became suddenly human again: "Get in, Laura, and let's get away from here," he muttered.

"Let me first find something that will do you good—you always have some kind of pain-killer in your car, haven't you?"

Even as she spoke she was opening the door giving into the back of the motor. She heard him say: "There's nothing of the sort there to-day—" and she saw that this was true, for there was only a square box clumsily wrapped in a large sheet of white paper standing on the floor of the car. Something, however, was written on the paper, and she bent forward and read it: "DIPHTHERIA GERMS. IF AN ACCIDENT BEFALLS THIS CAR AND I AM INJURED OR KILLED,

PLEASE BURY AT ONCE IN A DEEP PLACE." This injunction was written in block letters, and above in larger characters was inscribed the word "*Danger.*"

"What are you doing?" he called out suddenly in a loud, discordant voice. "Come and get in, Laura."

When she had obeyed him they drove on in silence for what seemed to her a long, long time, till they came to the side of a beautiful wood situated under the downs. There he stopped the car, and getting out stood still for a while, listening, with his face set and stern.

But there was no traffic in that lonely place, and without looking at her he explained: "I've something to do here—a patient to see in the wood. So will you wait in the car? It won't take long, my dear."

And as he uttered the words "my dear" there came across his mouth what seemed to her burdened heart a spasm of pain.

He opened the door at the back of the car, and she watched him in silence while he took out the box containing—what did it contain? The awful seeds of physical death, or something far more terrible—than that. Something, maybe, which betokened the spiritual dissolution of their love?

Leaving her with her face filled with questioning anguish turned towards him, he strode off, down a narrow path which she knew led to the heart of the wood, for they had come here three Sundays ago, and Mark had said: "Why not have lunch in this delicious place, my darling?" Without waiting for an answer he had taken the rug and a book of verse, while she had held the basket containing their mid-day meal and some needlework. They had walked on and on, side by side in happy silence, till they had seen to their right a clearing where half a dozen young trees had been uprooted. There they had spent most of the afternoon; she sewing, and restfully content in a way she could never feel during their brief daily meetings, while he read aloud to her now and again.

And now, with her heart full of fears which were the more terrifying because they were still vague and unsubstantial, she recalled what had happened when she had made a half-laughing declaration that she would like to "stay put" in this green wood, and with only the birds and squirrels to keep them company, he reading poetry to her while she sewed, "for ever and for ever."

"I want more than that!" and he had flung down the book in his hand, and leaping up he had gone off alone into the depths of the green shade, leaving her troubled.

It was then, though she had said nothing to him at the time, for she possessed the rare gift of silence, that she had decided to fling convention aside and marry this man who loved her, as soon as was in any way possible, given this work on which he was now engaged. The reply to the pleading letter she had received yesterday morning, had been her answer to his cry in yonder wood.

How strange that during the long afternoon they had spent together here he had said nothing of any patient living near? Then she reminded herself that there had been time for dozens of sick and ailing folk to have sent for him since then. There was something about Mark Scrutton that inspired a feeling of confidence and strength. The practice he had taken over had grown steadily, and would be found by the man who was about to take it back inconveniently large—the more so that many of the new patients were working folk.

The waiting, the solitude, for the road where she now

began pacing up and down was a bye-way and, as they had found when there before, led only to the downs, suddenly became intolerable. The more intolerable because more and more was her heart filled with secret, dark, and terrible imaginings. All at once she turned into the path he had taken, telling herself piteously that surely he could not mind her coming to meet him on his way back from what she tried to believe must be a lonely woodman's cottage the other side of the wood?

After a while she found herself approaching the place where they had been so happy during one of the few peaceful times they had spent together since she had returned to Silchester. Suddenly she stopped, for coming from the undergrowth which encircled and hid the clearing from the path where she now stood, she had heard sounds which for a moment she thought must be moans made by some wild creature caught in some fiendish cruel trap.

Overwhelmed with sensations of wrath and pity she listened—and then she sensed that those awful sounds were wrung from the extremity of suffering now being endured by some poor human being. Yet a moment later, and she knew from whom were coming those stifled groans.

Mark Scrutton, in his misery, did not hear the rustling made by the parting of the low branches, and neither did he see the affrighted eyes which gazed through them.

His long lean figure lay prone, close to a spot where the earth, already disturbed by the uprooting of a sapling, had been dug in, and then filled up again and smoothed over. By his outstretched clenched right hand was the small iron scoop with which had been accomplished that which this man had come so far, and in such secrecy, to do.

Laura saw his face set as if in frozen lines of agony and

stark despair; his eyelids were red and swollen, but even while she looked at him, he so far mastered himself as to close his lips, tightly.

She straightened herself and, having regained the path, she began stumbling along further into the wood, for her decision had been taken the instant she had seen the look on his face.

He would not find her on the bye-road where he had curtly told her to wait; for by the time he had returned there to say he now knew what manner of woman it was he had once loved, she would be safely hidden in the great stretch of undergrowth and thick bushes. Unless by a fortunate chance for her, there happened to be a deep pond ahead, of the kind often found in a primeval bit of woodland in southern England. Indeed, as she hastened on and on, she looked now and again to her right and left for the gleam of water.

But his hoarse voice suddenly smote her ears. "Laura! Where are you going? Come back—that's the wrong way."

"I know, I know—" she gasped, and then she began to run.

After all he could not force her to obey him, and to "come back" to take her punishment? Though he would never know it, she had suffered already more punishment than mortal woman, however wicked, should be made to endure. One poor thing remained to her, of all else she had been stripped. This was the power of death. And she told herself that nothing should make her look into his face again. Rather than do that she would blind herself with one of the branches which reached across the narrowing path before her.

"Laura? Stop!"

His voice was close behind her now, and it was a cold, passionless voice. "Are you mad!" asked that stern voice.

She stumbled, and his arms, closing round her for a moment, prevented her from falling to the ground. But quickly those strong arms released her.

She stood still, and without turning round she answered his question: "I am not mad, Mark. I am what you have now discovered me to be, bad. I beg you to leave me. I'm quite all right, and I shall get a lift home on the other side of the wood. There are a lot of cars and vans always going along the road over there."

"We can't part like this—"

"Of course we can, and shall. You know now that I am quite a different woman to what you supposed me to be. My life for a long time has been one long lie."

"Surely not since we have known one another?" he asked the half question in an almost inaudible voice.

"Yes—more than ever a lie since then," she answered in a loud voice.

He took her by the shoulders and swung her round, "D'you mean you never loved me? Tell the truth!"

She kept her eyes fixed on the patch of ground between them. "How could I love a man who did not know the real me?" And then defiantly she added: "I must go now."

"No!" he cried violently. "Not like this."

"There's nothing more to say, Mark."

But her voice faltered as she spoke, for she had seen his hands. Those hands were earth-stained, and clasped together so tightly that the knuckles showed white.

He came closer to her. "Do you really wish us to part like this, without a word, Laura?"

"You once said to me, just after I first knew you loved me, 'You can tell me anything,' and I nearly told you the truth then. But I knew if I did that it would kill your love, and your love—fool and coward that I was—was already precious to me."

He groaned aloud, and then she muttered: "Don't think I've escaped punishment, Mark. Hanging by the neck till I was dead would have been merciful to what I have lived through many hours of each day."

She saw his hands fall apart, and breaking the secret vow she had taken she raised her head, and looked at his ravaged face, and made up her mind what she would do. He should not feel her death had been on his head. She would do her best, and she knew her best could be very good, to make the way in which she would take her life appear a real accident, when and where she decided it should take place.

In a quiet, resolute tone, she said: "I will tell you all that I feel I can tell you, Mark, and then you must drive me back to Loverslea. I'll explain to John and Alice Hayward this evening that I stayed on to say I've made up my mind, at last, about Canada." She added as if to herself: "He'll be so pleased that even Alice will welcome me back, for one night at any rate, and from there I'll go to London to-morrow."

They began walking side by side, and all at once she exclaimed: "Let us go and sit down where we were that Sunday! It's close here—somewhere on the left."

He hesitated perceptibly, and then, "Very well," he answered, and made a way for her to pass through the undergrowth.

They both remembered that he had said three weeks ago, "I wish I had the rug for you to sit down on. You mustn't spoil that pretty white dress, my darling," and that then he had bent down and kissed the hem of her woollen frock.

"I shall be all right here," she said as if to herself, and she slipped down on to the mossy ground, close to where he had lain in an abandonment of horror and misery half an hour ago.

He walked restlessly about the small clearing for a few moments.

"Mark?"

"Yes," and he came and stood before her.

"How did you find out?"

As he made no answer, she gave a sudden cry: "Does anyone else know?"

He sank down by her, and took her hand. "Of course not, and never will—"

She drew her hand away, and stared stonily at nothing, while he told her in quick broken sentences what he had done early that morning.

"And now it's my turn," she said, and sighed. "Do you want me to tell you everything?"

"Yes. Everything—"

What he wanted her to tell him, what he had always longed, with a fearful longing to know, concerned her relation to her husband. Since he and Laura had become lovers that commonplace, mean-looking, elderly masculine entity had haunted him each night, and filled him with an agony of retrospective jealousy. What manner of human being had been the real Fordish Dousland? Till this moment he had tried to stifle his horrible curiosity. But now every barrier had fallen. It was no longer what Laura had done, it was what had brought her to do so awful a thing, that made him exclaim: "Yes! Everything—"

But the unhappy woman did not know what was in his mind as she said: "I will tell you everything—indeed I will. But I don't know where to begin."

He wanted to exclaim: "Begin on the day that man first kissed you—" but he was afraid, ashamed, too, to say that.

"There were times, but not since you and I have come to know one another, when I used to feel that it couldn't be true, and that I couldn't have done it," and it was as if she was talking to herself.

He looked at her. That was no answer to his unspoken question. When was she coming to the only thing that mattered to him?

"Dr. Grant suspected me from the first, and I think Angelo Terugi did, too."

"That Italian fellow?" He felt suddenly fearfully afraid for her.

"Of course he knew the truth. He knew—"

And then she broke off what she had been going to say.

"Knew what, Laura?" he asked harshly, knowing that the Italian must have known what were the real relations between his master and mistress.

"He knew that the Chianti flask had disappeared. But I suppose he couldn't quite make up his mind whether it was I who had hidden it."

Mark Scrutton looked at her fixedly. There rose before him a vision of Laura as she had stood in the witness-box giving the lie direct to Angelo Terugi. For a brief moment he forgot Dousland.

"Then the flask was on the tray after all?"

"No, no, *no*!" and her voice rose almost to a scream on that last "*no*."

She was telling Mark Scrutton the truth, and the doing of it was searing her heart. Why put herself to the torture if, when she told him the truth, he did not believe her?

"Do you mean the flask was not on the tray?"

"Not till I myself put it there! That day, after lunch, Fordish, who knew that there was no wine coming for a day of two, determined Angelo should not drink the little of the Chianti that remained. So he hid the flask, as he had done once before—but not in the same place."

"I see."

"You don't believe me, Mark, do you?" she said piteously.

"I want to believe you."

But even as he spoke those words, there had come back, like an enveloping flame, fierce retrospective jealousy of the man to whom Laura had belonged for four years. When she had uttered Dousland's name, "Fordish," he had felt a tremor of sick pain as well as of disgust.

"What made you marry that man? I've never spoken to you of him, but that's not because I haven't thought of him."

"It was Alice Hayward made me marry him. She judges all men by John Hayward. She thought Fordish Dousland was like him. Instead he was—"

"Go on!"

Her head fell on her breast. "He made me loathe the word 'love.'"

Mark Scrutton turned his head away. He was remembering that moment in the early dawn, by the sea, when she had moaned: "Never speak to me of love."

"Why didn't you leave him?"

"Because I thought, because I had been taught, that a woman ought never to leave her husband. Also, I felt I ought to make up to him," she looked at him woefully, "for not being what he wanted me to be and—and what he believed the normal woman becomes as a matter of course, once she is—she is—"

"Is what?"

"Married."

"So you stayed with that beast, and did your best—in other ways?"

He was staring at her woefully now. She had said so little, yet she had said everything.

"Yes, but it was of no use. He thought me a bad manager, and I expect I was, though I spent all my savings over trying to make him comfortable."

She was looking down, avoiding that intent questioning gaze while she went back, and lived again the life she had led as Fordish Dousland's wife.

"I think what I minded most was having nothing to read. When I had no more money, and so couldn't subscribe to a book-lending library, I went to the public library. He was very angry when he found that out." She looked up: "That may seem a little thing to you, Mark. But by that time, I mean by the time I had become literally penniless, reading seemed the one thing that made life possible. Of course he didn't understand that."

She stopped, and then tonelessly she said: "And now I'll tell you what happened that last night."

"D'you want to tell me?" he muttered.

"Yes, I do want you to know it all—" and she nearly added the words, "—before I die."

"There were times, after I was arrested, and before my trial, when I longed to scream out everything that had happened. But everybody, even in the prison, believed me innocent. So I began to act the part of one wrongly accused. All the same, I never really forgot, even for one moment, what I really was, though as time went on it did seem incredible, even to me, that I could have done what I did do."

Mark exclaimed, suddenly, explosively: "It must have been dreadful going back to that house?"

"It did bring it all back, of course," and she sighed as she went on: "The first night I was there I dreamt I did it all over again, and I nearly told you the truth when you came the next morning. I had made up my mind to do it. Then, do you remember, you thanked me for coming there, and said it was noble and selfless of me to have come back."

Did he now say: "So it was?"

Looking at his pale set face she did not believe that she had heard aright.

Staring before her, as though there was something there—a vision of the past which only she could see, she said hesitatingly: "I suppose, without knowing it, that I had come to a kind of breaking-point. And yet nothing was really different, Mark. For a long time I had known Fordish hated me. And yet though he hated me I felt—"

Mark bent his burning eyes on her, "—that he wanted—" his voice died away.

Did she say "Yes," as she averted her head?

She went on speaking quickly, breathlessly, now.

"It must have been about eight o'clock when I warmed the spaghetti and took the tray up to his room, for he had already got into bed. And then he was angry because I had forgotten to grate some cheese."

"He seems to have treated you like a slave."

She said listlessly: "When I left off being what he used to call his odalisque, I became his slave."

"Go on about that night."

"As I was leaving him so as to grate the cheese, he told me he had hidden a Chianti flask which still had some wine in it in a locked bookcase in the dining-room. He handed me the key, and said I must get it as I went downstairs, as otherwise I would forget the wine as I had the cheese."

She waited a moment. "If I had remembered the cheese, Mark, none of what happened would have happened."

"How d'you mean?"

"Angelo Terugi had left the tin of poison on the kitchen table. He never told the police that, he let them believe the tin was in the garden shed that night, and I suppose that made a difference."

Mark nodded, remembering what play Sir Joseph Molloy had made of the fact that Mrs. Dousland would have had to go out and look for the poison in that dark and stormy night, were she what the Crown averred her to be, a calculating secret poisoner.

She went on, now speaking in a low firm tone: "As I looked at it, and at the flask, too, I remembered all you had said when you told us about that poison, and how Fordish had asked you if it was true that a man or woman taking a spoonful of that powder would die without pain."

"You longed to be free?" he put the words into her mouth.

"No, no!" she cried violently. "It was more than that. I had come to loathe Fordish—I longed for him to die. I used to lie awake at night, shivering with fear. He never allowed me to lock the door between our rooms, and that, though he hadn't come in there, excepting once to hide a flask of Chianti, for over a year. The last time I had told him I would leave him, and tell Mrs. Hayward the reason why, if he ever tormented me again."

She stared before her again as if she again saw something there no one else would ever see.

"I put a spoonful of the powder into the wine, and then I took it upstairs and left him without a word."

She waited a moment.

"He rang, and I went up and brought down the tray. I

waited till ten o'clock and then I went out into the garden. In the darkness and rain, for the great storm had begun, I hid the flask of Chianti where you found it."

Once more she stopped, and it was in a low, listless voice, that she went on again.

"I did not feel I could go up to my room, so I sat on in the sitting-room in the dark. Terugi came into the house at last, and for a moment I felt terrified, fearing he might open the door and put on the light. But of course he went straight up to his room, and as I stayed on, wide awake, down there, I began to feel as if I couldn't have done what I had done. It seemed incredible that Fordish would die. Isn't that strange? I remember knocking at his door in the morning, and feeling surprised he didn't answer. Even then I couldn't believe that I had killed him. But soon I knew I had, Mark, for he lay there, dead."

"And then you tried to telephone to me?"

"Yes, and if you had come that morning I think I should have told you the truth. I knew I had done a very wicked thing, and I thought everyone would come to know it. But I was too unhappy to care."

"And then Grant came, as I was away?"

"Yes, and suddenly I felt afraid of Dr. Grant. He was rough and rude, and—and asked me questions that disgusted me. But he hadn't been gone very long before Alice Hayward arrived, for Angelo Terugi, without telling me, had telephoned to Loverslea. After I had seen her, it seemed impossible for me to confess what I had done."

"I understand that."

She looked at him searchingly. "Do you really understand that, Mark?"

"Yes," he said firmly. "I do really understand."

"And then—queer, wasn't it?—during the time I was in prison, and while the trial was going on, as I told you just now I almost came to believe that after all I hadn't done that awful thing—and that Fordish had done it himself! I remember Alice Hayward saying to me: 'Even if you'd said you had done it, I wouldn't have believed you.' But of course, deep in my heart, I knew that I was—"

"Don't say it," cried Mark Scrutton violently.

She looked at him mournfully. "Nothing seemed real to me during those weeks, or afterwards, while the trial went on, day after day. And I made up my mind that if I was brought in 'Guilty' I would never confess the truth because of my father. Till I met you, no one but my father had really cared for me, and I couldn't have brought shame on his name."

She sighed, "I've told you everything now."

They both got up. But neither moved away.

"Laura?"

"Yes, Mark?"

"I think it is better I should know the truth. I hope you feel that too?"

What did he mean by this question? How could she feel that too?

She began walking towards the thick bushes beyond which lay the path, and he heard her say: "I've changed my mind again, and I'd rather walk alone to the other side of the wood, and get a lift on the high road we found the Sunday we were here before."

He strode after her. "I can't give you up, Laura. You're flesh of my flesh, and bone of my bone. If I'd been a woman, I might have done what you did. What has to be expiated we can and will expiate together."

Mystery in the Channel
by Freeman Wills Crofts

Mystery in White
by J. Jefferson Farjeon

Portrait of a Murderer
by Anne Meredith

Santa Klaus Murder
by Mavis Doriel Hay

Secret of High Eldersham
by Miles Burton

Serpents in Eden
edited by Martin Edwards

Silent Nights
edited by Martin Edwards

Smallbone Deceased
by Michael Gilbert

Sussex Downs Murder
by John Bude

Thirteen Guests
by J. Jefferson Farjeon

Weekend at Thrackley
by Alan Melville

Z Murders
by J. Jefferson Farjeon

Praise for the British Library Crime Classics

"Carr is at the top of his game in this taut whodunit... The British Library Crime Classics series has unearthed another worthy golden age puzzle."

—*Publishers Weekly*, STARRED Review, for *The Lost Gallows*

"A wonderful rediscovery."

—*Booklist*, STARRED Review, for *The Sussex Downs Murder*

"First-rate mystery and an engrossing view into a vanished world."

—*Booklist*, STARRED Review, for *Death of an Airman*

"A cunningly concocted locked-room mystery, a staple of Golden Age detective fiction."

—*Booklist*, STARRED Review, for *Murder of a Lady*

"The book is both utterly of its time and utterly ahead of it."

—*New York Times Book Review* for *The Notting Hill Mystery*

"As with the best of such compilations, readers of classic mysteries will relish discovering unfamiliar authors, along with old favorites such as Arthur Conan Doyle and G.K. Chesterton."

—*Publishers Weekly*, STARRED Review, for *Continental Crimes*

"In this imaginative anthology, Edwards—president of Britain's Detection Club—has gathered together overlooked criminous gems."

—*Washington Post* for *Crimson Snow*

"The degree of suspense Crofts achieves by showing the growing obsession and planning is worthy of Hitchcock. Another first-rate reissue from the British Library Crime Classics series."

—*Booklist*, STARRED Review, for *The 12.30 from Croydon*

"Not only is this a first-rate puzzler, but Crofts's outrage over the financial firm's betrayal of the public trust should resonate with today's readers."

—*Booklist,* STARRED Review, for *Mystery in the Channel*

"This reissue exemplifies the mission of the British Library Crime Classics series in making an outstanding and original mystery accessible to a modern audience."

—*Publishers Weekly*, STARRED Review, for *Excellent Intentions*

"A book to delight every puzzle-suspense enthusiast"

—*New York Times* for *The Colour of Murder*

"Edwards's outstanding third winter-themed anthology showcases 11 uniformly clever and entertaining stories, mostly from lesser known authors, providing further evidence of the editor's expertise...This entry in the British Library Crime Classics series will be a welcome holiday gift for fans of the golden age of detection."

—*Publishers Weekly,* STARRED Review, for *The Christmas Card Crime and Other Stories*